Praise for Lc

Cinematic in scope, ambition and execution, Nighthawks zips along at a breakneck pace.
Pajnewman.com

Bursting with intrigue. A highly addictive thriller.
Readandrated.com

An enthralling read that I highly recommend to anyone who enjoys crime thrillers.
Splashes into Books

This novel has strong potential for screen adaptation.
Norma F, Educator netgalley.com

NIGHTHAWKS

LAMBERT NAGLE

Lambert Nagle Media

For the other Ginny, our Rocky Bay collaborator and wonderful friend.

And when he was entered into a ship, his disciples followed him.

And, behold, there arose a great tempest in the sea, insomuch that the ship was covered with the waves: but he was asleep.

And his disciples came to him, and awoke him, saying, Lord, save us: we perish.

And he saith unto them, Why are ye fearful, O ye of little faith? Then he arose, and rebuked the winds and the sea; and there was a great calm.

New Testament (Matthew, 8:23-26)

Chapter 1

London, England

When he was ten years old, summoned to see Father Jack and waiting cold and alone in the school corridor, he had felt this way. Sitting outside DCI Reynold's office, Stephen Connor felt defeated. Through the glass partition, Reynolds was frowning as she dragged angrily on an e-cigarette. This wasn't going to go well.

'Come in Connor,' she called. As Stephen went in, he saw her hastily moving a stack of papers from her desk onto a table behind her. She glanced up at him. 'I hear from your superior officer that organising rosters isn't your thing.'

'I'm sure there are others better qualified for that than I am, Ma'am.'

'Something's come up, which might interest you.'

Reynolds said this without a hint of sarcasm. He half-hoped she was about to offer him a redundancy deal that was too good to turn down.

'I see you got pulled in on a job with Europol.'

'A joint people-trafficking raid in Belgium, Ma'am.'

'Good. I'll put "has experience working with teams across Europe,"' Reynolds said.

It was a slight exaggeration, but he wasn't about to contradict her.

'We've had one of their experts in counterterrorism on secondment. Now it's our turn to return the favour. You speak Italian, don't you? The Italian police need help with a case.'

'Can I just stop you there, Ma'am. I haven't spoken a word of Italian for ten years.'

'Don't worry, you'll soon get back into the swing of it. I've told them you'll be there by next Wednesday. Pack for three months. That's when the money runs out.'

Three months—and the rest. In all the time he had served on the force not one case had been wrapped up in less than six.

'But I'm getting married in July.'

'You'll have to reschedule. And if you can't, they've got churches in Italy. By then you'll be due a weekend off.'

'We've booked the reception, and paid—at least her father has. He hates me enough as it is. This is going to send him ballistic.' And Ginny, he thought.

'Tell him to claim on the insurance,' she said, barely looking up from her paperwork. 'If you wanted to play happy families, why did you join the Metropolitan Police, Connor?'

Stephen's gaze landed on a small, framed photo Reynolds kept on her desk. It showed a Detective Sergeant, the same rank as him, wearing a uniform long out of date. He'd heard rumours around the canteen about this young officer who had taken a bullet meant for her during an armed siege.

'How are you going to afford a wedding if you don't have a job?'

'You were going to have me suspended last time we met.'

'If it was up to me I would have done.'

He drew in a sharp intake of breath. Reynolds didn't mince her words.

'The only reason I didn't was because the PR department sent a photo of you receiving that bravery award from the Prime Minister to every bloody school kid who expressed an interest in joining the Met.' Reynolds sighed. 'This isn't personal. I've been ordered to axe thirty per cent of my staff, just so the new Home Secretary can put officers back on the beat that her predecessor sacked.'

'If I don't take this job I'm going to be selected for redundancy?'

'Help me out here, Connor. Who else can I send? I don't have any spare coppers, let alone Italian speakers. Here's the personnel spec if you're interested.' Reynolds slid the document towards him.

Stephen read the top line: Native English speaker to assist the carabinieri in an undercover operation to retrieve stolen art and antiquities.

'There's another reason I can't do this,' he said, looking up. 'My girlfriend works at an auction house. She sells antiquities. It's a bit too close to home.'

'Then you'll have something to talk about on your honeymoon, won't you? There's more to this case than a few broken pots so it should keep you occupied.'

'And I would report to?'

'The Italian art unit officially. But it depends on what you find out. If the case turns out to be bigger than art looting, then the other agencies will want to know.'

'And when there's a conflict of interest?'

'You'll have to make that call. Play your cards close to your chest.' Reynolds leaned back in her chair and looked directly at him. 'You're good at thinking on your feet. Why do you think I picked you?'

All that stuff about Italian speakers and having no one else to send was a smokescreen. After his last big international case, Reynolds had told him that mavericks like him were more of a hindrance than a help in modern police forces and that she'd be glad to see the back of him. Yet all of a sudden, she was putting him forward for another one. He read on: Surveillance experience. Well, yes, but he wasn't able to do that alone—he relied on his unofficial IT help-desk, his mate Tariq, for advice.

But what he was most afraid of wasn't work related. It was how the hell he was going to tell Ginny. It wouldn't matter which angle he came at it from—she was going to be mad at him.

'I'll let you know by Monday.'

'I know you'll make the right decision. Here's the rest of the briefing documents. My neck's on the block as well as yours, so don't screw up, will you, Connor?'

He gathered the papers and his dignity and took a deep breath. It was going to be a long week.

'I'll do my best not to, Ma'am.'

As he was about to step out the door, Reynolds looked up from her desk.

'One more thing, Connor. I had a call from the Australian Federal Police this morning. They've found clothing and personal items belonging to that missing eco-terrorist.'

'Activist,' he muttered, the colour draining from his face.

'No forensic evidence. But they're calling off the

search, winding down the case and they've taken her off the wanted list.'

'Very good Ma'am. Thanks for letting me know.'

He walked out of the office in a trance and had no memory of getting back to his desk and sitting down in front of his computer. He heard chairs scraping and muffled laughter as his colleagues gathered round.

'You alright Steve?'

'Where's she sending you?'

'Are you going to be our man in Moscow?'

His phone buzzed. He looked down. Three missed calls from Tariq and a voicemail message. Shit. Tariq must have heard by now. It would be all over social media.

'Steve, you promised me that as soon as you got news about Cara I'd be the first to know. You lied to me, mate.' He sounded deflated. It was uncharacteristic, Stephen thought.

Stephen pressed Return Call: no answer. It went to voicemail. He'd go round there, straight after work. If he was lucky, he'd get out by six.

But by seven that evening he was still at his desk. He'd planned to nip over to Ginny's office at lunchtime to tell her in person, but she was in meetings all day. He'd left a phone message but immediately regretted it. She'd been on his case about the job offer in a series of increasingly hostile text messages all afternoon. And he'd had to avoid Reynolds for the rest of that day while he tried to decide whether to take the Italian job or chuck the whole thing in.

Stephen tried Tariq one last time and left a message.

'I'm stuck at work. I heard the news this morning when I was hauled into the boss's office ' The phone clicked, and he heard Tariq pick up.

'This morning at eight there was a knock on my door. I

thought it was one of my couriers, but no, it was a journalist from one of the tabloids. She shoved a phone in my face asking if Cara Robertson had worked for me as a courier? I was half asleep, so I garbled that not only had she been one of my best bike riders, but that I'd looked out for her.'

'I didn't know they'd made a statement to the press. I'd have been round at yours like a shot if I had.'

'And then she said, "did I know she was a wanted terrorist in Australia?"'

He'd never heard Tariq this upset.

'It's okay. I'll pull myself together in a minute. Thanks for listening.'

'Go on,' Stephen said.

'I told her that Cara had been set up and that the real culprit had got off scot-free. But she wasn't interested in that.

"Hadn't I heard? The police had found her clothes in the desert. They were winding down the case. Would I like to comment?" And then the photographers let rip. So your mate here is going to be splashed all over the tabloids tomorrow. And you can be sure that woman will come up with some sob story of a pathetic man in a wheelchair, in love with one of his staff, when all we were was good mates.'

His voice lowered to a whisper. 'Cara's dead, isn't she Steve?'

'This is doing my head in, believe me. But the one thing I'm hanging on to is that so far, it's only clothing and personal items.'

Tariq cut in.

'So you're telling me she throws away her clothes because she fancies some new ones? This is Cara we're talking about here—always the first to give us a lecture about the environmental impact of the rag trade.'

'But there's been no…' Stephen struggled to find the right phrasing.

'Body?'

'No actual forensic evidence. I'm not giving up hope. I wanted to come and see you earlier, but there's stuff going on at work.'

'What stuff?' Tariq was grumpy now.

'Reynolds wants to move me on.'

'You got promoted?'

'No. If I agree to it, it's a transfer.'

'Like a football signing then?'

'I wish. No Golden Handshake for me.'

'I hope it's not somewhere out in the sticks.'

'Rome. I have to let the boss know by Monday.'

'What's the missus got to say about that?'

'I haven't been able to talk to her about it properly yet. All I've had is a barrage of angry texts:

"Why can't you stand up to her?" "What's wrong with the word no?" "Why are you letting her walk all over you?"

'It's going to be a yes, though. I can tell by the tone of your voice.'

'I've not made up my mind. I'm sorry about the way you found out about Cara.' He could hear the whirr of Tariq's wheelchair as he moved around his office. Tariq wasn't about to forgive him. He'd always been protective of his couriers. None more so than Cara. Like it or not, he also believed that Stephen hadn't done enough to help her when they were out in Australia.

And now it seemed his best mate didn't want to know about his move to Rome. It was Stephen's turn to be grumpy. 'Better get going. Lots to do.'

'Stay in touch, eh?'

'Maybe you can come visit for a weekend?'

'A wheelchair in Rome? It'd be a nightmare.'

'Think about it,' Stephen said as he hung up.

Chapter 2

One Week Earlier. Northern Territory, Australia

Scrubby trees dotted the landscape. In the distance, a rust-coloured escarpment rose out of the vast flatness. A heat haze shimmered from the roof of an indigo-blue transit van, parked in the middle of the outback.

On the ground a rusty sign proclaimed:

YOU ARE ABOUT TO ENTER A MINING LEASE. THIS AREA CONTAINS SHAFTS AND OTHER MINE WORKINGS. UNAUTHORISED ENTRY IS PROHIBITED.

Abandoned shovels and pick-axes lay rusting across the sandy soil. Nearby, a faded yellow metal hazard sign with a black triangle and a radiation symbol read: Radiation Area. No Camping. Do Not Drink the Water.

Stripped to the waist were two men; the younger of them baby-faced with a hairless chest, mid-twenties but could pass for younger. The other, hirsute and sweaty and a generation older.

'Nothing but sand out here and you had to pick the place that's radioactive?' the pale one said. The sweaty one examined the rusty tools, picked up two shovels and a pick-axe and threw them on the ground in front of the pale one.

'Who's going to look for her out here? Now get digging.'

The pale one sighed. Shovels dug into the soft sand.

Inside the van was a young woman, gamine, her short, cropped hair dripping with sweat. Bound and gagged, her fingers and lips were the only part of her body that could move. Slumped over, barely conscious, she roused at the sound of metal on stone, faint inside the van, but unmistakable. She heaved herself upright to peer through the front windows and saw the two men. One rested on his shovel seeming to look straight at her with a leer on his face. She shrank back and started to breathe rapidly, in shallow, panicked bursts.

She wriggled sideways so she could feel along the van's floor with her fingertips. They touched a metal box, big and bulky. She tried to turn the handle one way. It refused to budge. Then the other. It yielded a millimetre, maybe two. She tried again. One sharp tug and her index finger-nail tore off. But the handle yielded, just as the quick where the nail sat started to bleed.

She felt her way around the toolbox, testing each item. The effort of turning her body sent salty sweat stinging into her eyes. Through the tears she saw a crowbar, pliers, screwdrivers, spanners. And then a mini saw, which she grabbed, then the crowbar, which slipped through her fingers and clattered down beside her. The sound ricocheted around the bare panelling. She froze.

Outside, the two men appeared to hear only their shovels digging ever deeper into the soft ground.

Inside her stifling prison, the temperature over fifty Celsius, the woman adjusted her position, struggling to avoid the metal side panels, the searing heat burning through her thin T-shirt. She started to saw away at the cable ties that bound her, her hands slippery from the blood from her torn nail.

Outside, the pale one stopped digging and threw down his shovel. His skin was now an angry red. He grabbed a plastic water bottle, took a swig, then moved towards the van, the sweat running off his body. He pulled up his shirt and wiped his face with it.

'Hey, we haven't finished yet.'

'Just giving her the rest of this.'

'She won't need that where she's going,' the sweaty one said, pointing at the trench.

'It's better than chucking it. Who knows, I might get lucky.'

His accomplice shook his head, his hair dripping. 'Dirty bastard.'

The desert sunlight caught the chrome handle of the rear doors. The pale one grasped the handle, dropped it and let out a howl. He flicked his hand back and forth and stared at his fingers as the skin started to peel away.

'Bugger!'

The young woman's eyes darted left and right before she pushed herself towards the back of the van, wrapping the discarded cable ties loosely round her wrists.

Still nursing his injury, the kidnapper opened the back and peered in, his eyes adjusting to the darkness as he crawled in beside her. He flipped the lid of the water bottle, spat in it and pulled the gag off the young woman's mouth.

'Open up,' he said. She looked at him with contempt, but opened her parched, cracked lips and swallowed. 'Now, how about a bit of thanks.' Before he could wipe the smirk off his face, she pulled the crowbar from beside her and lunged at him like a cornered Death Adder. She tugged on the van door to close it, but it wouldn't pull shut.

'Give me the keys.'

The pale one held his hands up, protecting his face.

'Screw you.'

She pulled his trousers and his underwear so hard, he winced and scrabbled around in his pocket, feeling for the car keys. Cutting the ropes binding her ankles with the mini-saw, she crawled on her belly, commando style, to the driver's seat. As soon the key hit the ignition, the van roared into life. The wheels spun in the soft sand.

Outside, the gravedigger dropped his shovel and grabbed his AR-15, disengaging the safety as he aimed at the driver's window.

As the young woman scanned the ground in front of her, willing the van forward, the back door swung open. In her rear-view mirror, she saw her daypack fall out and in the next moment, the face of a killer. He mouthed obscenities at her as she put her foot to the floor. A burst of gunfire, bullets smashing the passenger window, through one side and out the other.

Blown sideways, the young woman held her hands up in front of her face and slammed her head against the side of the van. As the blood trickled down her temple, she pulled herself upright, shoved the vehicle into drive and gunned the motor.

The young woman crouched over the steering wheel, her eyes scanning the landscape for tyre marks; a track, or any sign of human habitation. Looking out over the vast emptiness towards the horizon, she saw a faint trail in the distance.

With one hand on the wheel, the young woman reached underneath her T-shirt and pulled out a pouch, slung around her neck. She glanced down to see that tucked inside was her burgundy-coloured passport.

Seizing his moment, her assailant crept up behind her on his knees, bleeding from his gums where the crowbar struck him. He lunged at her and jammed his forearm under her neck. She fought him off with her left hand and tried to steer with the other. The van lurched drunkenly from side to side. She slammed on the brakes, knocking her attacker sideways. She went for the crowbar next to her and aimed for the side of his head. He recoiled and slumped to the side, barely conscious.

She flicked the switch on the radio. Just static. She pressed the play button on the music system. Thrash metal blared out of the speakers. She turned it off and stared at the nothingness ahead.

In the distance, a large shape moved along the horizon like a mirage. It was a three-truck road train. It tracked ahead, roaring at speed along what must have been the highway. She pulled up before the junction, ran around to the back of the van, dragged the man out and pulled him into a sitting position. She grabbed a water bottle from the cool bag inside the van and threw water on his face. As he came round, he stared at her with hatred in his eyes. She spat in the water bottle and rolled it just out of his reach.

She made a run for it and jumped back into the van. As she wound the windows up, the thug at the side of the road screamed after her.

'You bitch. When I find ya, I'll do more than kill ya.'

* * *

Darwin, Australia

With the cash from selling the van and a new haircut and colour, Cara Robertson walked down to the waterfront and started asking around amongst the yacht skippers.

'Need any crew?'

'Where you headed?'

'Indonesia,' Cara said in her best New Zealand accent.

'We're going to Bali in a week. That do you?' Cara shook her head.

'I need to get there quicker than that,' she said.

'Try the fishermen. They might take you.'

'Thanks.'

She walked away from the yacht moorings to the commercial end of the harbour where the fishing boats were tied up. A man padded around his boat and glanced up as she headed towards him.

'Any chance of a lift to Kupang in West Timor?' Cara said.

The man looked her up and down, taking in her petite frame and slim shape.

'Why does a nice Kiwi girl like you want to go there?' he said, winking at her.

'I'm an aid worker.'

'Sure you are. What's your name?'

'Natalie,' Cara said.

'Not the sort of name an aid worker would have.' He gave her the once over again.

'What name would you prefer I had then?'

'I didn't say I didn't like it. It sounds more like a singer or an actress, that's all. Natalie Wood, she was a looker. I'll take you as far as Timor for a thousand dollars. Five hundred if you're, you know, nice to me. If you catch my drift.'

'That's not the only thing I'll catch by the sound of it,' Cara said, looking the lech up and down. 'I'll try somewhere else.'

* * *

Megalong Roadhouse, Western Australia

Sitting at a table, the two kidnappers nursed their beers. The hirsute one lowered his voice.

'I told the boss it was all good, okay?'

The younger one sported a bruiser of a black eye.

'He's going to kill us when he finds out that the mad bitch is still out there,' the pale one said, spilling his beer.

'I threw her stuff on the ground, made it look like there'd been a struggle. Then took a photo of that and the grave and sent it to him.'

'He didn't ask to see a body then?'

'Nah. Some guy in a suit on the other side of the world. You could tell him she was dragged away by a Tasmanian tiger and he wouldn't know any different.'

'You'd better be right,' the pale one said, eyes darting around the bar, looking for anyone who might have been listening. The truth was nobody seemed to be taking any notice of them: they were more interested in the cricket on the big screen TV and the droning commentary.

'If we keep our shit together we'll be good. The cops will close down the case. Another lone female tourist, dumb enough to go walkabout.'

Chapter 3

The present. Rome, Italy

Stephen had looked at his phone and willed it to ring. Nothing. The moment he'd decided to punch in Ginny's number, his taxi had gone into the Heathrow road tunnel as a jet was taking off. By the time the scream of the engines had subsided, she'd hung up.

As he suspected, Ginny had taken the news of his hasty departure badly and avoided him the entire week. She wasn't there this morning when he packed and left. There hadn't even been a falling out: the worst of it was that there hadn't been anything.

He'd vowed that as soon as the plane took off, he'd push all thoughts of Ginny aside. But as the wheels hit the tarmac at Fiumicino, pinpricks of tears welled up in his eyes. He made his way through passport control like an automaton.

Stephen pushed a luggage trolley loaded with his bags out into the arrivals area. His name was on a placard, held up by a taxi driver. He hadn't expected to be picked up from the airport. As he made his way towards the driver, his phone buzzed. Anxiety welled up inside him. But it wasn't Ginny, it was a text from his new colleague, Elisabetta di Mascio. He struggled to decipher it. His Italian was rustier than he thought. From what he could make out, the driver was going to take him straight to the office. Elisabetta wanted to talk to him about researching auctions. Did that word mean "auction"?

No time to get his feet under the desk then. Talk about being thrown in at the deep end. There would be a hell of a lot to absorb in an afternoon. New city, new force, new crime, in a language he hadn't spoken in years. He just hoped he was up to the job.

A uniformed receptionist ushered Stephen into the office of the Carabinieri for the Protection of Cultural Heritage and handed him a sheaf of paperwork. He was going to need help translating. It looked like standard HR stuff, red tape he'd have to wade through. Was he expected to fill out all these forms now?

He hated asking, but he didn't know whether they were soft or hard on rules here. Hell, he didn't even know the correct way to greet the woman in the next door office, who was standing while talking on the phone, deep in conversation. She had dark brown hair scraped neatly on the top of her head, medium height, athletic build, late thirties, early forties. He guessed she was Elisabetta or Lieutenant di Mascio. Which one was it?

Just as he was deliberating whether to wait for her to get off the phone or go to collect his ID and entry pass, she popped her head around the door.

'Stephen, come on in,' she said in English, in a broad Australian accent.

Before he'd had a chance to reply she held out her hand, 'Elisabetta.'

Stephen greeted her in Italian. Her grasp was firm and business-like.

'Bravo. Your Italian's pretty good.'

'It's the reading and writing I struggle with.'

Elisabetta glanced down at the forms in Stephen's hand and groaned.

'We don't have time for that now. I'll get someone to help you.' She looked at her watch. 'Except they finish early today.'

'We call them jobsworths back home,' Stephen said.

'Jobsworths,' she repeated, a puzzled look on her face. 'Wowsers, that's what we called them in Melbourne.'

Before he'd had a chance to reply, she ushered him into her office. 'Before I forget, these are the keys and the details of your serviced apartment. It's fifteen minutes from here. Not that I expect you to walk there with all your luggage.' She broke off and looked around.

'I left it at the front desk.'

'I'll try not to keep you too late. To give you a chance to settle in.'

'Thanks. It's more important that I get up to speed on the case.'

Elisabetta nodded and switched into full work mode, before Stephen had a chance to draw a breath.

'That was my contact in Traffic. They've found evidence at the scene of a fatal that might be relevant to our investigation,' she said, perching on the edge of her desk and offering Stephen her chair. 'I'm waiting to get more details.'

The phone barely rang before she picked up.

'Lieutenant di Mascio,' Elisabetta said, switching into Italian. Stephen leaned forward in his seat, worrying he wouldn't be able to keep up with the speed of the conversation.

'Superintendent Costa's office,' said a booming voice. Elisabetta tapped the button for the speakerphone. It hardly seemed necessary. 'The boss wants you to take a look at some photos,' the caller went on.

'What's in these photos?'

'Vases. Statues. Knick knacks. The kind of stuff rich people stick on their patios.'

'Any intel on the driver?'

'Antonio Sanzio, known as Tony. Small-time crook. Fencing mainly. And a former cop in the Guardia di Finanza.'

'Hang on a second, will you.' Elisabetta pressed mute on her phone and turned to Stephen.

'That's the financial crimes unit. They had a purge of corrupt officers after it was infiltrated by organised crime. Our dead driver might have been part of the clear out.'

Did she expect him to keep up with the events as they were happening and read the case notes later? Was that how she operated?

'Has the cause of the crash been determined yet?' Stephen asked, hoping this would give him some breathing space.

Elisabetta shook her head. She took her finger off the mute button and ploughed on. 'Carry on, officer,' she said.

'The photos are old-school Polaroids.'

'Scan them to me first.'

'On their way.'

'Stay on the line, will you?'

Stephen adjusted his chair to get a better view of the computer monitor. Elisabetta leant over and clicked open the first attachment. It showed dirty and broken pottery, covered in soil, smashed into a dozen pieces, each one roughly the size of a man's hand. As she clicked through the remaining photos, there were images of what looked like a lion, and then a winged figure with the head of a woman attached to a lion's body. Elisabetta clicked back to the first picture of the broken pottery.

'What background colour would you say those broken pieces are?'

Stephen peered at the screen. 'Sort of clay coloured, but they're covered in earth, so it's hard to tell.'

Elisabetta clicked in for a close-up. She did a double-take.

'What is it?' Stephen asked.

'Look here.' Elisabetta pointed to a fragment that appeared to be two-tone. 'What's different about that one?'

'The colour. The background's black and the engraving's a dirty red,' Stephen said, hoping he'd got it right.

She perched on the edge of her seat. 'Let's compare them with mass-produced ones.' She opened up another window on her screen of a garden centre and clicked on a link to the factory-made pots.

'What about these?'

'The decoration on each one is identical and they're all the same size,' Stephen said.

'Go on.'

'The one at the crash site has been glazed and painted. You can see the black there, and the drawing seems to be in a shade of um, clay.' *There was a technical name for that tone, but Jesus, Mary and Joseph, what was it?* 'Terracotta?'

'You're right. It's "red figure" vase painting as opposed to "black figure". Anything else?' Elisabetta asked.

Stephen hesitated. He peered at the photos again. 'It's as though the vase is telling a story. And that each painted section is like a scene.'

The contact at Traffic interrupted. 'Lieutenant di

Mascio, I've got another call coming in. Do you want me to send the rest of these photos over?'

'Yes, please,' Elisabetta said. She looked up at the clock and turned to Stephen. 'You need to get down to the firing range so that they can issue you with a pistol. Then we can go through the rest of these photos.'

* * *

Stephen was relieved to go and do something physical. Firing a weapon at a target was easy compared with trying to understand the finer points of ancient Greek pottery. By the time he got back from his firearms test it was gone five. As he made his way back to Elisabetta's office, he spotted a man in leathers holding a crash helmet walking into reception carrying a large envelope. Elisabetta strode purposefully towards him, calling out behind her, 'Stephen, take a seat, I'll be right back,' and turning to the courier, 'I think those are for me.'

As he sat down, Stephen noticed a framed photograph of Elisabetta in a karate uniform, at an awards ceremony receiving her black belt, Third Dan.

She walked back into her office with the envelope. She opened it and laid out a series of Polaroid photographs on her desk.

'*Madonna*! Traffic made them sound like patio ornaments. But look at these. It's a treasure trove.'

There were necklaces, brooches, a sculpture of a Roman centurion's costume, as well as a bust of a Roman head. It looked like the collection of an amateur archaeologist with pots and vases in various states of disrepair—some in pieces with earth still on them and others restored.

'You can even see the room the photos were taken in. The table looks like it's in someone's kitchen. That red baize fabric they're displayed on is a tablecloth,' Elisabetta said.

Stephen felt out of his depth. It had been a long day. 'Do you think they're fakes?' he ventured.

'A broken head and that sculpture would be difficult to fake. They look like one-offs,' she said, her jaw dropping as she pulled out the final photograph in the pile. It was distinctly different, a scene in a gallery with someone standing by a backlit display case containing an urn, a whole, undamaged one.

Stephen stood transfixed. The scene depicted in the broken fragments had been fully restored. It was the story of a giant and a warrior, fighting to the death. The drama was played out in front of two terrified onlookers, both women.

'It's the same as the broken one,' Stephen blurted out.

'I know. But it can't be. There is only one krater in existence that tells this particular story.'

Stephen frowned. 'Krater?'

'An urn, used in ancient Greece to dilute wine with water,' Elisabetta said and pointed to the signature: Euphronios. 'That signature belongs to the painter, not the potter. Euphronios was one of a handful of highly sought-after vase painters.' The name didn't mean anything to Stephen, but even in a photograph he could see that the vase was something extraordinary.

'It's one of the finest pieces of painted pottery in all of the ancient world and it's every bit as dramatic as the Sistine Chapel. Here we have Antonio Sanzio standing proudly next to this perfect krater, in a museum in the Vatican. What's he doing there?'

'As though he was the archaeologist who discovered it. And look, there's someone else hiding behind the plinth, trying to get out of the shot,' Stephen said.

'So there is. I'm going to get down to the Vatican Museums before they close. If this confirms what I'm thinking, I'll need a warrant to search the dead guy's apartment.' Elisabetta scribbled down a name and number on a scrap of paper. 'Call them for me, will you? Ask them to hang on until I get there. I'm going to leave you in the hands of a colleague.'

She picked up the phone. 'Pasquale, can you get down to my office and look after Stephen, our new colleague from London. I have to go out. Thanks.' Elisabetta grabbed her keys, phone and the bundle of photographs, and strode towards the exit, issuing a series of instructions. 'I want a digital version of that photo of the two men, something we can zoom in on. And we need to find out who the other person is. Have I forgotten anything? Can you find out if there are any upcoming antiquities auctions across Europe? That's in the file on my desk, as well as the case notes of this current investigation on the table. I'll let you know about the raid on Sanzio's apartment.'

'Tonight?' Stephen called, but Elisabetta had disappeared out the door.

As instructed, he phoned the contact at the Vatican Museums, who was angry at having to wait for Elisabetta to get there.

'Why can't it wait until tomorrow?' he had asked.

'Because it's urgent police business,' Stephen had replied, which had shut the man up. As he waited for Pasquale, Stephen felt his head spinning.

⁂

The security guard on the desk glanced up as a woman hurried through the staff entrance to the Vatican Museums, flashing her carabinieri badge at him. He looked at his watch. It was past 6.00 p.m.

'I can't stay here all night,' he said, crossly.

'Ten minutes is all I'll need. Come with me if you want to make sure I'm out of here on time,' Elisabetta said.

'I wasn't going to let you loose in there on your own.' Elisabetta started to say something but he cut her off, speaking into his walkie-talkie. 'Staff entrance, now.' A second guard appeared. The first guard turned to Elisabetta. 'Let's go.'

Their footsteps echoed as they walked through the deserted galleries.

When they reached the room with ancient Greek pottery on display, the security guard sat down on a bench seat in the middle of the gallery and started playing with his phone.

The krater was on a raised plinth in the centre of the room inside a glass case. Elisabetta photographed it from every angle, concentrating on the broken pieces of pottery and how they had been fused together.

The second security guard was monitoring the CCTV from the staff desk. He pulled out his burner phone from his pocket and made a call. 'We've got an art cop in here.'

'What does he want?' The male voice on the other end of the phone sounded irritated.

'She's only interested in one thing. The big pot in the glass case in room 10. Sending you a photo now.' The guard zoomed in on Elisabetta's face, took a still photo of the monitor and pressed send.

* * *

It was gone seven and Stephen was surviving on adrenaline. There was a knock and Pasquale popped his head around the door. His lank hair and John Lennon glasses reminded Stephen of a student rather than a police officer.

'We're ordering in. Want something?' He passed the menu over.

On the go since early morning, Stephen had managed to down numerous coffees with a few biscotti, but still hadn't eaten anything substantial. 'I'm starving. What's good?'

'They do a great pizza with potato and fontina cheese.'

'I'll try that. And thanks for blowing up the photo.'

'Any luck?'

'The man he's with is wearing a suit and a tie. And if you look here, he's wearing a distinct tie pin.'

Pasquale peered at it.

'You can't see much of his face, just a reflection. I'll try the Europol database to see if they can get anything from it. If Tie Pin Man has been arrested or has a criminal record there'll be a mugshot. You never know.'

'Thanks,' Stephen said. 'I appreciate it.'

'I'll give you a shout when the food arrives.'

Stephen had gone as far as he could on this one tonight. He'd see if Elisabetta could throw any light on it tomorrow.

'What else have you got?' Stephen asked.

'The messages and call log on Sanzio's mobile. Here, listen to this.' Pasquale pressed the message button in the local memory.

'We're down here doing your dirty work, Tony, and we want our money. Don't give us any of your usual bullshit.' Stephen struggled to understand the accent.

'That was left half an hour before the crash. If I can track the caller, we'll know where Sanzio was headed that day,' Pasquale said.

'You recognise the accent?'

'Naples.'

'Thanks Pasquale. Keep working on it.'

'I'll let you know,' Pasquale said with a shrug. If he read his body language right, Stephen wasn't high on his new colleague's list of priorities. He'd have to earn his respect first.

He turned his attention to the police report of the fatal car accident. As he typed in the name Antonio Sanzio on the police database it brought up a string of convictions. There were bent cops, and there was Sanzio. From extortion to racketeering, he was in on it.

Stephen skimmed through the notes from the accident report:

"At 2.54 p.m. a grey Peugeot estate, heading in a southerly direction on the Rome to Naples autostrada just south of Monte Cassino hit the crash barrier. Traffic medium to heavy. No adverse road or weather conditions. Sole occupant of car pronounced dead at the scene. The attending officer noted the victim was so heavy it took four people to lift him onto the stretcher. The post-mortem and the vehicle test results will be available in 24 hours."

He was interrupted by an incoming text from Elisabetta.

Back-up for Sanzio search sorted. Go and get settled in to your apartment. Take the morning off to buy whatever you need. I'll see you after lunch.

Stephen grabbed the stack of papers Elisabetta had left him and his bags from reception and fell into the waiting taxi, exhausted.

Chapter 4

As he turned the key to his apartment, Stephen's heart sank. It wasn't so much the size—he'd expected it to be small, and at least this had a bedroom separate from the kitchen and living room. But it was the corporate beige carpet and walls that made him glum. This was never going to be home. He wished now he'd been bolder with Reynolds. Why didn't he just come out with it and tell her he'd consider redundancy for the right offer? Her opinion of him couldn't get much lower.

The next morning Stephen got up early and went for a run in the Borghese gardens. He grabbed a coffee and pastry on the way back and to kill time until Ikea opened, he took a walk to the nearest supermarket. Elisabetta had given him the morning off to settle in, but the truth was the less time he spent in his apartment the better. It just brought it home how alone he felt. Done by midday, he headed into the office.

He was due to meet Elisabetta in an hour and a half. She'd asked him to research upcoming antiquities auctions. Ginny planned her diary round them. And if the auction was on a Friday, would tack on a weekend away. Last year they'd gone to Liechtenstein. Another time it had been Brussels. Antiquities was a specialist area and there weren't many auction houses left that dealt in them. He had no luck with Sotheby's and Christie's. As he searched Denham's website, he couldn't help but feel like it was an act of treachery.

* * *

The following Tuesday, Stephen walked alongside Elisabetta towards the departure gate.

'What brought you to Italy?' Stephen ventured. He hoped it didn't sound like he was prying.

'One parent wanted sun and surf. The other wanted pasta and ruins. I got caught in the middle,' she shrugged, turning away from him to glance over her shoulder, abruptly ending the small talk.

'We keep our suspicions about the Vatican krater between ourselves, right?'

What did she think he was going to do? Talk to his new colleagues about a hunch they had, with nothing for evidence except photographs?

'Of course. We have to prove it first. No mean feat.'

'Precisely.' Elisabetta's smile was open, even warm. They broke off their conversation when the boarding call was announced and they made their way to the plane. Once they'd sat down, Stephen glanced at the empty seat beside them, before pulling out an envelope and passing it to Elisabetta. It contained the enlarged photo of Sanzio and the reflection of the unidentified man he was with.

'What do you think about that tie pin?'

'Hard to say. He's a member of an exclusive regiment or some religious order?'

Elisabetta looked as worn out as Stephen felt. She pulled out an eye mask and shrank down into her seat, leaving Stephen to read the notes he'd made ahead of the auction.

Once he'd found out that Denham's in Geneva were offering ancient Greek vases for sale, he'd worked quickly. The expensively produced auction catalogue showed off some remarkable pieces. He couldn't even detect where the joins were in the pots. There were beautifully drawn figures around the base, depicting scenes from Greek mythology. But what had struck him most was their remarkable similarity to the restored vases in Antonio Sanzio's amateur-looking photos.

When he'd told Elisabetta that the items were being sold by a company registered in the Cayman Islands, she'd mentioned that one of the reasons he'd been hired was to help them unravel these sorts of complex financial connections.

Either she'd been misinformed about his experience, or Reynolds had talked him up to the Italians. What they seemed to need was a forensic accountant and he certainly wasn't that.

When they touched down at Geneva, Stephen still had his briefing notes on his lap, as well as the auction catalogue with the Denham's logo. He was glad Elisabetta still had her eye mask on and couldn't see his reaction, if the turmoil he felt inside was reflected on his face. He couldn't help but associate the city with Ginny. He tried and failed to push away the memories of the birthday weekend they'd spent there last summer.

As they were taxiing, Elisabetta pulled off her mask and turned to him. 'These are for you,' she said, handing him a clutch of business cards.

His cover was Stephen Walsh, relationship manager for a boutique art insurer.

'Sounds suitably vague,' Stephen said.

'No-one's going to ask for a quote. But if they do, we've got it covered. Here's your phone,' she continued in a low voice. 'There's a messaging service should anyone call the company.'

Pulling up to the gate, Stephen switched his own mobile on. No message from Ginny, then. But Pasquale had sent a text:

The voicemail on Sanzio's phone was left by a Geppo Corri, a small-time thief and petty criminal.

Stephen texted back: *Can we track him?*

I'll see what I can do. No luck with a match for Tie Pin Man's face by the way.

It would have been a stroke of luck if the technology had been able to identify the mystery man so early in the case, he thought as he shoved his phone back into his pocket. As they walked down the concourse he glanced back at the other passengers. A mixture of business types and tourists, he guessed from their attire. He noticed a middle-aged man, phone glued to his ear in one hand, dark blue overcoat slung over his other arm. The man glanced at Elisabetta. Stephen wondered if they knew each other.

As they walked up the elegant steps to the auction house, Stephen was overawed by the plush surroundings. He tried to push aside the feeling that he was a gauche outsider pretending to be at ease. This was Ginny's world, not his. There would be people here who she would know, if not in person then by reputation.

Elisabetta, catalogue in hand, turned to Stephen. 'The two lots we're interested in are quite far down the list but we can view them first. I'll meet you at the Greek pottery at quarter past, down on the next floor. You might want to check out the bronze figurines first while I look at the other artefacts.' Stephen nodded. Elisabetta pointed to the items of interest, which she had circled in the catalogue. He remembered seeing similar figures in Sanzio's photos.

Stephen studied his floor-plan. The place was packed. He could barely make his way through the crowd. Now that he was standing cheek-by-jowl he was able to get the measure of who was here: men in well-cut suits with expensive watches, accompanied by toned and tanned women, talking excitedly in a dozen languages. One or two stopped to admire the artworks, but many in the crowd who were milling around appeared to be art tourists, whiling away a couple of hours.

Moving along the exhibits, Stephen spotted Elisabetta's admirer, still hanging on to his coat. Why hadn't he checked it in? It was hot in the room. The space was so tightly packed it was hard to see, but it looked like he was quietly observing an older man, who looked as out of place among the moneyed types and the flunkeys as Stephen felt. He was early-seventies, he guessed, with a few strands of auburn left in his grey hair. He was understated, dressed in what looked like an ensemble from a smart department store: chinos, a sweater, and a jacket but no tie. On closer inspection Stephen saw that he was discreetly holding what looked like an asthma inhaler.

It was difficult to tell from this angle, whether they were being watched, but as the catalogue the scholarly looking man was perusing was in English, he decided to take his chance.

'Are they bronze, the little figures there?'

The man turned to him, his face lighting up.

'Yes, I believe they are.' It was from the way he ran the "they" and the "are" together so it sounded to the untrained ear that he was saying a soft "d" where the "th" should be, that Stephen guessed West Cork. It was faint but still audible, despite being overlaid by a strong accent from the east coast of the United States. Stephen shook the man's hand.

'Stephen Walsh.'

'Michael McCarthy.'

'You can take the boy out of Cork…' Stephen said.

'But yours is a sophisticated city accent, whereas mine, well, it comes from the countryside, let's put it like that.'

'I'd recognise it anywhere,' Stephen said.

'When I've spent the best part of thirty years trying to lose it?'

'It follows you round, doesn't it?' Both of them nodded. Stephen seized his chance. 'Are you here to bid?'

'Alas, my interest is purely academic. I've done a few art history courses, but I'm very much an amateur collector. Now and again I get lucky at car boot sales and markets. I love these little pieces. The Greeks used them as offerings. To thank the gods for granting them a wish.'

'What kind of a wish?' Stephen said, trying his best to keep the conversation going.

'The pragmatic kind. Healing a sick relative, that sort of thing. And you, do you have a particular interest?'

'I've just started a new job. I'm trying to learn as much as I can before anyone finds out that I know so little.' Stephen pulled out his business card. 'You live locally?' Stephen said.

'No, Rome.' Maybe he had time on his hands? Stephen tried not to look too curious, but that hadn't worked.

'I come to auctions for the chance to see rare works of art.' McCarthy examined Stephen's business card. 'The burden of having a modest collection like mine is that it's rarely worth insuring. Still, I know where you are,' he said, before putting the card away in his pocket and fishing out his own.

Elisabetta had been astute in choosing his cover. Insurance wasn't exactly a conversation starter.

Stephen turned his attention instead to McCarthy's card. He'd guessed retired academic. But his title— Monsignor as well as the address in Rome made sense to him now. He struggled to remember the ecclesiastical hierarchy from his distant Catholic past. Monsignor was only one down from a cardinal. And a cardinal was a Prince of the Catholic Church, nominated by the Pope.

Without missing a beat, Stephen said, 'I've recently relocated. It's vast, Rome, isn't it?'

'I still get lost.'

'Once I've done my crash course in the art history sites, I'll be able to show you round,' Stephen joked.

'Interested in classical or Renaissance?' McCarthy said.

'Both.'

'Then we must meet.'

Was Stephen meant to reply that he would like that, but then never follow through? He didn't know anyone in Rome. What was the harm? And the man must have known something about art, more perhaps than he was letting on, if he was prepared to travel all the way from Rome to Geneva to attend an auction, when there was enough art on public display in Italy to satisfy the most ardent art enthusiast. What was it, he wondered that attracted someone to rare and beautiful objects that would most likely end up locked away in some rich person's private collection?

'And I can buy you lunch so that you can show me where to eat,' Stephen said.

'As long as you aren't expecting gourmet food.' McCarthy's response had been warm enough.

'Good, I'll call you.' Stephen's phone vibrated in his pocket and he excused himself.

It was a text from Elisabetta:

They just announced our lots have been withdrawn. I had my suspicions—they weren't on display.

Time to get out of here. Stephen texted back: *I'll be out the front.*

He slipped the phone back into his pocket and walked casually over to the Greek pottery. Elisabetta had been right. Instead of the advertised pots, there were two empty glass cases, photographs and a note where the items were meant to be. He stopped to look at the photos. In the reflection, there was a flash of dark blue—a raincoat slung over an arm. Him again. The way the man swept past him reminded Stephen of the time he'd gone to Fortnum & Mason looking scruffy, to buy Ginny a present and he'd been followed by a store detective.

He turned away to look at another display case containing pots. They were decorated with what looked like the letters from the Greek alphabet, a similar form and shape to the letters in the photograph of the tie-pin. He got out his phone and took a couple of photos before heading off to meet up with Elisabetta.

'What happened?'

'A delivery problem is all they would say.'

'Someone's keeping tabs on us. I just saw the same guy who was sitting two seats back from us on the plane.'

'People have flown from all over Europe to come to this,' Elisabetta said, shutting him down. Just then her phone rang. She pulled a face, and answered it, holding the phone close to her ear. When she finished her call she hailed the first available taxi. Stephen had to sprint to catch up with her.

'That was the boss. He's not happy,' she explained as

they jumped into the taxi. 'He wants to see us. To the airport please, driver.'

The taxi sped off.

* * *

Geneva, Switzerland

Michael McCarthy was walking out of the auction house when a tall, grey-haired man pushed past him. McCarthy's instinct was to keep walking. He hoped he hadn't been spotted.

'McCarthy, what brings you here? Something in the catalogue I missed?' The man was so loud.

McCarthy spun round and acted surprised to see Robert Hurst looking down at him. How long had it been since they'd seen each other now? Six months?

'A tourist trip, here to take in the scenery, mainly,' McCarthy said, gesturing to the backdrop of mountains and Lake Geneva shimmering in the sparkling sunshine.

'I'm only sorry we couldn't have carried on working together,' Hurst offered.

'You're still there?' McCarthy had asked the question, despite knowing the answer.

'They love their meetings don't they? Getting approval to acquire anything these days seems to entail tons of them. Not how I like to work at all. No wonder you decided to call it a day. Next time you're in town give me some notice. I'm sure Maris would love to meet you. She was a big fan of the museum. Still is. If you'll excuse me, I have a plane to catch.' And with that, McCarthy was dismissed.

He watched as Hurst got into a black Range Rover,

engine running. Behind the wheel was a woman, Hurst's age, her face in a tight knot. If she was Maris Hurst, she didn't look like the sort who would love to meet anybody.

* * *

Stephen and Elisabetta were walking across a pedestrian crossing outside Geneva airport, after their taxi driver had dropped them at the wrong terminal, when a Range Rover, with headlights on full beam, hurtled towards them, its engine roaring.

'What the?' Stephen said, pushing Elisabetta so hard, she sprawled onto the pavement, leaving him stuck in the middle of the crossing. He felt the impact as the vehicle clipped his hip. Limping, he tried to give chase on foot, but fell to his knees before he got very far. The Range Rover disappeared into the distance. As Elisabetta came rushing up to him, Stephen called out.

'I didn't get the number.'

'Me neither. Reflective plates.'

'Let's pull the CCTV,' Stephen said.

'Let's get you seen to by a paramedic first. You're bleeding,' Elisabetta said.

'I'll be fine. I want to go and talk to security.'

'There's no point. Those reflective plates don't show on CCTV.'

Stephen fretted as he limped off to first aid. 'Whoever was behind the wheel of that Range Rover knew we were here.'

Chapter 5

Rome, Italy

Stephen winced every time they hit an air pocket on the flight back to Rome. Landing had been excruciating and he struggled to walk off the plane unassisted. Elisabetta insisted he go to Accident and Emergency. 'What about Alberti?' Stephen said.

'I'll deal with him,' she said firmly. 'See you tomorrow.'

There seemed little point in arguing with her. And if hospital waiting times were as long as they were back home, it wouldn't be worth going in to work. It took two hours to get through triage. And another two before he saw a doctor. Apart from a surface wound that needed cleaning up and a vivid purple bruise down one side, he would live. They sent him on his way with a prescription for painkillers. By the time he got back to the apartment, it was after six. He rang Elisabetta.

'What did Alberti say?'

'Nothing yet. He wants to see us both tomorrow. '

The following morning, Stephen did his best to get out of the way as Elisabetta's boss, Superintendent Alberti, strutted around, waiting for her to get off the phone.

He caught Alberti looking over his shoulder as he got on with sifting through the evidence bags found at Tony Sanzio's apartment. He felt sorry for Elisabetta. At least his boss at the Met hadn't been a micro-manager.

There was a receipt from a garage in Switzerland. He glanced down at it. It was for a replacement tyre. He'd been about to put it back into the evidence bag, when he got a call from traffic.

'The vehicle report on the grey Peugeot estate you asked for is ready. Sending it over to you now.'

'Thanks,' Stephen said. He clicked on the link and skimmed through the report. There were white paint scrapes on Sanzio's Peugeot suggesting he'd been side-swiped by a white car. A witness reported seeing a white Fiat that failed to stop at the crash scene. Was it worth trying to find the driver? The Peugeot's tyres weren't balanced and the treads were uneven. One of the four was new. Why replace one and not the rest?

Stephen picked up the phone.

'Lieutenant Connor, carabinieri in Rome. You did a job on a Peugeot estate with Rome plates two weeks ago,' Stephen said. 'I've got an invoice number.'

There was a sharp intake of breath on the other end of the phone.

'That asshole!' the mechanic said. 'He kept moaning about being forced to pay Swiss prices when tyres in Italy cost fifty percent less.'

'Why didn't he wait to get the job done when he got back over the border?'

'He got caught with a bald tyre by the traffic police.

You'd think we were the ones who'd given him the fine, the way he carried on.'

'Okay, thanks. You've been very helpful.' If Sanzio had caused a scene at the garage, the local police who had pulled him over might remember him. He dialled again. There was a delay while the officer on the duty desk pulled up the incident report.

'Yes, Antonio Sanzio was pulled over for routine questioning and became abusive. He refused to tell us what he was doing in Switzerland. We read him the riot act and told him he was welcome to sit in a cell while he cooled off. Grudgingly, he told us he was delivering goods.'

'Did the story stack up? The guy's dead, killed in a fatal.'

'He was a terrible driver. Changing lanes all the time.'

'You tailed him?'

'We wanted to know what he was delivering. This scruffy guy in his muddy and dented ten-year-old Peugeot turns out to be taking antiquities to an auction house.'

'Let me guess. Denham's in Geneva.' Stephen said.

'Correct.' There was a pause on the other end of the phone. 'Something about that guy didn't add up,' the officer observed.

'You're right there. Thanks for your help,' Stephen said and hung up.

While Stephen was trying to figure out what his next move was, Alberti popped his head around the door.

'You first, di Mascio,' he said. Stephen winked at Elisabetta. She raised an eyebrow in reply. They went into conference room and shut the door. It was an old building with poor soundproofing. Alberti talked at Elisabetta, raising his voice until it became a tirade. Stephen couldn't make out what he was saying—he didn't have to. The tone said it all. When Elisabetta finally did get the chance to say her piece, she spoke quietly and deliberately. This seemed to enrage her interlocutor. He started shouting over her and interrupting until something in Elisabetta snapped.

Stephen made out a few of Elisabetta's shouted words and what he heard worried him. It sounded like she was saying something about Alberti being the one who had fobbed Stephen off onto her.

As the din of the argument reached a crescendo, Stephen no longer wanted to listen. He went back to the evidence bags from the raid on Sanzio's apartment when a slip of paper with some scribbled notes on it fell out. On it was a list of names: Don Corleone, The Great Gatsby, the Lawyer, the Sales Rep, the Guardian, the Accountant, the Fixer (with three exclamation marks and a smiley face) and lastly, Nighthawks. Before he had a chance to consider what these names had to do with the case, Alberti strode out of the office and headed for the door. He glared at Stephen, with a face on him the colour of an Atlantic storm. Elisabetta came quietly out of the boardroom and pulled up a chair beside him. She looked drained.

'I thought he wanted to see me,' Stephen said.

'I dealt with it.'

'I'd rather know. I won't be offended.' He was quaking as he said that.

Elisabetta hesitated. 'You sure?' He nodded.

'He asked why we'd gone "gadding off" to Switzer-land, as he put it. Then he proceeded to dismiss my explanation that you'd found those restored pots up for auction. Then he got angrier still that they were pulled from the auction at the last minute. And accused us of wasting money on a wild goose chase.'

'I heard the shouting,' Stephen said. 'If I was in your position, the last thing I'd want is to have to babysit a new colleague.'

'You heard that? You weren't meant to. Sorry. Your Italian's better than I thought.'

There was an awkward moment between them.

'No offence taken,' Stephen lied, trying not to show his feelings.

'As you heard, he barely let me get a word in. He wanted to know why you'd hurt yourself. I told him you'd deliberately put yourself in harm's way on my behalf. And that he should be thanking you for what you did instead of going on about budgets and deadlines.'

Stephen glanced up.

'You said that?'

Elisabetta nodded. 'And I meant it.'

Reynolds didn't want him and neither did Alberti. He really was stuck between a rock and a hard place.

'I owe you one,' she said. 'And that's why I stuck up for you. He even had the gall to ask what would happen if you'd suffered a more serious injury. I don't know why but he's got it in for us. Every cent we spend he's promised to scrutinise. And if we don't get results fast…'

'Let me guess. He'll send me home anyway?' Stephen said.

Elisabetta grinned. 'That pretty much sums it up.'

Maybe coming here had been the right decision after all.

'This might cheer you up.' He slid the receipt from the Swiss garage across to her. 'Our colleagues in the Swiss police pulled Sanzio over for a traffic infringement near Geneva a couple of weeks ago.'

Elisabetta raised her eyebrows one after the other in a so what gesture.

'He wouldn't tell them what he was doing there so they followed him. All the way to Denham's where he was delivering antiquities for a forthcoming auction.'

'Good work,' she said.

"There's something else,' Stephen showed her the hand-written list of names. 'What do you make of it?'

Elisabetta shrugged. 'By the smiley faces and the exclamation mark, it looks like Sanzio was rather pleased with himself.'

'He could be bigging himself up, of course. To make himself appear more influential than he actually is. Or was, rather.'

'I'd rather you pursued the Sanzio connection to the auction house,' Elisabetta said.

'I think it's worth chasing.' Stephen held Elisabetta's gaze. 'And Pasquale has triangulated where the call left on Tony Sanzio's phone came from.'

'Can I listen to it?' Stephen played the recording.

'Play it again?'

The accent was distinct, almost staccato. Stephen struggled to make out the words.

'Pasquale traced the phone to a Geppo Corri. A small-time thief and petty criminal from Naples.'

'Secondigliano to be precise,' Elisabetta said, a frown creasing her forehead.

'Something happen there?' Stephen said quietly.

'Someone close to me got caught in the cross-fire. I'll tell you another time,' she said. 'Let's just say it's a rough part of town.'

'I'm sorry,' Stephen said, awkwardly. It was a platitude, but he didn't know what else to say. 'Corri could be one of the names mentioned in the list. Here,' he pointed. 'He could be the Sales Rep.'

'Or he could be Batman. We need a good reason to justify spending money. Long investigations are expensive. That's what the boss just said.'

Stephen felt the tension.

'We need to be focusing our efforts at the top of the

food chain, not going after the low-hanging fruit.' Elisabetta stabbed the scrap of paper with the nail of her index finger so forcibly, Stephen thought she was going to tear it.

'You get to the general by finding a weakness in the ranks.'

'But these are the spear throwers,' Elisabetta said, sighing.

'You just heard the man. He hasn't been paid. He'll talk for money. And even with the Swiss intel about Sanzio delivering antiquities to the auction house, we don't have any physical evidence of suspect looted items. Corri might be our only chance.'

'I'll give you one week. And you'd better come up with results or Alberti will be on my case.'

'That's what he said?'

'No, but that's what will happen. And I want no part of it. I've got enough to do as it is. Here's the number for the Naples office. They'll put a tail on him.'

Stephen felt elated and terrified at the same time. His fingers trembled as he made the call. They were polite and a little world-weary in Naples when he put in his request. It didn't take long for them to get back to him.

'Geppo Corri has got previous. As a minor,' the officer in Naples said. 'Juvenile detention at fifteen. Breaking and entering, burglary. That's nothing compared with the kind of shit that goes on now in that part of town. What do you want me to do?'

'Follow him. Every time he goes out. And keep me in the loop.'

'Will do. What's the authorisation on that?'

'I'll send it through.' As Stephen put the phone down he realised that this was another department of the Italian police who would know if he messed up. He'd better be right.

Chapter 6

Near Naples, Italy

Paolo wrapped his scarf around his nose and mouth to quell the stench of diesel fumes. As he tried to straighten up, he hit his head on the earth above him. Even his slight, one-metre sixty frame was too big for this dank, fetid burial chamber. The visibility was barely more than half a metre in front of him in the ghostly half-light filtering from his head torch.

He switched off the engine of the mechanical digger. It spluttered to a stop. His fingertips were blistered from the effort of trying to keep hold of it, a machine as wild and unpredictable as a frightened animal; lurching off in one direction, then again in another.

An older, shorter version of him came over to check up on his work.

'Not bad,' Geppo said.

'Not bad? It must be at least twenty square metres,' Paolo grumbled.

'You're not getting extra money, if that's what you're thinking. If you don't like it, you know what you can do.'

'Get another job you mean?' Paolo's tone was bitter. 'Except I can't, thanks to you. If you'd kept your mouth shut about the cheap concrete, we'd both be in work.'

'I didn't have a choice. I owed it to the families. Ten people died on that bridge. And I'd do it again,' Geppo said.

'Do me a favour, Uncle. Next time, think of your own family first. It was you who got us blacklisted from every building site in the city.'

'You were the one who hung around home, smoking weed, getting into fights. I gave you a chance, you cocky little shit. Or did all that skunk give you memory loss? Back to work.'

Paolo shrugged his shoulders, turning his back on his uncle and kept on digging, wiping the sweat off his face.

'Guess how much they made selling that statue of that fit bird we dug up in November?'

Geppo shrugged. 'You're going tell me anyway.'

Paolo raised one eyebrow and gave his uncle a disdainful look.

'A million dollars. And the same for that big vase with the handles. The one they glued together.' Geppo's lips moved, but he couldn't seem to get the words out. He gulped and got a mouthful of dust churned up by the digger, lingering in the still air.

As his uncle started to choke, Paolo pulled the cap off his water bottle and passed the bottle over, but in his haste, managed to spill most of it all.

'Two million dollars? We got 2000 euros for those two jobs.' Geppo could barely get the words out, he was coughing so hard. As the fit subsided, he stared at his nephew.

'How did you find out?'

'The internet, Uncle. You've heard of that, right? Fat Tony better watch out. I'm going to give him so much shit for that,' Paolo bragged.

'Piss Tony off and we'll have no takers for our stuff.'

Listening to Geppo and Paolo's conversation, trying to pick up the odd word of Neapolitan dialect, was a group of young African men, barely out of their teens. Their job was to go over the newly dug ground, touching the surface area, feeling for any dips or mounds. Just at that moment, one of the workers hit the bottom of the tomb with his shovel. It sent out a sharp clang that reverberated around the cave in surround sound.

Geppo squatted down and pressed his hands into the dusty red clay. Paolo gestured to the kid, who passed him the shovel. As the sharp edge hit the ground, there was the unmistakable sound of steel on stone.

'Pick-axe,' Geppo said, pointing. It was passed silently, from one hand to another. Kneeling now on the hard ground, Geppo winced, as his knees made contact with the dry earth and stones. After three sharp blows in quick succession, he started to scrabble with his bare hands. He felt the outline of a large, raised circle. 'If this is what I think it is, payday could be sooner than you think. I hope it's intact, though Tony doesn't seem too bothered if they're in one piece or two halves. Just not too many bits.' A chink of daylight penetrated the dark tomb. 'Damn these summer mornings. I'm not leaving here until we've dug this little beauty out. Get the guys to hide the digger and all the tools in the usual place. And we'll need two of them to carry out that head. It weighs a ton,' Geppo said, pointing to a large carved bust of a man with curly hair and a beard they had dug up the night before. 'I'll take the rest of the stuff.'

'Okay, we'd better hurry,' Paolo said.

Sweat was pouring off Geppo now as he cleared a space around the bottom of the mystery object.

'It's a big one; it must be nearly half a metre wide and the same deep. Tony's going to piss himself when he sees this. But I'm going to need some help to drag it out of here.'

With one mighty tug, Geppo loosened the earth, and as the soil fell away, it revealed an urn, cracked into three pieces. Exhausted from the exertion, Geppo sat down to rest.

'Wrap them separately or they'll break,' Geppo said hoarsely.

'What with?'

'The shirt off your back, you twat.'

Paolo took his shirt off, quickly tore it up and bound the fragments as best he could before bundling them into a sack.

'We need to get the hell out of here,' Paolo said impatiently. Geppo rummaged in his pocket and pulled out a handful of euros.

'Give this to the guard. Stall him for ten minutes. I need to clear up before those museum creeps find out we've been here and come down and seal up the tomb.'

Paolo hurried away, walking as fast as he could through the tunnels, his precious cargo slung over his shoulder.

As he stumbled out into the daylight, temporarily blinded by the brightness, Paolo reached for his money. The Somalis were right behind him. The guard looked at his watch.

'You've gone over by two minutes. No, make that three. An extra ten euros, so you owe me twenty.' He held out his hand expectantly.

Paolo swore under his breath, pulled the crumpled

notes from his pocket and threw them in the guard's general direction and walked away, the sackful of pottery cosy against his back.

* * *

Stephen was back at his desk first thing, when his phone buzzed.

'Lieutenant Renzo Bianconi here from the Naples unit. It's about Corri.' He was off again, before Stephen had the chance to respond. 'We tracked him to the migrant camp where he picked up three Africans in a van at around nine p.m. last night.'

Stephen was playing catch-up, not quite sure that he had understood correctly.

'You think Corri's a people smuggler?'

'No, he's using them for muscle for a job. When he drops them back, what do you want us to do?'

'Where did he take them?' There was an awkward silence on the end of the phone.

'We tailed him as far as Pompeii and then got turned around by the boss for an urgent job. You know how it is.'

They had him and they lost him?

Stephen took a moment. It was pointless getting angry. He needed the guy on side.

'What's in it for the migrants, Bianconi?'

'Renzo. Stephen, isn't it?'

'Yes.'

'They're here with no papers. If we go and lean on them, they're going to co-operate,' Renzo said. 'But it's your call.'

Was he hearing right? His colleague was bragging about blackmailing an asylum seeker into becoming an informer.

'Then what?' Stephen said.

'We tell them to move north to the next country. That they'll have better luck in France or Germany.'

'Do whatever you have to do. See you in a few days,' Stephen said.

'I'm looking forward to meeting you,' Renzo said. He lowered his voice. 'By the way, can you thank your colleague, di Mascio, for putting in a good word for me. I got an interview.'

'Will do,' Stephen said, as he scribbled down the message. As he put the phone down, he reflected for a moment. He'd been so eager to avoid confrontation with a new colleague that he'd allowed him to get away with stand-over tactics. What was he turning into?

* * *

Lieutenant Renzo Bianconi was parked close to the migrant camp in an unmarked car with Police Lieutenant Vittorio Sironi. Renzo, short and muscular, tore into his doughnut in two big gulps. Vittorio, who was taller and leaner, laid out a paper serviette on his lap and nibbled at his pastry while sipping daintily at his coffee.

A burst of static came from the police radio.

'Corri's van on the move, over.'

'Roger that,' Vittorio said, as Geppo Corri's dirty grey van rolled slowly down the street. The van pulled up and three Somali lads jumped out.

Vittorio scattered crumbs all over the seats and then tried to clean up before Renzo snatched the paper bag out of his hand and threw it into the footwell.

Vittorio grabbed his camera and fired off a series of photos of the three men.

Renzo spoke into his microphone, 'Alpha One, paying

our friends at the migrant camp a little visit. Alpha Two, tail Corri.'

'Alpha Two, Roger that. Fiat Ducato in sight.'

Renzo and Vittorio jumped out of the car and started walking purposefully towards the migrant camp.

* * *

Naples, Italy

Paolo slept past midday, got up and turned on the television. When the lunchtime news came on, he muted the sound. He made himself a quick espresso, opened the window and leaned out and lit a cigarette. He glanced back at the TV. On the floor next to it was the looted stone head, decorated with a pair of mirror shades.

There was an old story about a car accident and footage of a grey car that had hit the crash barrier on a motorway. The police were putting out a further appeal for witnesses. None had come forward. He shrugged and turned over to watch Lazio play Roma.

His phone rang. The caller ID was Geppo. He declined it.

He slumped down on a chair and his head lolled from side to side as he dozed off. He was woken by a hammering on the door. Sleepily he opened it to find an agitated Geppo—his forehead creased and his hair wild and straggly.

'What's up with you?'

'Didn't you see the news?'

'Roma lost. So what?'

'I'm not telling you out here where all the neighbours can hear.' Geppo stepped into Paolo's messy apartment.

He caught sight of the stone head with the mirror sunglasses. 'Show some respect. That thing is at least two thousand years old.'

'It was giving me the creeps with those dead-looking eyes. What did you want, Uncle?'

'Tony's dead. In a car crash on the autostrada between Rome and Naples.'

'I saw that. It happened last week.' Paolo said.

'No wonder he didn't return my calls,' Geppo said.

'They could have told us before we dug up all that new stuff.'

'You mean the cops, ringing all of Tony's contacts?'

'Yeah. Why not? He owes us money. Then goes and dies on us. We work for another week with no pay. And now we're stuck with all this gear we dug up for him. How shitty is that?'

'You don't think I hadn't thought of that?' Geppo waved his arms, pacing around the room like a chimp in a too-small enclosure. 'We need to find a safe place to stash the gear. Away from prying eyes.'

Paolo shrugged and glanced around at his cramped apartment.

'Not here. Or at mine. What about your mum's garage?'

Paolo laughed in Geppo's face. 'What about it? She'd know I was up to something. She's your sister. You ask her.'

Geppo deliberated for a moment. 'Here's what we'll do. I'll tell her I need some temporary storage while I'm trying to sell stuff on eBay.'

'It'll cost you.'

'What do you mean it'll cost me?'

'Rent for the garage is fifty euros a week.'

'You cheeky bastard! It's not even yours!'

'Fifty euros to buy my silence,' Paolo said, casually lighting another cigarette.

'I'll be deducting that from your wages you little shit. Or else you can find yourself another job.'

'Suit yourself.'

'Not a word to the guys at the site. It's business as usual, okay?'

Paolo shrugged.

* * *

The following morning Stephen was asleep when the phone rang. He looked at the clock. It was 7.00 a.m.

'Stephen Connor.'

'It's Bianconi in Naples. Sorry for the early call. But you might want to hear this. Geppo Corri has just arranged a meeting at a lock-up garage for midnight tonight.'

'That's an odd time of the night to be doing business.'

'Even for Naples. Do you want to come down for that? The fast train from Rome gets you here in an hour.'

'Sure. I'll ring you when I know which train I'm catching. And thanks.'

Stephen rung off and texted Elisabetta about where he was going, then padded into the kitchen. He dropped two teabags into a cup while he waited for the kettle to boil. It was going to be a long day.

* * *

Stephen arrived at Naples Central Station in the early evening as the light was fading. The place was modern, clean and bustling, with earnest commuters and harassed families making their way past inviting brasseries, but as soon as he left the concourse the atmosphere changed. A well-dressed couple went to help an elderly tourist with his suitcases. A young lad moved swiftly forward and in less than ten seconds had slipped his hand into the unsuspecting traveller's hand luggage and pilfered his credit cards and his wallet.

'Hey, stop thief!' Stephen shouted. As he did so, a hand reached out. A voice from behind him said,

'Stephen?'

Stephen turned around.

'Renzo.' A short, dark and stocky-looking man in his early thirties in leather jacket and jeans went to shake his hand. 'You don't look much like your police mugshot. The car's this way.' As they walked towards the vehicle, Renzo was quiet and matter of fact.

'It might look like an opportunist theft, but it isn't. It's a tried and tested scam run by organised crime gangs. That young kid who grabbed the wallet ripped the cards out and passed those along to the teenage girl with the baby, who gave it to another kid who hopped on a motor scooter. In the time it takes to make a phone call, they'll have spent two thousand dollars on the credit cards in stores in on the scam. Welcome to Naples.'

The culture shock Stephen felt on arrival in Rome was nothing compared with Naples. Rome seemed like London now, with its wealth and high culture, whereas Naples felt like Liverpool—charming and friendly people who radiated a cheerful energy, in a city with an astonishing amount of poverty and a criminal underclass. Everything that had just gone on had been recorded on CCTV, yet the brazen way the gang had gone about its business took him by surprise. 'We're round the corner,' Renzo said, glancing around.

'How did it go with the guys down at the migrant

camp?' Stephen asked as they passed stall after stall of counterfeit goods, which seemed to be manned exclusively by teenage boys of African descent, who were packing up for the evening.

'They know the score: inform on Corri or end up working for the mob,' Renzo said, indicating the wretched kids who were trying but failing to entice them to buy a selfie-stick.

Thirty metres away was what looked like a surveillance van, with its engine running.

'I haven't told any of them here yet, but I've been offered that job. And I'm going to take it,' Renzo said.

'Understood.' Stephen wondered if Alberti had hired him, as Elisabetta hadn't mentioned it. Did she even know? 'Congratulations.'

'Thanks.'

As they got closer to the van, there was another officer sitting in the driver's seat.

'Hop in,' Renzo said.

Stephen slid into the middle next to the driver, who held out his hand and introduced himself as Vittorio.

'We've got some time to kill before Corri's meeting,' Renzo turned to Stephen. 'How about we go and get something to eat?'

'Fine by me.'

They were tucking in to bowls of pasta less than twenty minutes later when they got a call from the officer monitoring Corri's phone.

'Corri's contact now wants to meet at quarter to eight.'

'Okay, we're on it,' Renzo said, finishing off a mouthful of pasta, pulling out some notes from his wallet and leaving them on the table. 'Let's go.'

* * *

The back of the surveillance van was hot and uncomfortable. Half-eaten chocolate bars and empty coffee cups lay strewn on the floor. Cables of various colours snaked towards a large silver box, the size and shape of an amplifier.

Connected to that was a laptop, where Vittorio, wearing headphones, stared at the screen.

It was the waiting around Stephen disliked the most. His only job was to pick up the camera with the telephoto lens as soon as Corri showed up. They were parked up with the lights off down a side street. To any passer-by it looked like a trade van locked up for the night.

'It's him,' Renzo said.

Stephen grabbed the camera as Corri's van pulled up outside a set of run-down lock up garages, spray-painted with graffiti lit by a forlorn-looking street light, its yellow sulphurous glow casting eerie shadows.

Corri waited inside the van with his sidelights on. The sound of an approaching car triggered him to get out and make his way towards the roller door of a single-car garage.

As he unlocked it, a short barrel-chested man with tousled dark hair approached him. Corri opened up the roller door and switched on the light. He jumped back and seemed to yell something, as though he'd got an electric shock. It was empty, apart from a single plastic box sitting forlornly in the corner. He picked up the box and pulled out its contents.

It was hard to see what was inside. Stephen focused his telephoto lens on what appeared to be ornaments and jewellery. He fired off a series of pictures.

The buyer seemed angry and stalked off, jumping into his car and driving away, leaving the unfortunate Corri with his head in his hands, rocking from side to side.

'Oh shit.' Stephen looked at his fellow officers.

'Shit is right,' Renzo said. 'Looks like he's been cleaned out.'

'Except for that box of ornaments. Probably because they're not worth much,' Vittorio said.

Stephen's heart pumped a little faster. He'd zoomed right in on the items stashed in the bag, hadn't he? Some of the shots he'd taken had to be in focus.

'I got close ups. Here, look.' Stephen tried to keep his hands steady as he viewed the images of a series of figurines in various poses. He handed the camera to Renzo first, then Vittorio.

'They're the kind of thing you'd see on a mantelpiece,' Renzo said. 'Or maybe in a glass case in a museum.'

'Or at an auction,' Stephen said. 'I'd swear I saw identical pieces to these on sale in Switzerland.' He remembered his conversation with the retired priest about similar-looking pieces. What was his name again? He had his card somewhere. As he was about to rifle through his wallet to find the business card, Renzo whose turn it was to photograph the suspect, pointed the camera through the glass of the van window towards Corri. He motioned to Stephen.

'Looks like he's making a call.'

Vittorio switched on the speakerphone.

'Paolo you little shit. We've been robbed. Who the hell did you tell?' Stephen struggled to understand the broad dialect, but got the gist of his outburst.

'Uncle, don't get mad. Mum changed her mind. I was in the middle of calling you when you rang. I had to move the stuff out of there.'

Stephen signalled Renzo.

'What did he say?'

'His nephew is trying to cover his arse.'

There was a crackle, and the connection failed.

'Shit. Loose connection, sorry,' Renzo said, jamming the wire into the machine.

'I've just been down here with a buyer who was willing to take the lot, no questions asked. You've screwed that up,' Geppo said.

'Don't blame me, she's your bloody sister,' Paolo shouted.

'Where is everything?' Geppo said.

'My apartment. I tried calling you. You didn't pick up.'

'Your apartment? Where anyone can see who's coming and going?'

'I did it in the middle of the night. The Somali guys helped me.'

Renzo turned to the others.

'They kept quiet about that one. We need to get back down to that camp first thing. Tell them that we mean business,' Renzo said. 'I gave them a burner phone. Every time Geppo hired them they were told to let me know.'

Stephen felt alarmed. He wanted no part in roughing up teenagers.

'Maybe there was a misunderstanding. It was the nephew who hired them, right?' Stephen said.

'So what?' Renzo's tone was aggressive.

Vittorio put his hand up to shush the argument.

'Keep it down will you, I can't hear them.'

'And don't worry, nothing got broken that wasn't in bits already,' Paolo continued.

'Paolo you idiot! You'd better make sure nobody saw you. And that those guys didn't steal anything.'

'Why would they do that when I'm paying them good money to guard the stuff? They're taking it in turns to do eight-hour shifts, so we have round the clock security,' Paolo said.

'What are you paying them with? Fake Rolexes? Tony

was meant to pay us, and he never did, remember,' Geppo said. 'And until the new Tony makes contact, we haven't got any money.'

'You got a better plan, Uncle?'

'Thanks to you screwing up that deal with the trader, I'll have to sell the smaller items online.'

'Good luck with setting up that stealth eBay account,' Paolo said with youthful superiority.

'I'll be there in twenty minutes,' Geppo said, sheepishly, before hanging up.

Renzo looked at Stephen expectantly. 'What do you want to do? If we follow him to the nephew's, you can get a search warrant to raid the apartment.'

Elisabetta had been adamant. She wasn't interested in the low-hanging fruit, but Corri was their only lead so far. It was too early to bring him in. Better to watch and wait, especially if the new Tony showed up.

'Stand the surveillance down and keep tracking his phone and monitoring the calls. And pay another visit to our informers.'

'Okay boss.'

'I'll keep tabs on eBay, ready to bid, the moment Corri lists his items. If anyone new makes contact to arrange to pay Corri or to meet him, call me,' Stephen said.

He looked at his watch. If he was lucky, he'd get the 8.45 p.m. train.

'Any chance of a lift back to the station?'

'I can't. I've got a kid,' Renzo said.

'We've all got somewhere to get to,' Vittorio snapped. 'I'll take you.'

Stephen hadn't noticed it before but there was definitely an air of hostility between the two of them.

'Drop me off first, will you,' Renzo said. 'Here will do.'

'Suit yourself. I could take you to the door.' Vittorio

drove fast and braked suddenly. 'Thanks,' Renzo said, glaring at him. He walked off towards a row of bars and cheap restaurants.

'So much for getting back to the wife and kid,' Vittorio observed.

'What's up with him do you think?' Stephen said.

'Trouble at home by the sounds of it. His partner's nagging him, wanting a bigger apartment. It comes down to money. He was talking about asking for a transfer up to Rome. They're better paid up there.'

'Ah that makes sense. I think he got an interview,' Stephen said, keen not to get involved.

'If he gets it, we'll all breathe a sigh of relief down here. Then he'll be your problem. Here you go,' Vittorio said, as he pulled up.

Those two really don't like each other, Stephen thought, as they arrived back at the station.

On the train back to Rome, Stephen reached into his wallet and pulled out the business card belonging to the retired priest. Monsignor Michael McCarthy, that was it, the self-described amateur collector of the exact same figurines that Geppo Corri was trying to offload. Or, at least that's what they appeared to be to his untrained eye. Maybe McCarthy could set him straight on whether they were fake or the real thing. He turned the business card over. I wonder, he mused, then thinking better of it, he slipped the card back into his wallet. Had he seen something of a kindred spirit in the priest from his homeland, that he was prepared to trust him, without knowing anything about the man? He pushed the thought away.

Chapter 7

Naples, Italy

Renzo, a beanie pulled low over his ears, sat on a barstool, huddled in front of a slot machine. He picked up his ticket for 200 euros and went up to the cashier.

'Another 200 please.' The woman looked him up and down and shook her head.

'You're at the end of your credit.'

He pulled out what he thought was his credit card from his wallet. The cashier glanced down and saw that it was a police ID.

'Cash only,' she said handing the card back. 'I wouldn't flash that around here if I were you,' she said, indicating a group of men playing poker at a nearby table.

'Shit,' Renzo said, under his breath, before shoving the ID back into his wallet and pulling out a handful of hundred euro notes. 'One more game for the road?'

'One only and don't come back here until you've

settled your account. I mean it,' the woman said looking at him. 'Got a family?'

Renzo nodded.

'Thought so. If you blow this and you can't pay, we'll send in the bailiffs.'

Renzo shook his head, muttered under his breath, 'I'll show you,' as he slipped away back to his seat.

He ignored the warning sign about playing more than one machine, slid across onto the adjacent seat and started shovelling money mechanically into the slot.

The cashier watched him then got up and marched over to the barman. She whispered in his ear, 'He's a cop. Do you want me to throw him out?' The barman shrugged.

'Cop with a gambling habit. What's new?' Suddenly the room was ablaze with light, a medley of bells and sirens. Above the noise, a woman gave out a loud shriek of delight.

'Right, who wants a drink,' she said.

* * *

Rome, Italy

The eBay alert pinged on Stephen's computer. A listing in antiques brought up what looked like not just old but museum-ancient jewellery consisting of a dull gold bracelet, a hair comb inlaid with mother-of-pearl, a matching hand mirror, a necklace and a set of earrings.

To the uninitiated, they looked like junk shop finds. Stephen, thanks to the intensive tutoring he'd received in ancient art at Villa Giulia this past week, knew better. But what caught his eye was the name of the seller. Oppeg

Irroc. How original. Geppo Corri written backwards. An avatar a kid would use.

As he scrolled through the items for sale, he searched again. Where were the figurines? He started typing a message:

Anything else for sale?

A reply came straight back.

Plenty.

And sure enough, Corri sent through a list, including two small statues, one which he described as men dancing. Stephen got out of his seat and punched the air.

'He's our man, I'm sure of it.'

Cash only. Collect at 9.00 p.m. tomorrow. Here's the address.

'I haven't even bought them yet, and he's already giving me the address.'

Elisabetta, who was at the desk opposite him, pushed the hair out of her eyes as she looked up.

'Who?'

'Geppo Corri. The looting suspect in Naples.'

'How much is he asking?'

'He's listed them individually, but I'm going to offer him 400 euros for the lot. I'll say I'm in the trade. Come and take a look.'

Elisabetta slid out of her chair, walked around to where Stephen was sitting and peered over his shoulder.

'The comb and the mirror you'd find in a Roman noblewoman's tomb.'

'You think we're on to something?' Stephen felt a rush of excitement.

'The stones in the necklace are different in shape and colour. And they're held together so delicately. It wouldn't take much for them to disintegrate. They can only be real.' Elisabetta got up and started pacing up and down the room, twisting her hands together.

'They must have plundered a tomb. Whoever it was has been lying there undisturbed for thousands of years until these bastards came along. It's our heritage they're stealing.'

If he read her correctly, it sounded like she was having second thoughts.

'We're doing this to stop him selling to anyone else,' Stephen said. 'And if we don't buy, someone else will.'

'You're right. I don't think we have a choice. Offer him 425.'

While he'd been listening to Elisabetta a dozen new watchers and a rival bidder had come online. He clicked onto the bidder's avatar: He (or she) called themselves *Nosce te ipsum*.

Not enough, came the message back.

'There's a rival bidder. But according to their profile they've got no track record.'

'We can't be outbid.' Elisabetta said.

The bids went back and forth like a game of cat and mouse. The rival bidder got to 500.

'What do you want me to do now?'

'Talk up your glowing reviews and top buyer and seller rating and offer him 550.'

600 and it's yours. Cash only.

'He's got us where he wants us and he knows it,' Elisabetta said.

Agreed, Stephen wrote back.

Meet here. Stephen wrote the instructions down and passed it over to Elisabetta.

'Mind how you go. Take one of the local undercover officers, in case it's a set-up.'

'Will do.'

'And one more thing,' Elisabetta said, looking at Stephen's chinos and open neck shirt.'Don't dress like that.

You look like a cop. They crucify cops in that part of town. I'm not joking,' she said looking Stephen in the eye.

He felt a knot in the pit of his stomach and mumbled, 'point taken.'

* * *

Naples, Italy

Stephen felt uncomfortable in a perfectly good, if slightly worn grey suit he'd found in a second-hand clothes store, which also sold him an office shirt and a tie. He recalled that the last time he'd worn that kind of outfit had been at a funeral.

As he looked around at the desolate concrete tower block, rubbish strewn everywhere, he couldn't get over the sinister quiet of the night. On closer inspection, there were a few youngsters around, junkies mainly, sitting around stoned or openly shooting up. All his instincts told him to get out of there.

They'd had to park the car three blocks away so as not to draw attention to an unknown vehicle. Vittorio had been the one to boast that they hadn't been spotted, but then a boy who looked no older than ten had appeared from nowhere and asked,

'Mind your car, Mister?' Vittorio had told him where to go. Stephen wasn't so sure that had been a good move but it wasn't his patch. Now Vittorio didn't look too happy either.

'Ready?' Stephen said.

'I just want to get out of here alive,' Vittorio said. 'See those little kids over there?' Stephen nodded.

'They're the lookouts. They know we're here.' With a

feeling of dread welling up inside him, Stephen got out a burner phone and sent Corri a text.

We're outside.

They heard footsteps running down a concrete set of steps, which echoed into the night. Then a man, who Stephen recognised as Corri, appeared from the shadows. He pointed towards the stairwell and led the way. Stephen went second and saw Vittorio looking round to check they weren't being followed, before falling in behind. Stephen counted four flights, then they went across a concrete walkway, which stank of piss. He could see that the door to one of the apartments was ajar. Corri pushed it open. A younger man barred the doorway, giving him and Vittorio a long, hard look, before letting them in.

'Bag search.' As Corri's accomplice spoke, Stephen recognised his voice from the surveillance audio. It was Corri's nephew, Paolo, he was sure of it. Paolo pointed to the large sports bag Stephen had slung over his shoulder, which he opened for inspection.

Stephen's eyes darted towards a folding table in the middle of the sparsely furnished living area, where the sale items were set out. Stephen held the printout of the eBay listings in his hand and then promptly dropped it.

As he bent down to pick it up, he silently cursed himself for his nervousness, but Paolo was too quick and got there first, giving him the side-eye as he handed it back to him.

'All good,' Stephen said. He drew out 600 euros and was about to pass them over to Corri when Paolo stepped in.

'I'll take that. Just in case it's funny money.' He made a big deal of holding each note up to the light.

'Call me if you have anything else. I sell antiques.'

Stephen passed over another of his fake business cards. Corri took it and passed it to the nephew.

'I might have. Give me until the end of the week.' The nephew shook his head firmly.

'Or we might not,' he said, glaring at his uncle. 'Not Italian, then,' the nephew said, looking at Stephen's business card.

'No, English,' Stephen said, calculating that Paolo wouldn't be able to tell the difference between an Irish and an English accent. Paolo looked him up and down, and then again at Vittorio.

'I've seen you before.'

Vittorio didn't flinch. 'Maybe you have.'

Stephen, ignoring the stand-off between the two of them, turned to Corri.

'I could do with getting these pieces cleaned up before I show them to clients. Know anyone?' He tried to make the question as casual as possible on the off-chance that the two treasure-hunters were aware that the stuff they looted was given a make-over before it was sold.

'Grab my phone Paolo, will you. There was that contact Tony gave us.'

Tony? As in Sanzio?

Paolo shuffled over and gave Corri his phone, not taking his eyes off Stephen.

'What's up with you?' Corri mouthed.

Paolo rolled his eyes.

'I don't trust them,' he mouthed back.

Stephen looked from one to the other, doing his best to appear bored.

Corri, who was apparently desperate to do the deal, ignored his nephew and passed Stephen a scribbled note with the name and phone number of one Aniello di Lauro.

'We'll be off then.' Stephen felt his anxiety beginning

to build. He packed up the treasures as carefully as he could, using the tissue paper he'd brought with them. Vittorio was as ham-fisted as he was. They ended up shoving everything into plastic shopping bags, before putting the lot into the sports bag. Elisabetta would be horrified when she found out how they had man-handled the delicate, historical treasures in their hurry to get out of there.

He counted every step back across the walkway and down the four flights. The fluorescent lights cast cold blue shadows. The piazza where the kids had been shooting up had gone quiet. Stephen peered through the dark and saw shapes, like discarded bags of rubbish, lying on the ground. As they made their way past, he could see they were rough sleepers.

Three blocks felt like a long way. Stephen started to speed up. Just then, he heard a staccato whine approaching from behind. Vittorio grabbed Stephen by the arm, and they started running at full tilt. A driver on a motor scooter, with a passenger on the back, mounted the pavement and gave chase.

'You take the back,' Stephen shouted, turning around to face their assailants. As the rider drove straight towards them, the pillion passenger leant over to try to grab the bag of antiquities. Vittorio was on him and yanked him by the collar of his cheap leather jacket. He screamed as he was lifted into the air. The driver swerved and lost control. As the bike toppled over, Stephen went for the driver, but Vittorio pulled him back.

'Leave it.' The would-be muggers, wearing full visors, picked themselves up and started limping away. The pillion rider spat the words out over his shoulder.

'Filthy cops.'

At least the car was still there. Or most of it was.

Stephen heard Vittorio cursing and looked down to see that all the tyres had been removed. And smirking as he disappeared into a nearby alleyway was the same young kid who Vittorio had refused to pay to mind the car.

Vittorio swore and then phoned for a tow truck. As he and Stephen waited beside their immobile car, the urchin who had arranged for the street mechanics to steal their wheels, swerved around the corner on a bicycle. He lifted it up by the handlebars and the bike reared up, like a trick done by traveller kids back home in Cork on their coloured ponies. The kid proceeded to ride around them in ever tighter circles, never taking his eyes off the two of them. Out of the shadows appeared four other boys, ranging in age from what Stephen guessed was nine or ten to sixteen.

'Careful, he's got back up,' Vittorio said. 'If I have to, I'll make a run for it.' Stephen held the hard-won eBay items closer to his chest.

'They'll outrun and outmanoeuvre you. Just have to hope the tow truck gets here soon.' Stephen heard the fear in Vittorio's voice. The last thing he needed right now was for him to lose control of the situation. He had brought Vittorio along because he worked these streets. If he couldn't deliver, Stephen was going to have to find a way of imposing his own authority.

'They're kids. And kids are the same, whether it's a sink estate in north Dublin or a run-down neighbourhood in Naples.'

As the eldest boy stepped forward, he called out.

'What's in the holdall, mister? You rob someone?'

'No, but I think you did. How much for the tyres?' Stephen said.

'I'll trade you for what's in the bag.' The kid was calm now, bored even.

'I'll tell you what we've got in the bag. A taser. So piss off, the lot of you,' Vittorio shouted.

The boy spat at Vittorio's feet. Vittorio attempted to take a swing at him, and Stephen stepped in, careful to keep the holdall away from flailing limbs. And then in the distance, a sound that was music to Stephen's ears: the chugging of a truck, changing down a gear.

'Just in time,' Vittorio said, as from around the corner, the tow truck appeared. The driver pulled up, jumped out, saw the kids and shouted at them to back away. He seemed to have better control of the situation than Vittorio. The gang melted away into the darkness as quickly as they appeared. The tow truck driver shook his head wearily. He winched the car up onto the truck and opened the door to the cab. They couldn't get in quick enough.

'We're going to get hell for this.' Vittorio muttered.

Stephen turned to him. 'You are, mate. I'd have paid the kid the protection money.'

Vittorio scowled and said nothing for the rest of the journey. Stephen stared straight ahead. He glanced at a building with a clock face. Eleven o'clock. Ten in London. He'd promised Ginny he'd get in touch that evening. She'd still be up.

* * *

Naples, Italy

Renzo eyed the slot machines as he walked through the dimly lit club. He stood outside a door marked Private and knocked twice. There was the sound of a key unlocking, and as the door swung open, Renzo was engulfed in a pall of cigarette smoke. He coughed and the five players seated at the table, three of whom were smoking, looked up at the interruption. One man, thin but with muscled arms, seemed to be the one that the others deferred to. His face was expressionless.

'You'd better get used to it if you want to win your money back. Now, where were we gentlemen?' the muscle said as he displayed his hand. He laid down a five, a six, a seven, an eight and a nine of clubs. There was a collective groan from the others as the winner leant over and scooped up a pile of cash.

Renzo took his seat. The winner looked him in the eye, throwing his money right back into the middle of the table.

'Well my friend,' he said, turning to the new arrival. 'What else do you have to play for?' He took out a photograph of a woman and her baby taken outside a modern apartment block and threw it onto the cash. Renzo blanched.

'Leave them out of this.'

'It's too late for that. It's up to you whether they have a roof over their heads or not. Are we ready?' the muscle said. The seconds ticked by as one of the other men dealt the cards. Holding them close, the rookie glanced at his hand. Beads of sweat trickled down his forehead. The muscle discarded three cards and picked three new ones off the deck. Renzo turned over his hand to reveal a queen, a jack, a ten and a nine of hearts.

'It's your lucky day,' one of the card players said.

The muscle smirked, throwing down an ace, king, queen, jack and ten of spades. Renzo sat there, unable to move.

'What have I done?'

'There, there,' the muscle said as he scooped up the money.

'You got a problem. I got a solution.' He turned to the

others. 'You lot, make yourselves scarce.' They nodded, grabbed their jackets and headed out the door.

* * *

Naples, Italy

At the so-called twenty-four-hour garage, the mechanic who had been called up in the middle of the night, swore down the phone at Stephen, before he could get so much as a word out.

'Why couldn't it wait until morning? You cops are all the same. You screwed up my night,' he said, cutting Stephen off. Vittorio had refused to even get out of the tow truck, insisting the driver drop him off home, leaving Stephen well and truly stuck, waiting for the mechanic. The truck driver had unlocked the door but then shoved off. With no idea how long he'd have to wait, Stephen glanced around the repair workshop. It was divided into three: a repair bay sunk into the floor with room for two cars, an office to the side, and a holding area with tyres and three cars in various states of repair.

As he was looking around his phone buzzed. He glanced down. Ginny.

What the hell? Something must be up.

She texted: *Miss you. I'm in Milan on Friday. Meet up in Rome on the weekend?*

What was she doing, messing with his head like this? He'd convinced himself that her father would have persuaded her to call it off. He wanted to write back straight away but he was distracted by the sound of a key scraping in the lock. He looked up. Tucked away in the corner of the workshop was a Fiat of a style at least ten years old. The car was a dazzling metallic blue. He wasn't a car-obsessive but he knew that model had never come in a shade like that. It had to be a respray. And as he walked over towards it, he wondered why, when the respray would cost more than the car was worth. A set of keys clanked, startling him as he turned round. The bleary-eyed mechanic was eyeing him suspiciously.

'This better be good, getting me out in the middle of the night.'

'I didn't plan to be here at this time either. Get this done now and I'll buy you a beer.'

The mechanic shrugged.

'A beer? I was getting down and dirty with the missus when you called.'

'Mine just got in touch. It's been a month. I was texting her when you came in.' Stephen looked down at his phone to avoid the look of scorn the mechanic was giving him after his blatant lie. 'She lives in England.'

'Who does?'

'My girlfriend. We were meant to be getting married.'

'It's not all it's cracked to be. Here, make yourself useful.' The mechanic chucked over a form and a pen for Stephen to fill in.

'Fill in where the incident happened and why.'

'Will do. Mind if I have a look round while you sort out the car,' Stephen said.

'Help yourself. I'm just the monkey who works here.'

'Know anything about that blue Fiat. Looks like it's had a respray.'

'Maybe I do, maybe I don't. Who's asking and what's it worth?'

* * *

It was 1.00 a.m. by the time Stephen delivered the repaired vehicle back to the Naples base. The duty officer was waiting with a message from Renzo.

Comms recorded a conversation between Geppo Corri and a potential buyer. I left an audio file for you.

'Thanks,' Stephen said wearily, helping himself to a coffee before sitting himself down and listening to the tape.

'I'm the buyer who lost out on eBay. Do you have anything else for sale that wasn't advertised?' the caller began. Stephen nearly fell off his chair. He knew that voice, he was sure of it. He called the duty officer over.

'Does this guy pronounce his Italian a bit like me?'

'More like an American.'

'Thanks.' Stephen turned up the volume so he could listen again. There was an unmistakable wheezing at the end of the sentence. He was ninety-five percent certain that *Nosce te ipsum* was none other than Michael McCarthy.

Chapter 8

Rome, Italy

As he sat waiting, Michael McCarthy was kicking himself. Why hadn't he been firmer with that young art insurer?

He was on one of his regular visits to Villa Giulia and had been discussing with a curator about the way the ancient Greeks worshipped figurines when he saw out of the corner of his eye the young Irishman hovering in the background, pretending to examine some little bronzes, like the ones in Geneva. Walsh had told him he was there on an art history course. Why he was a suitable candidate for a job as a fine art insurer, McCarthy didn't understand, but if he'd passed the right exams, who was he to judge?

He was at the back of the restaurant, not his usual table. Walsh had requested somewhere quiet where they could talk. Was he going to ambush him? He'd agreed to meet because he felt sorry for him: struggling with a new job in an unfamiliar city, playing catch-up with the language. Walsh been fishing for a personal tour of the galleries, but McCarthy had been firm, using his upcoming travels as a get-out clause. He'd rashly suggested lunch, forgetting that conversations over meals when there were only two of you could be awkward when you didn't know each other. At least he had an excuse to leave early—his flight was that night and he hadn't even started packing. He sat there trying and failing to quell his mounting anxiety about what was waiting for him on the other side of the Atlantic.

* * *

The exit from the Metro at the Coliseum was packed with tourists, posing for selfies. Stephen pushed his way through the crowds towards the Monti neighbourhood. There was no logic to the higgledy-piggledy layout of these ancient Roman streets. His GPS struggled. And as he looked at his watch, he saw he was running late.

He'd been at a crash course in art history with fellow police officers when he'd bumped into McCarthy and over-heard him engrossed in a highbrow discussion about ancient art. McCarthy seemed to be the type who could talk to anyone—an art expert one minute, a layman, like him, the next. But even so, it was a stretch to go from discussing art in a gallery to dealing with shady types on eBay. And why would someone of McCarthy's standing risk being caught with fakes or looted items?

There it was, Trattoria via Panisperna.

As Stephen strode into the restaurant his eyes took a few seconds to adjust to the change in light levels from the bright noonday sun to the darkened interior. He looked at his watch again. He was fifteen minutes late. He felt the colour rise from his neck to his cheeks. He looked around and hurried over, flustered, when he spotted McCarthy.

'I got my timings wrong. Sorry.'

McCarthy got out of his seat and grasped Stephen's arm.

'Good to see you. Welcome to my humble little local.'

Once Stephen had sat down, a waiter came over with a basket of bread and a half litre carafe of red wine.

'Anything you don't eat? I forgot to ask. The chef usually brings me whatever he wants to cook that day,' McCarthy said.

'I'll eat anything that's put in front of me except for offal.' As the wine glasses were filled, McCarthy spoke to the waiter, then when he'd gone, leaned forward.

'The smell of liver and bacon frying on the hob takes me straight back to my childhood. Different times.'

'My dad has a thing for liver. But Ma refused to cook it. She'd send him home to my grandma's while we went to the chipper.' As he spoke about his mother, it occurred to Stephen that because Ireland was a small place, she might have heard via the Catholic grapevine of the priest from Cork who was high up in the Vatican. But was he brave enough to ask her, when all she would want to talk about was how his wedding plans were going?

Stephen glanced down as the waiter slid a plate in front of him. There appeared to be a bone with a hole in the middle, oozing with fatty liquid, and sprinkled with parsley. It looked distinctly unappetising, but the aroma was Sunday roasts with Yorkshire pudding.

'I grew up on bread and dripping,' McCarthy said.

Dripping. Ma swore by it for roast potatoes. This, he guessed, was bone marrow. He hadn't the first clue how to eat it. He took his cue from his guest, who prised the marrow out with a deft flick of his fork.

"My grandma fried tinned corn beef in dripping and then mashed it with potato and onions. Even washed out plastic bags and stuck them on the line.' Stephen was trying too hard.

As if on cue, McCarthy spoke.

'We're both a long way from Cork.'

And we didn't come here to talk about food memories.

He was beginning to regret bringing the photos of Corri's hoard with him. But it was too late now, he'd have to plough on, regardless.

He waited until the waiter had cleared their plates.

'Coffee?'

'Yes please. Even though I know there is some law against drinking cappuccino after lunch,' Stephen said. He paused, told himself not to screw this up, and launched straight in.

'A new client got in touch about insuring what to me looked like almost identical artworks to the bronzes at the auction. There's some provenance, but it's incomplete. And I can't insure them until I know they're genuine. I figured you might know someone who would help authenticate them. I hope you don't mind me asking.'

'No, of course not.' McCarthy's breath was wheezy. He took a puff on his inhaler. Had bringing up the bronzes caused his guest's asthma? McCarthy shifted in his seat. 'I'm fine,' he said, as if in answer to Stephen's unspoken question.

Stephen slid over the photographs of the bronze figurines from Tony Sanzio's crashed car.

'I'm flattered you value my opinion. But I'm no expert.'

Stephen begged to differ. And if he could read McCarthy's body language correctly, he'd swear he flinched when he saw what they were. Then his face lit up and he seemed to come alive.

'This one,' McCarthy said, trying to contain his excitement as he pointed, 'is a Dancing Lar, or Lars Familiaris, a protective deity or votive, if you like, that Romans liked to keep in their homes to ward off evil spirits. The green patination is the bronze oxidising, and looks to be even, as far as I can tell in this photograph. Could be first to second century AD. I have a number of these in my own humble little collection. And I'm always on the look-out for them.'

'I've never had the house room to collect anything. What was it that got you interested?' Stephen said, curious to understand what made McCarthy tick.

'I started out with a pair like these—a gift from a grateful parishioner who wouldn't take no for an answer. And it built from there. Of course, they weren't worth anything like they are now.' McCarthy's pale neck started to redden.

Perhaps McCarthy was an innocent collector. Or perhaps he was an addict, needing a constant fix, neither asking nor caring where the supply came from.

'Could it be a fake?'

'Unlikely. The patina is a sign of age but I'd have to have the object in front of me rather than a photograph. I'd question the point of faking something worth not more than two or three thousand euros.'

A small-time crook could earn a living from selling those.

'If there are just one or two, they might not be worth insuring.' McCarthy looked Stephen in the eye.

Your man was sharp.

Stephen searched for a plausible response.

'We'll insure them as part of a collection, rather than individually.'

As he said this, Michael McCarthy slid back the photographs to Stephen and in doing so glanced down at his watch.

'I'm so sorry, but I have to go. Duty calls and I must go

home to pack a bag. You know what it's like flying to the States. They expect you to be there two hours early.'

Stephen had been saving the eBay items he had bought off Geppo Corri until last. But from the reaction on McCarthy's face to the photos of the deities, he had clearly touched a nerve. He seemed rattled. And what was that bit about "duty calls?" It didn't sound like he was going on holiday.

Stephen couldn't afford to alienate McCarthy. It was going to be difficult enough to keep him on side, if he hadn't blown it already.

They said their goodbyes and Stephen got up and made his way towards the bathroom.

McCarthy had left by the time he got back. Outside the restaurant, he saw McCarthy in the distance.

As McCarthy was walking along, a tall, thin figure in a hoodie came running up behind him and ran into him, knocking him over. It looked deliberate. Stephen started running and gave chase. The assailant darted between passers-by and ran down a side-street.

At the far end of the street, Stephen saw a black four-wheel-drive pull out and the mysterious figure hop in. He ran after it, but by the time he dashed between the long line of slow-moving traffic it had disappeared.

By now McCarthy was nowhere to be seen. He made his way back to the restaurant, to check if he'd gone back there. He tried the front door but it was locked and the place was deserted. He tried phoning, but the call rang out. Was McCarthy hurt? If so, he could file a police report and Stephen's testimony as a witness would have added weight to any investigation. Or had he put that one down to experience and gone home with nothing more than bruises, to get ready for his trip?

Was Stephen the intended target and the mugger had

made a mistake, assaulting the wrong man? No, given that the attacker had an accomplice, he was left with a lingering feeling that whoever was behind this might have been using McCarthy as a way of warning Stephen off.

* * *

Michael McCarthy had picked himself up from the pavement. He'd suffered nothing more than a grazed hand and a few bruises. He patted his jacket pocket. He still had his wallet. What then was the point of assaulting him?

When he got home, he rushed around, throwing his belongings into a suitcase. Once he was done, he took out Stephen Walsh's card and turned it over. That business with the photographs. Was Walsh that ill-informed that he expected McCarthy to be able to tell whether they were fakes or the real thing from photos? Was he in fact who he said he was? He dialled the number. When a receptionist answered the phone, name-checking the company on the business card, McCarthy couldn't help but be surprised. Mr Walsh was out of the office, but if he cared to leave a message, the receptionist would be sure to pass it on.

'Please thank him for taking me to lunch, and I apologise if I appeared distracted. I'll be sure to give him a call on my return.' Now that Stephen's story had checked out, initial suspicion had been replaced by an overwhelming sense of self-doubt. As he put the phone down, McCarthy felt guilty.

* * *

Later that afternoon, Stephen was with Elisabetta, alone in the canteen, the last two stragglers waiting in line to collect their coffees.

'Would you happen to have come across Monsignor Michael McCarthy?' Stephen asked.

'Of course. He used to be director of the Pio-Clementino, one of the Vatican museums. I don't know the new guy at all. If McCarthy had still been there, I wouldn't have had any trouble arranging a visit after hours. Why do you ask?'

'It turns out the man I was making small talk with at the auction in Geneva was him. We were looking at the bronze figurines together. He passed himself off as an amateur collector. Why would he do that?'

'Maybe he doesn't have a big ego. I don't know. Why are you asking now?'

'I wanted to see if he might know whether the figurines Corri sold me were genuine or not. I'd tell him that a client was asking about getting them insured.' Stephen said. He took a breath. 'That's if he deigns to speak to me again. I think I came across as someone who knows practically nothing about the subject matter.'

'He'd be the one to tell you.'

'And you would be okay with that?'

'I don't see anything wrong with it. In fact, he could be a useful contact. Just keep up the cover story, that's all.' Elisabetta said.

Phew. 'Okay, that's good to know. You want me to cultivate him?'

'The museum bought the suspect krater under his watch,' Elisabetta said.

'You don't think McCarthy had anything to do with it, do you?'

'What I think doesn't matter.'

She had a point.

'If he lived and breathed art as he obviously does, why did he leave the job?'

'The official line was that he retired. But it was all rather sudden,' Elisabetta said. 'I hadn't really given it much thought before now.'

'I looked on the Vatican website to see if I could find out anything about him but there was just a short biography and nothing else. Is that their usual style or could they be hushing something up?' Stephen said.

'I'll give my contact there a call to see if he can throw some light on it. But in the meantime, befriend McCarthy. He could be useful,' Elisabetta said.

Stephen kept his mouth shut. He wasn't going to risk telling her he already had.

Chapter 9

The day started badly. Alberti called a meeting, which Renzo had turned up from Naples to attend.

'I'd like to introduce you to our latest hire,' Alberti announced.

Stephen looked at Elisabetta and mouthed, 'Did you know?'

She shook her head.

'Renzo Bianconi is a distinguished officer from our Naples office and he's going to split his time between there and here to begin with. He'll be on rotation and will be helping out di Mascio and Connor for now. He reports directly to me. Any questions?' Elisabetta started to say something, but must have thought better of it.

Stephen felt it best to keep out of her way for a while so slipped out of the office to double-check all the panel beaters and car body repair workshops in Rome. Not one had repaired or resprayed a white Fiat. He was visiting the last garage on his list, head down, deep in thought.

'Where have you been?'

He looked up to see Elisabetta was standing beside her car.

'If you insist on going off pursuing leads without talking to me first why did you join the art unit? We're meant to be a team.'

Stephen's gaze was steady.

'Because you'd say no.'

'You're damn right I would.' Elisabetta shook her head and sighed. 'Maybe you've been looking in the wrong place,' she added, with a nonchalant shrug.

'If you know something I don't,' Stephen looked straight back at her.

'If the accident happened between Rome and Naples and the driver did a runner, there's a fifty per cent chance he took it to a garage down south. Somewhere where they don't ask too many questions.'

'That's just it. I think I've found it. By accident. I just wanted to be sure. Down south as you said. And thanks. I promise I'll keep you up to speed with what I'm doing from now on.'

Elisabetta nodded and opened the passenger door of her car.

'Okay. Want a lift?'

'Yeah. Thanks for the offer,' Stephen said as he slipped into the passenger seat.

Elisabetta glanced over at him. 'I didn't come here to have a go at you. I wanted to get your advice.'

Stephen nodded. 'Hit me with it.'

'It's here,' Elisabetta said, reaching into her bag. She handed the letter over, started the engine and drove off. Stephen scanned the contents. It was a letter from the Vatican Museums, politely refusing Elisabetta's request to take a sample of the Euphronios krater in their possession.

'Why would they say no if they had nothing to hide?' Stephen said.

'That's what I thought. I called them, saying that I understood that the krater was extremely delicate. Instead of taking a sample, could I come down and take another look at it? I was put on hold for ten minutes. Then they told me some rubbish that it wasn't available to view because it was undergoing restoration. Before I had a chance to say anything they'd hung up.'

'What the hell's going on there do you think?' Stephen said.

'I don't know but something's not right. Someone there knows where that krater came from and when,' Elisabetta said.

'McCarthy must be keeping secrets. Maybe they made him sign a gagging order?' Stephen asked.

'I wouldn't put it past them to put a non-disclosure clause in his contract. I spoke to my contact. It turns out McCarthy was fired from his job. He'd been accused of stealing deities from the Vatican. An anonymous whistle-blower in the gallery tipped them off. They raided his home and found a dozen figurines that didn't belong to him.'

'On the face of it that sounds reasonable, doesn't it?' Stephen was curious now.

'He wasn't given the opportunity to explain. He was fired on the spot. Not even allowed to collect his things. And the irony was he was the one who had catalogued the figurines in the first place. Before his time nobody else even knew they existed,' Elisabetta said.

'But he crossed a line He took them home. Even if he was planning on returning them.' Stephen responded.

'He just wanted them to be admired, according to my

source who knew him. The pieces they made such a song and dance about went straight back into storage.'

'I'm surprised. I thought you'd be on the side of the law on this one,' Stephen said.

'Normally I would be, but I think it's a disproportionate response. It wasn't even an internal enquiry. They employed a private investigation agency to go after him.'

'That's the kind of dirty trick that a corporate company would do so they wouldn't have to pay out any entitlements due,' Stephen said.

'And you'd only do that if you really wanted to get rid of somebody. My contact thinks there was more to it.'

'The question is why? Could the new management be more compliant than McCarthy was and were prepared to keep quiet about the provenance of some of their recent acquisitions?'

'You don't mess with the most powerful church in the world,' Elisabetta warned, locking her gaze with Stephen, who felt at that moment the weight of the task he'd taken on.

* * *

A young mother balanced a briefcase, a bag of shopping and a baby in a buggy in the entranceway of an apartment block. Struggling with the key to the mailbox which refused to budge, she gave it a firm tap and across the floor spilled a pile of bills addressed to Giulia and Renzo Bianconi.

A neighbour clearing her own letter box reached down to help.

'Thank you so much. I have butterfingers today,' Giulia said, her face flushed with embarrassment. As if on cue, her baby girl made a cooing sound. The older woman's face lit up.

'You're blessed,' she said, before turning abruptly and disappearing up the stairs. As the sound of her footsteps receded, Giulia shuffled the letters and tore open a bank statement addressed to the joint account holders. At the sight of the words "rent arrears" and "eviction," she became agitated, clumsily shoving all the letters into her briefcase. She pressed the lift call button. The baby started to cry.

The buggy took up all the space in the tiny, cramped hallway. There were shelves crammed into every horizontal surface. On the back of the front door hung a makeshift coat rack, laden with scarves and bags. Although it was tidy enough, the one-bedroom apartment was bursting at the seams. The tiny kitchen had no more than two feet of bench space. The mother put her baby, who was fractious and tired, into her high-chair.

'There, there, dinner's coming right up,' she said, as she took a labelled plastic container from the fridge-freezer and popped it into the microwave to defrost. The baby was impatient, thumping her chubby fists onto the tray table.

At that moment there was a knock on the door. The woman got up and opened it and before she could say anything a legal document was thrust into her hand.

'Giulia Bianconi?'

'What the?'

The man's foot wedged itself between the door and the door frame. Giulia, desperate to keep him out, stamped on the intruder's foot. He swore loudly and squirmed, but kept his foot firmly in place. The baby wailed in loud sobs. Giulia gave one last shove, but then seemed to crumple under the pressure, as though the fight wasn't worth it. She hurried away to her baby. The bailiff stepped inside the apartment, his two accomplices following behind him, one of whom nearly tripped over the buggy.

Giulia spooned food into her baby's mouth, her hands shaking. She started to sing in a sweet voice to try to comfort her child.

'If you're happy and you know it, clap your hands.'

She interrupted her song.

'You can take the TV and the sound system but leave me the fridge and microwave. Otherwise, I won't be able to feed my baby.' The man stared at her.

'You should have thought of that before you racked up all these debts,' the bailiff said. 'I'm just doing my job.' Ten minutes was all it took to clear the apartment.

'That sofa you're sitting on. Has it got a fire safety label attached to it?'

Giulia got up and looked underneath.

'I think so. Yes, there it is. We're very safety conscious because of the baby.'

'Good,' the bailiff said. 'We'll have that as well. Move your stuff, will you? I haven't got all day. I'm double-parked. And talking of cars, hand over your keys. Where's it parked?'

'What car? It was stolen, involved in an accident and written off. If you don't believe me, ask my husband when he comes back.'

'I don't have time for that today. He can call this number,' the bailiff said, handing Giulia a business card. 'Unless you can prove that it's a write-off, we're still going to chase you for it.'

By the time the men left, Giulia and her baby were sitting on the bare floor. She got up and looked around at the emptied flat. They had left her a mattress, clothes, the buggy and the baby's cot. She started to cry. Just then the key turned in the lock and Renzo, who was drunk, lurched forward.

'What have you done?' Giulia whispered. 'Please don't wake her. You owe me that at least.'

He looked away.

'I've texted Mamma, and she said to bring the baby over straight after work tomorrow,' Giulia said.

'I'll find the money somehow, pay everything back. Then we can make a fresh start.'

'I can't do this anymore, Renzo.'

'I just got a new job, that's why I was out celebrating.'

'I'm happy for you. But in the meantime, where are me and Ava supposed to sleep?' Giulia passed Renzo the bailiff's business card. 'How about sorting this one out? He's going to chase you for the money owed on the car.'

Renzo stared at the card, then shoved it in his pocket.

'It's more of a promotion. To the carabinieri in Rome, working with the art unit. When you add up the extra allowances, my take-home pay will be up twenty per cent,' Renzo said.

'Seriously? You were going to take a job in Rome without asking me?'

'I didn't want to tell you in case I didn't get it. I'm doing it for us. And Ava.'

'There's six months left on the lease. We can't afford to give our notice. And how are we going to find a comparable place in Rome. Apartments are twice the price. Then there's the cost of living.'

'They'll cover the moving expenses and any other relocation fees. As soon as I get the first month's salary, I can start to pay back everything we owe.'

'Renzo, that's what you always say. And I bet, before you've had a few drinks you mean it,' Giulia said, shaking her head. 'But the thing is, Rome has slot machines and every other temptation under the sun for people like you.'

'You'll be safe at your parents, so I don't have to worry

about you, and I'll be up there sending as much money back as I can.'

'On one condition.'

'What's that?'

'That you'll get counselling for your gambling habit.'

Renzo paced around the room, like a caged tiger in a small enclosure.

'I promise,' he said without conviction.

'Or I'll call it quits,' Guilia said, staring straight at him. Renzo let out a barely perceptible sigh.

Michael McCarthy stood on his balcony looking out onto the square below, turning a bronze figurine over and over in his hand. It was a Lars Familiaris, no more than six inches high, similar to the one in the photograph Stephen had asked him to identify. In a museum it would be dwarfed by bigger and flashier sculptures and earn no more than a cursory glance from a passerby.

But this tiny bronze statue of a male dancer, standing en pointe, holding a bowl in his left hand and a drinking horn in his right, was the reason he stood there today, his whole life flashing by before him. It was an odd sensation when he wasn't the one who was dying. Or not yet.

When he'd been a humble priest back in Boston, almost forty years ago now, a black stretch limo would pull up outside his church in Allston every Sunday at precisely five to ten. Out would spill the entire Russo entourage, who piled into the church and occupied the front three pews. Nobody else would dare to sit there. Giuseppe Russo was a well-known mafia boss with a large family and just as many hangers-on. They ruled the neighbourhood with baseball bats and guns as well as patronage and favours. They were hard people to say no to.

One day after mass, Giuseppe himself had cornered him.

'In your sermons, you talk about how painters in Italy featured Jesus in every single painting. I take it you like art, right?'

It had seemed a straightforward enough question. 'Yes.'

'You like art because you know how to look at it. Me? I don't know what I'm supposed to be seeing. I know jack shit about paintings, begging your forgiveness, Father. I was kicked out of school at fifteen. But Maria, my wife, she wants me to fill the house with beautiful artworks. I want you on the payroll as my art advisor.'

McCarthy had been offered an opportunity to show someone who dealt in death that art was transformative. If he could give a mafia boss a conscience it would be worth it, he reckoned.

'What are you interested in?' he'd asked

'Old stuff in churches. Like they have everywhere in Italy.'

'We could make a start right here. There's plenty to see in Boston. Then New York…'

Giuseppe gave a little chuckle. 'So I persuaded you,' he'd said.

The patriarch had found his weak spot and exploited it ever since. How stupid he'd been not to realise, until now, that he'd sold himself for thirty pieces of silver and that there was no going back.

In the square below, a taxi hooted its horn. McCarthy snapped out of his reverie, hurrying inside his apartment and hastily locking the balcony doors behind him.

Chapter 10

Boston, USA

Michael McCarthy tiptoed into the bedroom where Giuseppe Russo, or the shell of him, was propped up at an angle on an improvised hospital bed. His mouth and nose were covered by a transparent plastic mask attached to various tubes, which wound across his body towards a ventilator. The only sound, the rhythmic hiss of the machine. A nurse, dressed in grey scrubs, was monitoring the old man's vital signs.

McCarthy took the old man's hand in his and sat on the edge of the bed.

'Are you ready, Signor Russo?'

Giuseppe's eyelids flew up and down.

'Do you want me to write down your confession?'

'Not if you can hear me,' Giuseppe said, his voice hoarse and barely audible.

'I can hear you fine. May we have a few minutes alone

together?' McCarthy asked, turning to the nurse. 'I'll call you if anything on the monitor changes.'

'As you wish,' she said, looking at her patient. 'I'll be right outside.'

Once she'd closed the door behind her with a little click, Giuseppe indicated that McCarthy should come closer. He shuffled forward until his ear was an inch from the plastic mask.

'Don't write anything,' Giuseppe whispered. 'Bugs. Cameras.'

'Who would do such a thing?'

'My loving son. I had to pay off his lipreader.' The old man wheezed painfully.

McCarthy was on the point of calling the nurse back when he realised it was laughter.

'Now, to business.'

McCarthy understood the old man's impatience. A personality as big as a house striving to flee his frail and failing body. McCarthy stood, hung the purple stole around his neck, put on the biretta, and opened the little travel case, all neatly packed for the last rites to speed the deserving soul to heaven. Moving deftly, he spread a small white cloth on the nightstand, placed two candles on it and lit them, put the crucifix between them, and a glass he filled with holy water. Dipping the head of the little aspergillum into it, he sprinkled the bed, muttering the familiar prayers and finally asked,

'Do you wish to confess your sins?'

'I do, Father. Closer.'

'I'm listening.'

'I've ordered many killings in my time. Sometimes of rivals. Sometimes not. These guys. Nearly all of them had families.'

McCarthy had heard all this before.

'But that's nothing compared with the ones who died from drugs. They were only kids, Father and I killed them. God won't forgive me for that will he?'

A bead of sweat pricked the back of McCarthy's neck, part the strain of bending, part the sensation that he and Giuseppe were being watched and listened to by someone hardly feet away from the bed.

'I don't know what to do,' Giuseppe was suddenly speaking louder and more urgently. His eyes were feverish. McCarthy held his hand as he went on.

'You must do what you believe is right. It's not too late.'

'I'm sorry Father, it is for me.' Giuseppe shook his head. 'That's why I need your help,' he whispered.

McCarthy's job was to give absolution, to shepherd his parishioner into the next world. It was hardly the moment to ask what it was that so troubled Giuseppe that he could do no more than make an oblique reference to it.

'In the name of the Father, the Son and the Holy Ghost.'

'I have something for you. Over there.' A skeletal finger pointed to a chair, where a large plastic bag with an oblong object inside it, was propped up. McCarthy walked over and peered in. It was a painting, depicting the story of St Jerome and the lion, a favourite of Renaissance artists. 'It's from an artist's workshop. No attribution. Needs cleaning. All the paperwork you need to take it out of the country is there.' Giuseppe stopped mid-sentence and chuckled. Or at least made an attempt. 'Hey Father, I bet you didn't even think I knew words like attribution or artist's workshop, did you? That's all thanks to you.'

McCarthy squeezed Giuseppe's hand.

'You were a quick learner.'

Giuseppe looked directly at the priest. 'Be careful when you turn it over and remove the frame.'

If there was one thing McCarthy had taught the old man, it was that the back of a painting could tell you its entire life story—it was where galleries and exhibitors placed their stamps; owners put their waxed seals and signatures, all clues to a picture's provenance, providing you could decipher their coded messages.

As they made eye contact, the Monsignor nodded. 'You are too generous.' And then, the old man passed him a note. McCarthy could make out a name: Restauratori di Belle Arti and an address, just outside the centre of Rome.

'That's my conservator in Italy,' Giuseppe said, determined to get the words out, even though his breathing was erratic. 'He's done work for me in the past.' McCarthy knew the name.

Giuseppe had amassed a considerable art collection over the years, much of which he kept in the house. He had confided that while Maria was alive, he hoped that Joe would keep his hands off the paintings and sculptures. As the old man sank back, deep into the pillows he murmured, 'Luca. God took my son. And maybe I took the lives of a thousand other kids as payback. Retribution.'

A father's thoughts on his deathbed would be bound to turn to his favourite son, hoping, perhaps, to be reunited in heaven.

When McCarthy began teaching Giuseppe about art, the mafia boss had insisted that the priest join the extended family for lunch once a month. These were large, boisterous affairs that allowed McCarthy to get to know the rest of the clan. Joe was only interested in himself, baseball and junk food. Luca, on the other hand, was already showing signs of high intelligence and an interest in the world around him.

Giuseppe decided that he wanted to bring the boys

with them when they visited galleries and churches. 'It'll be good for them to have an all-round education,' he said.

But McCarthy's heart sank. The thought of dragging small children around an art gallery filled him with dread.

They'd been standing in front of Rembrandt's only seascape, Storm on the Sea of Galilee in the Stewart Gardner museum, when Giuseppe stopped, transfixed.

'I don't know what it is, but this…It's as if God himself painted it.'

McCarthy saw the light in Giuseppe's eyes. All his teachings about the power of art to move the soul had been distilled into this one painting, as the storm threatened to overturn the ship carrying Christ.

Luca, who was about nine at the time, stopped to look, equally taken with the drama in the piece.

As they were ready to move on to the next painting, Giuseppe looked round.

'Where's your brother?'

Luca had shaken his head and shrugged his shoulders. 'I dunno.'

Just then they heard a high-pitched scream and the sound of running feet. The commotion seemed to be coming from the internal courtyard which was visible from every floor in the museum. Visitors to the gallery were leaning over the balcony transfixed by the disturbance below. Another loud shriek drowned out the soothing sound of running water.

Giuseppe started to run towards the disturbance, muttering, 'Oh Jesus.' Chased by two security guards, Joe huffed and puffed his way inside a sarcophagus, lay down on his stomach and started drumming his heels and bashing it with his fists.

'Giuseppe Junior,' the father shouted. '*Vieni qui. Pronto.*'

It was on that third outing, to the Isabella Stewart

Gardner, that McCarthy felt the penny had finally dropped with Giuseppe—there was a raging monster inside his youngest son that he was never going to tame.

It was only now, years later that it occurred to McCarthy that the patriarch had also found out something else that day—that beautiful art was an addiction. And then it dawned on him—he had transferred his own infatuation with beautiful things onto Giuseppe.

From then on, Giuseppe began to use art as a way of escaping his lavish, but sordid life. Just before Luca died, Giuseppe had set off for Italy. It wasn't wholly a business trip, he confided in McCarthy. It was a surprise for Luca's birthday: Michelangelo's David in Florence, the Last Supper in Milan and the Sistine Chapel in Vatican City. Joe, though, had been left behind.

There was mystery surrounding the circumstances of Luca's death and Giuseppe had locked himself away for three months, refusing to see anyone, apart from McCarthy himself.

McCarthy stood, strangely sad for the old man who had trapped him in this beautiful, fraught relationship for so many years. He recited the words of absolution, and anointed Giuseppe's eyes, ears, nostrils, lips, hands, and last of all, lifting the sheet, his feet, already growing cold.

'May the Lord pardon you the sins you have committed.'

Giuseppe lifted his head one last time.

'I've done some bad things. But you can help me make amends.'

By the time he sank back and hit the pillow he had gasped his last breath. The machine by the bedside let out a piercing shriek. The nurse bustled back into the room, closely followed by Maria, Giuseppe's once glamorous wife.

When McCarthy had been promoted to Monsignor, Giuseppe had refused to call him by his new title. To the Russo's, McCarthy would always be known as Father. So it was Father McCarthy who gathered the tools of his trade, packing them swiftly but reverently into their travel case.

Maria elbowed the nurse aside and threw herself to her knees by the bedside, sobbing. McCarthy placed a hand on her shaking shoulder just as Joe walked in, his powerful shoulders moving with all the grace of a belligerent ox. He took his mother's hand and kissed it softly in the manner of a dutiful son, but he extricated himself when her fingers wound around his.

'Mamma, would you like to sit with him a while?'

Maria nodded, tears streaming down her cheeks.

'I need you in my office,' Joe said, gesturing McCarthy towards the door. 'Go get that painting the old man gave you. I want to take a look at it.' McCarthy went over to the corner of the room and picked up the painting. It wasn't very big, roughly seventy by seventy centimetres McCarthy guessed, but it was surprisingly heavy. He carried it carefully, not wanting to drop it, especially in front of Joe.

* * *

McCarthy followed Joe up the stairs. The exertion made him short of breath. While Joe wasn't looking, he took a couple of puffs on his inhaler. He walked into what was once Giuseppe's office, which appeared to have been taken over by the son while his father lay dying. He propped the painting up gently next to the desk.

Luca had been dead over twenty years, yet the place was practically a shrine. There had been pictures of him everywhere. Giuseppe had insisted on having a death mask cast of Luca's face so that he could commission an artist to recreate him in oils. The death mask was gone, and the framed photographs. Only the portrait painting was still in place, but someone, presumably Joe, had draped a sweat-shirt over it.

McCarthy, again moved by the old man's death and by the sacrament he had administered, began to ask what had happened to the pictures, when Joe, wanting to control this first conversation he was having as head of the family, interrupted him.

'The old man, he had a few sins to confess. Am I right?' Joe said.

'No more than anyone else about to enter the Kingdom of Heaven.'

'But Pop's done some seriously bad shit over the years. Sorry, Father.'

'In the eyes of God, we're all equal.'

'Don't give me that hypocritical bullshit, Father,' Joe said, as sat down behind his desk.

The premature rolls of fat protruding over his stomach made McCarthy wonder what his brother, the slender boy in the painting under the sweatshirt would have looked like, had his life not been cut short. Not like Joe, that was for sure. He looked so much like his father that every time Giuseppe looked at him, he would have been reminded of his younger self. And presumably, he hadn't liked what he'd seen. Luca had taken after his mother, with all the height and grace of her northern Italian heritage.

'Whatever he said to you goes no further,' Joe said.

'Confession is a dialogue between the penitent and God. All the priest does is act as a conduit.'

'Just keep it that way, okay.' Joe looked McCarthy up and down. 'Now let's have a look at that painting Pop gave you.' Joe picked up the painting and stared at it. His lip curled in distaste. 'It's dirty,' he said in disgust. 'I don't want it. But that note he gave you, I'll have that,' he said, snatching it out of his hand as McCarthy passed it over. He'd already memorised the name and the address.

'If this guy checks out, maybe I'll let you keep that crummy painting. For now.'

If there was one thing McCarthy knew about the patriarch, it was that he wouldn't go passing a name on in plain sight of Joe, if the man wasn't legit. Joe picked up the phone.

'Hey, call this number in Italy will you and tell them they can expect a visit,' Joe said, as he read out the phone number. He hung up and turned to McCarthy.

'Tell me, is it painted by anyone famous?'

Joe had never shown the slightest interest in art. So why now? Maybe he was jealous that it was McCarthy who'd received a gift from the old man and not him. McCarthy was going to have to be careful how he explained it.

'A famous artist took on assistants to learn to paint in his style. They needed to practise. This painting is likely to be one of those.'

Joe inspected his nails without once looking up while McCarthy was speaking.

'Why would he do that?'

'He needed help to prepare the paints, clean up after him, or to paint a background that you wouldn't notice when you viewed the artwork. The famous artist would only paint the parts that required a high level of skill, like the expressions on someone's face or folds in the clothes. Then he'd sign it, as a work approved by the maestro himself.'

Joe had started to pick off the hangnails one by one as McCarthy talked.

'You're saying that it's got no signature so it's a dud?' Joe lost interest at that point. 'Where were we? I remember.' Joe opened a drawer and pulled out an envelope. The old man wanted to give you these as well. He must have liked you.' He held up the envelope and opened it carefully and pushed the paperwork over to McCarthy. It was the deeds to his apartment.

McCarthy was lost for words.

'I don't know how to thank you both. I will forever be in your debt.'

Joe gave him a cold stare.

'You will, won't you.'

McCarthy felt a wave of fear sweep over him. Giuseppe had wanted to gift him the apartment years ago, but he had always politely declined. With the wildly unpredictable Joe now running the family empire, McCarthy was scared at what he was going to ask for in return.

'Okay, I'll relieve you of that burden,' Joe said, giving a tight little smile. 'I could do with a place in Rome. Be handy when I come over for business. Where is it again?'

'Trastevere, across the Tiber not far from the Vatican.'

Joe shrugged as though he didn't care.

'Would you like me to continue as the family's priest?' McCarthy ventured, hoping Joe would say no.

'I'll let you know,' he said, looking McCarthy up and down as though he was some lowly errand boy.

'It's been an honour to work for the family,' McCarthy said, in as sincere a tone as he could muster.

Joe waved away McCarthy as though he was a pesky fly.

'The damp air in Ireland won't do your asthma any good. Nor will hanging around with the wrong crowd.'

McCarthy felt fear in the pit of his stomach.

'If you catch my drift,' Joe continued, a curt smile on his lips. 'I'd hate for something bad to happen to you,

Father so be careful who you have lunch with, okay?' Joe said, leaning back in his chair.

McCarthy's face gave nothing away. It was a skill he'd honed after years of practice in the priesthood. Only, he couldn't control his panicked asthmatic breaths. His mugging had been Joe's doing and the guy had deliberately knocked him over to intimidate him, that much he understood.

But how had Joe had found out he was considering a move back to Ireland? He didn't recall telling anyone his plans other than estate agents he'd emailed and a few he'd had conversations with. Had one of them been gossiping, perhaps in the pub, and word had got back?

As McCarthy was leaving Joe's office, he turned around to see Joe take out a cigarette lighter and set fire to the deeds of the apartment. By the time he managed to extricate himself from the room, he noticed his hands trembling. He realised that no matter where he went, Joe's network of eyes-for-hire wouldn't be far behind.

Chapter 11

Rome, Italy

As soon as McCarthy arrived back in Italy, he put his new escape plans into action. He'd heard about a religious community for retired priests in La Paz, Mexico. It was within a monastery, where he could be alone or in the company of others when he wanted. When Joe did eventually catch up with him, there would be security and potential witnesses. Surely even Joe wouldn't be stupid enough to wipe out an entire brotherhood, just to get to him? McCarthy had intimated to the head of the order that it was a matter of urgency that he withdrew from public life. The response had been swift and astute. He didn't need to know in advance what his motive for the sudden move to La Paz was, as long as McCarthy would tell him once he arrived.

McCarthy started preparing for his departure, letting it be known that he was going on holiday, to brush up on his Spanish, before his retirement. But first he had to over-

come his dread of being parted from his beloved antiquities and the paintings he'd spent his life collecting. Could
he persuade the monastery to take them as a bequest? He
could offer to curate them as part of a visitor display
attraction, where members of the public would pay to
come and see them, and the income could go to funding
the religious community and all its good works.

Yes, this was the solution, he was sure of it. No-one
would turn down a gift like that. If the artworks were going
on display for others to see, rather than just for himself,
surely God wouldn't mind if he acquired a few more pieces
before he left? Despite all the fears and anxieties of the
past few days, those artworks Stephen Walsh had wanted
his advice on still intrigued him. He'd have to be careful.
Joe had specifically warned him off meeting the young
Irishman. Why?

And then of course there was the not so small matter
of the painting Giuseppe had given him. He regretted now
that he'd been distracted when they'd met six months
before the patriarch's death.

He'd gone to Boston to tidy up his financial affairs, but
Giuseppe found out and had pleaded with him to hear his
confession. He knew he was dying and wanted to put his
life in order. McCarthy had heard all his lies and excuses,
from the killing of innocent bystanders to murdering
informers in front of their children. McCarthy went
through the motions, knowing they were going over old
ground.

After confession, Giuseppe invited him back for a
drink. By then, Giuseppe's mind had started to wander,
which McCarthy put down to the powerful painkillers he
was taking. He talked about how the best place to hide
something was to hide it right under your nose. The way
they tried to hide the Jewish girl in the attic in Amsterdam,

even though there were Nazis everywhere. And in the midst of all this, he became suddenly lucid and began to tell McCarthy about his anguish at not being able to love his remaining son. McCarthy was taken aback: for once, it seemed, Giuseppe felt genuine remorse.

Was Giuseppe so over-medicated that he had confused their chat with the act of confession? Or did the old man know by then that the damage had been done and that it was pointless going through the motions of contrition, when no actual atonement would take place. As the jet lag washed over him, McCarthy had struggled to find connections in the patriarch's thought processes, made his excuses and left.

Whatever had happened in those following six months, it seemed clear now that relations between father and son had deteriorated even further. He'd overheard Joe's orders to his associates to pay his father's conservator a visit. They would have threatened him and forced him into reporting back if he found anything of interest. McCarthy would go through the motions of setting up a meeting, then reschedule, using his holiday plans as an excuse. But in the meantime, he would quietly contact one of his trusted former colleagues from the Vatican Museums.

The painting was still in its protective wrapping. He carefully removed the bubble wrap and, away from Joe's prying eyes, he was able to examine it closely. He was familiar with the iconography: St Jerome in a cave, removing a thorn from the paw of a benign-looking lion.

The drapery and folds of the saint's red robe had been competently executed and the facial expressions of the two subjects indicated that this was the work of a diligent pupil in a well-regarded studio of its time in fourteenth century Florence. McCarthy measured the painting. His guess at the size was right: seventy by seventy centimetres exactly.

There were no clues in the symbolism of the subject matter, or indeed the colours or the way the artist had applied the tempera. He couldn't tell, without having the painting examined in more detail by an expert, what material the pigment had been mixed with. He guessed egg yolk, but it could have been any water-soluble binder. Nothing so far alerted him to anything out of the ordinary, until he turned the painting over. Giuseppe's recommendation to have the painting restored was nothing of the sort. It was an instruction to remove the back and the frame. Joe who knew nothing about art, would have had no clue, even when he was listening in to every word of their conversation.

McCarthy's fingers trembled as he picked up his phone and punched in the numbers. He had his story ready. When his friend answered, McCarthy asked if they could meet. It was a delicate matter and he required the utmost discretion. He wanted to seek his advice over the authenticity of a painting. It had, he said, without being able to go into detail over the phone, a difficult provenance. They agreed a date and a time. His trusted colleague wouldn't ask, but if he did, McCarthy had a story all prepared that the painting had been seized by the Nazis during the Second World War and that the owner had left behind some information about the painting's history.

McCarthy felt sick at the thought of having to tell the man such a bare-faced lie. But that was the cost of protecting his friend from what Joe would do to them both if he suspected his father had double-crossed him and given McCarthy something of value. And if he did have a valuable artwork this was the time he would need an art insurer. He knew one of those, but Joe had specifically warned him off going anywhere near him.

* * *

Stephen was slumped in front of the TV, following the news or at least trying to. They were running a piece on an earthquake in Indonesia. He could see the emergency services pulling people out of the rubble with ambulance workers standing by. Then the usual press conference with a regional chief saying that they were doing all they could. He was about to switch over to another station when the focus shifted back to the disaster. A rescue team had just pulled out a child from the rubble, and they were rushing towards an ambulance with the kid on a stretcher. Next to it was a young Western woman who seemed to have been unaware of the camera until it was focusing on her face. A face that was in perfect proportion, a face he'd recognise anywhere. As she pulled a headscarf over her head, long, dark, tendrils of hair escaped. That was different. He'd never seen her with anything but a gamine crop.

Reaching for his camera, he fired off a few screen grabs. He was in two minds whether to call Tariq. He decided to sleep on it.

Stephen slept fitfully. In his dream, Tariq had come to Rome. They had sat in a restaurant in the Campo di Fiori.

'Like old times, eh?' Stephen said.

Tariq had nodded. Stephen had wanted to tell his friend that he wished he could turn the clock back. He felt pinpricks in his tear ducts and was doing his best to keep it together. Tariq, he sensed had more to say.

'I wanted so much to go with you to the other side of the world when you went running after Cara. You could go where you wanted when you wanted. I was a prisoner stuck in this damn chair. But it wasn't about you, Steve. It was for Cara.'

The only reason that Stephen knew it was a dream was

that not once in the whole time he'd known him had Tariq expressed a hint of neediness or self-pity.

'She's family to me and I love her.' Tariq paused and looked up at Stephen, his face etched with pain. 'And I think you do too. But not in the way I do. You're still in love with her.'

Just as Stephen was about to come up with a pat denial, he woke up. As he sat up in bed, it occurred to him that whatever excuse he'd made, Tariq wouldn't have believed him. They'd known each other too long.

As he drank his coffee, he went online. His scroll through the morning headlines was interrupted by an incoming video call. It was Tariq.

'Hi Steve, sorry for the early call but I needed to talk. I know you're going to tell me I'm paranoid, but I've been getting silent calls at odd times in the day and at night. They're routed through South East Asia. I think it might be Cara. I think she's alive, Steve.'

Stephen hesitated. He wanted to say he'd seen someone who he thought was Cara on TV. But Tariq would seize on it, he felt certain, if he had said it was footage from Indonesia.

'These calls. They could be a scammer, a fax machine, or a premium phone line.'

'No, I checked all that. Your lot think you're the only ones with spying devices?' Tariq chuckled.

'Talking of spying devices, what do you know about facial recognition software?' It was both a genuine question and a nifty way of avoiding being grilled about Cara.

'I saw what you did there. But I'll answer the question. The system you cops use has its limitations. The only reason that an individual would be on a police database is if the person has been arrested or has a criminal record.'

Stephen knew that bit but let it go. He wanted Tariq to talk.

'What if they're high profile and have been in the media, which I'm sure the guy I'm trying to identify has? It's just that I can't work out who he is,' Stephen asked.

'Maybe if he's on social media and there are photos of him all over the place, you might get a match. But it isn't as easy as they make it out on TV. Ideally you want them caught on CCTV.'

'This is just a face in a gallery.'

'You could always ask someone who works in the business.'

Stephen groaned. 'You're going to suggest Ginny, I can tell. Nice try but I can't. Even if she did give me a positive ID, I'd have to lie about why I wanted to know. She'd put two and two together. She's not stupid. Any other ideas?'

'Surely the gallery would have the CCTV? Or maybe it's been wiped by now.'

'Something like that,' Stephen said.

'So which databases have you tried?'

'Europol.'

'Interpol's is more comprehensive, get them to try that.'

'Thanks mate, I appreciate it,' Stephen said.

'Now can we get back to talking about Cara?'

Stephen sighed. 'If it is her, why doesn't she talk to you?'

'You know why, Steve. If ASIO is monitoring the calls, then they can track down where she is and send someone after her. She was a threat to national security, remember?'

Stephen veered between thinking that Tariq was right half the time and the rest, worrying that Tariq's conspiracy theories were clouding his judgement.

'But then she'd no longer be on Australian soil, would she, that's the difference. They're no longer actively looking for her.' Stephen lowered his voice. 'That find in the outback changed everything.'

Tariq looked at Stephen, mouth open in shock.

'You were the one who said they hadn't found any forensic evidence,' he said accusingly.

'No one knows how she got out to where she did. It was right in the middle of nowhere. The best theory is that she got lost, or she had heatstroke and got disoriented.' What Stephen didn't say was that she might just have run out of water.

Tariq turned away from the screen.

'Why would she bury her own clothes? She can't have been alone.'

How the hell had Tariq got hold of that information? There had been an embargo on it.

Composing himself, Tariq turned to face Stephen square on.

'You, a copper of all people coming up with this far-fetched theory. You should know better. Until there's conclusive proof, I'm not giving up on her. What they were trying to do to her out there, only she knows.' Tariq glared at him.

'I'm sorry Tariq. You know I…'

'I get it.' He looked steadily at Stephen. 'Got to go,' he said abruptly and hung up. *He deserved that.* Who did he think he was to crush Tariq's hopes like that? What to do? Stephen messaged Tariq, apologising. He left it at that. And heard nothing back.

Chapter 12

Ginny had left a series of texts. Stephen scanned them as he walked back into the office. There had been a last-minute change of plan and a meeting had been switched from Milan to Rome. Was he free for the weekend? *So far,* he wrote back, *let me know when you get in.* There was no time to dwell on why she'd got back in touch when relations had been so frosty. He had work to do.

Stephen slid an authorisation request across to Elisabetta.

'And this is for?'

'A tap on the antiquities restorer, Aniello di Lauro, known associate of Tony Sanzio's. I got his number off Corri. Tony had to have someone to clean up and restore the pots.'

'Yes to surveillance and background checks. The name doesn't ring a bell and the pool of art restorers, even in Italy, is small. But someone else in the profession will have had dealings with him. We should be able to find out about him fairly smartly. Call a meeting and we'll get the team onto it.'

'If it turns out he is legit, I won't have to answer for phone tapping someone on the right side of the law going about their daily work?'

'Exactly. Someone will know this guy, even if he didn't train here. You can't just come along and try your hand at art restoration. Not like that deluded parishioner in Spain, the one who botched up the face of Jesus in the fresco.'

Stephen supposed Elisabetta was trying to protect him from the wrath of Alberti in case he turned out to be wrong. If he was right, then he'd press her again for the phone tap.

The briefing was over in a few minutes. Less than an hour later, Pasquale had come back with intel that di Lauro's car had been caught on speed cameras in northern Italy, heading towards the Swiss border. And then crossing back into Italy a few days later.

'Anyone have a tame opposite number in Switzerland by any chance?' Elisabetta said.

'I do,' Stephen said. 'Leave it with me.'

'You might want to see this, boss,' Pasquale said, talking to Elisabetta and turning his back to Stephen. Maybe he was being paranoid, but the guy seemed to take every opportunity to try to undermine him.

'His workplace is in a rundown part of Marconi. We've triangulated CCTV. It's a nondescript building with a dry-cleaner's at the front.'

'It wouldn't do to advertise to thieves that you had priceless artwork on the premises,' Stephen said.

'You and I better pay him a visit,' Elisabetta.

'Now?'

'No time like the present.'

'What about calling my contact in Switzerland?'

'Pasquale can do it.'

'Okay,' Stephen said. As he passed the information

over, he heard himself telling Pasquale that his contact was a valued one who was doing them a favour.

Pasquale looked at Stephen over his John Lennon glasses with contempt.

I wasn't imagining it then.

'While you're at it, can you try Interpol to see if you can get a match with Tie Pin Man?

Pasquale was never going to like him. He had nothing to lose by making it known that the feeling was mutual.

'There's an admin charge. Sign here so I know which account to put it against.' Pasquale practically threw the paper at him.

Stephen signed it and shoved it straight back.

Elisabetta who had been observing their antics, shook her head.

'You two are as bad as each other.'

* * *

On the other side of the city, a skinny, wasted teenager, with track marks all the way up his arms, wandered from room to room in a building that looked like a cross between Willy Wonka's chocolate factory and a methamphetamine lab. There were white plastic benches, glass beakers, medical instruments laid out on metal trays, a series of magnifying glasses in assorted sizes, test tubes, and glass bottles full of liquids in an array of jewel colours from amber to verdigris to papal purple.

'Hey, will you look at this shit! I mean it, come over here will you ' A homeless guy, in his late thirties but looking fifty, his trousers held up by string and his teeth tanned from tobacco, seemed less enthusiastic, picking up a brass Bunsen burner and turning it over.

'Maybe if we could melt this down, it'd be worth something.'

The kid who was standing nearby, grabbed his arm. 'Hey, don't touch that,' he shouted.

'Okay, okay, I didn't mean to.'

'Don't you see? We can make our own meth. We won't have to pay a dealer.'

'You a chemistry teacher, now, like that guy, Walter White?' Tanned Teeth, scoffed. 'You've been watching too many TV shows.'

The kid was hyper, jumping from one foot to the other, punching his palm with his fist. 'Shut the fuck up.' His scream echoed around the deserted building.

His fellow addict wandered off to a storeroom, full of boxes, mainly empty. The labels read: statues, calyx, psykter, funerary vases.

'It's not a meth lab, it's a factory,' Tanned Teeth said as the junkie kid walked in, his face crumpled as if all his hopes had been crushed there and then. He turned on the older man and started throwing, wild, wilful punches. The man covered his face with his arms, trying to hide his fear. He started to creep away.

'Where are you going? You've ruined everything.' The kid tore open the last of the boxes. Inside was a delicate vase. In a rage, the young junkie picked up the vase to fling it to the ground. The target of his anger tried to stop him.

'Not that one.' The man had it in his grasp, but the young addict found the strength to tackle him from behind and push him until he toppled over, his body curled over the vase. Instinctively, he put his hand over his head to lessen the impact, before he hit the concrete floor. The 2000-year-old vase shattered into lethal fragments, and in the confusion, a shard of ancient ceramic punctured his carotid artery. The slash across his neck burst into a red seam of foaming, arterial blood. He tried to pull the jagged pottery from his throat, but his vocal cords were cut and blood filled his mouth. One hand was trying vainly to staunch the flow, with the other he made to grab the young man's sleeve, imploring the addict to help him.

The startled child froze. He began to blink, unable to process what he was seeing. A look of terror on his face as he rolled away to avoid the rapidly spreading pool of blood. He squatted down with his back to the dying man, clenched his eyes shut and put his hands over his ears to blot out the bubbling cries.

The dying man fell in and out of consciousness. In the moments when he was awake, he clawed at his shirt, trying to tear strips off, as though a make-shift bandage might save him. As the life ebbed out of him, his shirt was in tatters.

The young junkie cowered, counting the seconds. When he reached a hundred and eighty, he raised his head and listened. The man was silent.

Dry-retching, his hand held over his mouth, he stumbled past the now dead man lying in a pool of his own blood. He picked up an old rag lying on the floor and in a futile attempt at cleaning up, tried to wipe away the evidence. With the blood-stained rag in one hand, he grabbed as many of the bloodied fragments in the other, stuffing them into his backpack, then fled the chemical lab down the empty alley.

* * *

As they had crossed over the Tiber, Stephen had been struck by the clash of old and new: a magnificent domed church marooned between the autostrada and a concrete and glass block, in a part of Rome where tourists, he supposed, would find little to interest them. Elisabetta had taken the exit slip road closest to the river on the western side, bringing them into the middle of a working-class neighbourhood. The plane trees lining the streets did little to disguise the grey 1970s apartment blocks, the depots, repair shops and rundown cafes.

As the car slowed, Elisabetta spotted an empty parking space next to a tiny urban park where old folks exercised their lap dogs. She pulled in, turned off the engine and turned to Stephen. 'Shall we?'

They walked along the street until they came to a warehouse with a dry-cleaning business built onto its frontage.

'Let's try the back and see if there's a way in,' Stephen said. They went around the perimeter. There was a roller door pulled shut with an empty parking bay backing onto it. Stephen put his ear to the door. The sound of running footsteps. He motioned to Elisabetta and they crept down as an ill-looking slip of a lad carrying a bag, his face white as a sheet, ran out of the warehouse straight into the two police officers. Stephen tackled the white-faced boy and had his arm up behind his back and was leading him away. Elisabetta picked up the dropped bag and peered inside.

'Fragments.' She showed Stephen the contents.

'You're going to show us where you got this stuff right now,' Stephen said, leading the boy towards the warehouse.

'He's covered in blood.' She pressed the number for the emergency services. 'You call back-up,' she mouthed to Stephen. 'Someone has to go with him to the hospital and make sure he doesn't do a runner,' Elisabetta said. 'There's nothing we can really to do to stop him if he wanted to go. He's young.'

The boy pointed towards the building and started to shake. 'I didn't mean to,' he began.

'How old are you, kid?' Elisabetta had barely got the words out before the boy started trembling and foaming at the mouth.

'He's having a fit.' By now the boy was on the ground with his head back. Elisabetta had him in the recovery position and was trying to hold the boy's head straight as he was twitching from side to side, his eyes rolling. Just then the ambulance came screaming around the corner, followed closely by a police car.

'Stephen, you go in first. Once I'm done here, I'll be right behind you.'

Stephen followed a trail of blood, presumably the boy's, through the back entrance. He walked into the abandoned factory. He scanned the layout. In one corner of the room was an array of white benches, set up like a chemistry lab.

He followed the bloody footprints' trail as it headed off to a side room. In front of it, hundreds of pieces of a shattered pottery urn lay scattered in front of an open doorway, the door held ajar by a man's body lying in a pool of blood. The lethal shard of priceless pottery was covered in blood and chunks of flesh from the victim's neck. He reached over to check his pulse. Nothing. He was still warm.

He grabbed his phone and hit Elisabetta's number.

'Call homicide, I've found a body.' He heard the sound of running footsteps.

It was Elisabetta. She was panting.

'Nothing more we can do for him,' she said, indicating the corpse. She crouched down at the scattered pottery fragments.

'Now that it's a crime scene and homicide are going to

sweep up all our evidence, you didn't see me do this,' she said, picking up a clean, dry fragment from the broken vase.

Stephen was taken aback. 'Don't they need that to establish whether it was murder, manslaughter or an accident?'

'They've got enough to go on. It's just bad luck that two junkies chanced on the factory, and worse luck that they got into a fight. What went on here has nothing to do with our investigation. That blood-stained shard is all homicide will need to determine how the guy died. In any case, whether it was an accident or murder, the kid's too young to be charged with anything.'

Before Stephen could protest, Elisabetta was on the phone to homicide. As she hung up, she turned to Stephen.

'Ten minutes, tops, before they get here.'

'What about the boxes in here?' Stephen pointed.

Elisabetta glanced at the labels.

'We need those. There'll be enough evidence left in there for forensics to test them.' They gathered as many boxes as they could and moved into the chemistry lab area. Elisabetta put her hand over her mouth and nose as she moved from room to room. She pushed open a door. It was another storeroom. Inside were brushes and paints, chemicals and plastic tubs with warning triangle signs on them.

'There's another door here,' Stephen said. He crouched down and looked through the keyhole. 'There's a set of concrete steps. Let's see where they go.'

Stephen tried the door handle. It wouldn't budge. 'Did you see anything in the storeroom we could use?'

Elisabetta shook her head. 'I'll give it a go,' she said, taking a run at it. Stephen jumped out of the way before a swift kick sent the door clattering down the stairs. They followed it down, covering their mouths and noses as they were hit by a wave of acrid chlorine. It led to a basement where they found a small swimming pool, roughly ten by eleven metres and approximately one metre five deep. At the bottom of the pool were more pottery fragments.

'It certainly hasn't been used as a swimming pool in recent times,' Stephen said.

'It's restoration on an industrial scale. We need to bring that restorer in for questioning, ' Elisabetta said.

Just at the moment Stephen's phone rang. When he saw the caller ID he jumped. Ginny.

'I'm at the airport. Didn't you get my messages?' Stephen was speechless.

Elisabetta turned to go up the stairs to be met by the homicide team coming down. He heard them arguing.

'I'm still at work,' he said. 'Give me an hour. Get a cab and I'll meet you in the cafe across the road from where I live. Here's the address.'

'Okay, I'll see you soon,' she said, sounding tired.

'Bad news. Pasquale just called. Aniello di Lauro's car was caught on CCTV last night in a convoy of vehicles headed to an address in suburban Geneva,' Elisabetta said.

'Where we can't touch him? Stephen said.

'For now,' Elisabetta said. 'He could say what was going on here was legal, but he's going to have to come up with some good reasons for the sudden midnight flit to Switzerland. I think we're done here.'

'My girlfriend just turned up and I'd completely forgotten she was coming.'

Elisabetta looked at her watch. It was gone seven. 'Long day, huh?'

Stephen nodded.

'I suppose I'd better go and check on that kid, before he discharges himself,' Elisabetta said. 'Come on, I'll drop you off home.'

As they made their way back across the Tiber, Elisabetta turned to Stephen, her smile wide.

'We did okay.'

'We sure did.' Stephen, said, elated, feeling for the first time since he'd arrived in Rome, that he was, at last holding his own. Which was more than he could say about his private life. At least, he consoled himself, Ginny had come in person to say her piece and hadn't sacked him by text.

Chapter 13

As soon as Stephen walked into the cafe, he could tell Ginny was out of sorts. She gave him a cursory hug and turned away. He wanted to hold her, tell her how much he loved her, but he'd come straight from the chemical lab and probably still smelled of chlorine.

'Is everything okay?' Stephen said as he picked up Ginny's bag.

'You've got blood on your shirt,' Ginny said.

He caught sight of himself in the cafe mirror. So there was. No wonder she recoiled at the sight of him.

'No, don't explain,' she said.

'Okay I won't. The apartment's just across the street. It's not as tidy as I'd like it to be.'

'I've had a hell of a week. And a stinking headache to go with it.' Ginny managed a weak smile.

She'd had a hard week? Quite possibly, but it probably didn't include dealing with homicide victims and epileptic junkies.

Their conversation was stilted and superficial. He didn't know which was worse, inane chat or stony silence.

At the apartment, Stephen's suggestion of drinks and dinner out was rebuffed. All Ginny wanted was a shower and an early night.

'But you first. You look like you could do with it more than me,' Ginny said.

'Have a look around, it won't take long,' Stephen said as he headed off for the shower. Ginny would have plenty to say about his one-bedroom apartment, painted in two tones of drab, a desultory attempt to make the space more appealing. As he was towelling off, there was a knock on the door. He opened it and Ginny was holding a bottle of red wine in one hand and pouring him a glass.

'Thought you could do with one,' she said. 'For every feature wall, there's got to be a bathroom that has glass bricks. Am I right?'

'Correct. Come on in, let me show you,' Stephen said.

Ginny at least was able to raise a smile and for a moment there it felt as though they were still the same people they'd been two years ago when they'd first met. He walked out, towel wrapped round his waist, holding the glass of wine and sat on the sofa. He grabbed the takeaway menu sitting on the coffee table.

'Everyone's got to eat, don't they? We can order in.'

'Sounds good. Now where do you keep the towels?'

'Hall cupboard. Sorry, housekeeping is a bit slack.'

'I did spring it on you,' Ginny said and walked off to the bathroom.

While she was showering, Stephen ordered pizza and then texted Elisabetta:

Any advice on where we can go on a day trip?

Elisabetta shot back: *Lunch at Antico Ristorante Pagnanelli, Lago Albano. How's it going?*

He couldn't lie. *So-so.*

Sorry to hear that.

It was an act of disloyalty, he supposed, to confide in a colleague about your home life, but that was what work mates did, wasn't it? When the pizza arrived, Stephen tore into it. Ginny ate the middle and left the crusts. She talked a little about people he'd met once and didn't care for. Then she pleaded her headache and went off to sleep. He spent the rest of the evening fretting while watching Lazio play AC Milan, falling asleep on the sofa.

He woke at about six and crawled into bed. Ginny pretended to be asleep. He slept until eight when he was woken up by the hissing of freshly made coffee from the stovetop espresso machine.

'Sorry, did I wake you?' Ginny called out. She was up and already dressed, in what he would call beige jeans and a black tank top, which showed off her taut arms. God, he wanted her but pushed the thought away. He'd play it her way.

'Shall I go and get pastries?' Stephen stumbled out of bed, grabbing the nearest towel he could find, wrapping it around his torso.

'I'll go. You get yourself ready for the day,' Ginny said.

She was in a better mood. Perhaps the weekend wouldn't turn out to be a disaster after all. Just then his phone buzzed. It was Elisabetta.

'We're interviewing the junkie kid this morning. You'll be done by midday, I promise. Still time for a late lunch out in the country.'

Stephen groaned. 'What time?'

'Ten.'

He looked at his watch. 'I'd better get my skates on.'

'And by the way, after you left, Pasquale came back with a positive ID on Tie Pin Man,' Elisabetta said.

'He did what? Why didn't he tell me himself? Who is he?' Stephen was indignant.

'An American art and antiquities dealer called Robert Hurst. He was arrested in Cyprus in 2000 at the airport with a suitcase full of priceless icons. They were seized, Hurst was thrown in jail. Twenty-four hours later the charges were dropped and they deported him.'

'Jesus. We're getting somewhere at last,' Stephen said.

'That's what I thought. Pasquale was embarrassed that he screwed up in front of you.'

'So he should be. What was he thinking?'

'I'd cut him some slack. You certainly haven't made a friend there.'

Just then the key turned in the lock.

'Ain't that the truth.' He sighed. 'Better go, I'll get there as soon as I can,' he said, ending the conversation.

Ginny was standing there smiling, holding out the pastries as a peace offering.

He took one of the pastries and began to nibble it.

'I've got to shoot back into work for an hour, tops.'

Ginny rolled her eyes. 'Whatever.'

* * *

Michael McCarthy was out of the door by first light. He hurried across the square next to his apartment. The dome of St Peter's refracted the celestial light of the rising sun. If ever there was a moment for regret at his fall from grace at the Vatican, this was it. He pushed thoughts of that aside. He had lost his status, but he still had his pride and his desire to help those less fortunate than himself. As he looked around his familiar streets, he saw there were plenty of those.

An outreach worker he didn't recognise was bending

down to speak to the homeless in their sleeping bags, while her colleague was dishing out toothbrushes, biscuits and leaflets on shelters and the needle exchange. Staff from a nearby cafe bustled about with coffee and pastries.

A sex worker dragging on a cigarette nearly tripped over a comatose junkie lying in front of her apartment.

'*Vaffanculo*,' she said, with contempt, stubbing out the butt on the pavement with her heel. 'People like me do an honest day's work so that people like you can lie around all day,' she muttered under her breath as she made her way inside and slammed the door.

A chorus of disapproval rang out from the homeless.

'*Puttana*.'

McCarthy looked around, peering at the ones still sleeping or who were so out of it they were barely breathing.

'Anyone seen the young lad, Bruno? He missed our weekly outreach meeting yesterday.'

'Nah. Not for a while. Last time I saw him that kid had so many holes in his arms you could strain pasta through them. I worry about him.'

McCarthy recognised the grizzled looking grey-haired man, who was sitting up in his sleeping bag. He sat down next to him.

'And I worry about you as well. It's too cold to be out here at night, Ernesto. I know you hate the shelter, but at least it's warm.' Ernesto sat up in his sleeping bag.

'Father, I know you mean well. But I'm past saving. It's the young kid you need to help. Before he wrecks his life the way, I did.' Ernesto looked round as the street began to fill with commuters. 'I'd better get out the way before this lot walk over me,' he said, standing up in his sleeping bag, shuffling off to the nearest park bench.

'Try the hospital, in case he's overdosed again, or ask

the cops,' Ernesto called out as McCarthy walked back inside his apartment.

* * *

In the interview room, the gaunt, drug-addled teenager was trembling. Stephen wondered if he was going into withdrawal. As he sat down the kid's phone rang. Before he could switch it off, Stephen put it on speaker.

A softly spoken voice said, 'Bruno, are you alright?' The speaker struggled for breath. It wasn't so much a breath, as an asthmatic wheeze. 'It's Michael.'

As in McCarthy. What the hell was going on? Stephen scribbled a note and passed it over.

Talk to him.

'Are you with somebody?' McCarthy said.

The boy sobbed.

'I've been arrested.'

'That can't be right. You're too young. Put me on to the arresting officer.' There was an awkward silence.

Stephen mouthed to Elisabetta, 'you speak to him.' Elisabetta looked back.

'What's going on?' she muttered. Stephen shook his head.

'Not now,' he whispered.

'Lieutenant di Mascio here.'

'You do realise it's illegal to arrest a minor, don't you?' McCarthy said.

'We haven't arrested him. He's helping us with our enquiries. A man died today,' Elisabetta said.

'I'm his outreach worker. I'll be right over. Where are you holding him?' As Elisabetta gave him the address, Stephen turned to the boy.

'I'm going to ask you again. How old are you, kid?' Stephen whispered gently.

'Thirteen.' Stephen, Elisabetta and their colleague from crime gave a collective sigh of disappointment.

'Interview terminated at 10.35 a.m.'

* * *

Michael McCarthy sat in the waiting room while Stephen and Elisabetta had a furious exchange in her office.

'What's going on here?'

'I recognised his voice. It's McCarthy. He doesn't know I'm a cop, remember? And I want to keep it that way.'

Elisabetta hit her forehead with the heel of her palm. 'Of course.'

'You'll have to do it. I'll watch from the observation room.'

'Okay.'

As soon as McCarthy sat down in the custody suite where Bruno was being kept, he looked straight up through the one-way mirror to the surveillance room. Even though Stephen knew he couldn't be seen, it still unnerved him when suspects and their representatives did this, despite all the years he'd been doing the job.

'I want to talk to the boy alone, in a room that isn't bugged,' McCarthy said to Elisabetta. 'And I'll wait with him until the officer from juvenile crimes arrives. I don't care how long it takes.'

Once an advocate had been appointed to act for Bruno and McCarthy had left the custody suite, Elisabetta, joined by Stephen, went back and interviewed him again.

'We're here to talk about the broken pottery, which had your fingerprints. Tell us in your own words again what happened?' Bruno didn't look at Stephen but at the court-appointed representative sitting next to him. He shook his head.

'He's already told you, he found the man dead,' the woman said in a bored tone, looking at her nails.

Stephen held his ground.

'And if you'd been listening you would have heard, we're here about the broken vase, not the poor guy who ended up being sliced in two. That one we'll leave to our colleagues in juvenile crime. We'll take a short break while you confer with your client,' Stephen said, getting up and walking out of the room. He needed fresh air badly. He walked past the reception area, ignoring the half dozen or so people who were waiting on friends or family to be released.

* * *

Michael McCarthy had declined to go home until he'd found out what was going to happen to Bruno. Looking up, to his surprise he saw a man walking out of the custody area who was none other than art insurer Stephen Walsh. If indeed that was his name.

Walsh must have struck up the conversation at the auction in Geneva about bronze figurines deliberately. Of all the people there, why had Walsh chosen him? Did he spot a fellow Celt from his complexion and hair colour? Or was that nothing more than a lucky coincidence? If Walsh had made the connection with the Vatican Museums, he'd know about his fall from grace. Had he believed the lies put out by Hurst via the Vatican PR machine—that he was weak and vulnerable and had helped himself to their collection? No wonder Walsh had tried to set a trap for him at that lunch meeting.

McCarthy went up to the reception area and stood in

the line for the desk, looking over his shoulder every time the lift doors opened. At last, he was at the front of the queue.

'Can I help you?'

'I'm the community support for the young lad Bruno currently being questioned by Elisabetta di Mascio. Can you tell me the name of the other officer, please?'

'Stephen Connor.'

'Thank you, sir. I will wait at home until I hear news of the boy's release.'

'What makes you so sure he'll be released?'

'He's a kid,' McCarthy said and walked hurriedly towards the stairs. He was due at the art restorer's in less than thirty minutes and he still had to get home and collect Giuseppe's painting. As the lift doors opened Stephen Connor got out.

* * *

Ginny had been gracious about their interrupted morning and was happy to wander around the shops while he worked. They'd agreed to meet just after midday.

Stephen kissed her on the lips. 'I've arranged a little surprise.'

'You know I don't like surprises.'

'Maybe you'll make an exception for this one.' Stephen kept his tone light, even though deep down, he felt that the day couldn't get much worse.

'I was hoping we could talk.'

'Can it wait?'

'Okay,' she said as if it wasn't okay.

Stephen's car had a halfway decent sound system that helped bridge the silence. He stuck his playlist of driving music on as loudly as he thought Ginny could bear, as she looked out the window, taking in the scenery. As Lake Albano swung into view, Ginny couldn't help herself.

'Wow. Some view. You've kept this place a secret.'

'I asked a local.'

'He has good taste.'

'She.'

'I see.'

'It's nothing like that.'

'What is it like then?'

Not like this hostile bullshit.

'Day or night, we're at the office or in the car. We eat on the go; the car becomes a mobile dining room. No matter how many windows you open, it smells of takeaway. By week's end you can't stand the sight of each other.'

'Sorry. I've got a lot on my mind right now.'

'Is it something to do with us?'

'No,' she said, looking away. 'It's work. The auctions and the valuations I can deal with. Even chasing up provenance. But I'm having trouble with the office bully. All the usual stuff. Sorry, I won't bore you.'

'You're not.' Stephen was concerned now. But Ginny wasn't going to elaborate and quickly changed the subject.

'You said you wanted me to look at something for you.' She had remembered after all. He hadn't planned to talk shop today, but out of habit had slung the file with the photos from the raid on Tony Sanzio's apartment into his briefcase.

'I'd like your expert opinion on some artefacts,' Stephen said. 'There's photos in the briefcase under your seat.'

Ginny reached around, felt for the briefcase and lifted it carefully. 'You brought it with you?'

'Safer to have it with me than leaving it at home.'

'You're the cop.'

'It wouldn't look good if someone broke into the apartment and stole it. The combination is 4273.' Out of the corner of his eye, Stephen saw Ginny tap in the numbers on the padlock and pull out the photos. He could see she was studying each one intently.

'Where are they from?'

Stephen hesitated.

'Okay, I get it, you can't tell me that. What do you need from me?'

'I could do with knowing how they get from being covered in dirt, some in pieces, to fully restored?'

'I only ever see the end product, so I can't answer that. What's your theory?'

'I'm not an expert, like you or Elisabetta. And she's a stickler. She'd be furious if she found out I'd shown you them.' Why oh why had he said something so tactless? He braced himself for Ginny's retort.

'I guess I would be too if I were in her position.'

'Thought you'd like to meet her. You might hit it off. She's coming round later this afternoon.'

Stephen had parked up, and they were walking into Ristorante Pagnanelli.

'If that's what you'd like to do, that's fine.'

Why did she turn the words round like that? He was getting tetchy and could hear the sarcasm in his voice.

'I would like to do that, yes.'

Stephen picked up his menu and hid behind it. Ginny did the same. As soon as they ordered, Ginny excused herself. She seemed to take ages, and when she did return, she seemed flustered. As she slipped back into her seat, she barely glanced at the lake and instead fixed him with her eyes, those beautiful green eyes that had made Stephen's heart melt when they'd first met.

'That thing I wanted to tell you,' Ginny said.

You're not good enough. I've found someone else.

'I've been headhunted. For a new gallery.'

Stephen felt an overwhelming sense of relief. If it was ambition that was coming between them, he could take it. He wished he could find the words to articulate that.

'It's an opportunity that happens once in a lifetime. If you're lucky.'

'Where will you be based?' It had sounded like a lame question.

'I know I gave you a hard time about coming here.'

At least she admitted it.

She looked towards the lake as she said this. Why couldn't she look at him while she was saying her piece?

'And I'm going to sound like a complete hypocrite.'

Stephen braced himself for what was coming next.

She looked away and started fiddling with her napkin.

'The suspense is killing me,' Stephen blurted out.

'Denver. Before you say anything, I know. It sounds like a million miles away. But at least it's not West Coast. I'll be travelling most of the time so we'll get to see each other.'

Stephen knew he should be supportive, tell her what she needed to hear, yet deep down, all he wanted to ask was what about you and me?

'They won't ask again.'

No, he didn't expect they would. He watched her body language as she talked. He could tell by the way she was leaning forward that she was drunk on flattery and living on adrenaline. He put himself in her place. And yes, he couldn't help but feel a tad envious. His boss at the Met couldn't wait to get rid of him.

'What will you be doing?'

'Head of Acquisitions. They've got a massive budget and an ambitious director who told me that if there's anything out there I want to buy for the gallery I should pursue it. And he'll do everything in his powers to make it happen.'

'You've had the interview?'

Ginny did have the grace to blush.

'Not exactly. We met informally in London, where he sounded me out. Asked me if I was interested. I said I needed to talk it through.'

So that was the real reason she'd chosen this weekend. She was working to a deadline—to ask for his blessing, not his advice.

'Of course, you must go for it. I won't stand in your way. We can put our plans on hold. It's not like we've sent out the invitations yet.' The bit about the invitations was true. Everything else he'd told her was just to make her feel better.

'I hoped you'd say that. I've already given the venue the heads-up. They came back to say two other couples wanted the same date. And we can have the deposit back.'

That was a relief. At least he wouldn't have to listen to Ginny's father complaining about how much it had cost him.

She twisted her hands together, opened her mouth to say something, then thought better of it. She mouthed, 'I'm sorry,' and stared down at the table. She pushed her food away, got up and leaned over the balcony. From where he was sitting, it seemed like she was looking beyond the view, at something that wasn't even there. He decided to leave her be.

When she turned towards Stephen and made her way back to the table, tears were rolling down her cheeks. 'I've booked an open return. There's a flight late tonight. Might be best if I was on it, don't you think?'

Stephen wanted desperately to take her in his arms and tell her that what they had was worth saving, but at that moment he felt completely numb. Lost for words, he found himself meekly agreeing with her. Why was she doing this, he wondered. What had happened in the past four weeks? At least when he left she was angry with him. Now she was only distant, distracted. It didn't seem to be another man— she would have said so outright. He trusted her that much.

Chapter 14

Stephen and Ginny pulled up outside Stephen's flat. The drive back from the restaurant had been difficult and awkward. Neither of them had felt like talking. Stephen spotted Elisabetta's scooter parked outside.

Damn.

He'd invited her around as a thank you for suggesting the lakeside restaurant. With all the emotional fallout, he'd forgotten to message her that the trip had been an unmitigated disaster and that it was probably best they cancel.

She was staring at her phone and hadn't spotted them.

'That's Elisabetta. Sorry.'

'It's okay by me,' Ginny said, her tone softening. As they got out of the car, Elisabetta looked up, shoved the phone into her pocket and came towards them.

'You must be Ginny.' She kissed her on both cheeks. 'Shall we walk?'

'Why not?' Ginny's tone was friendly.

As they strolled along, exchanging pleasantries, Stephen spotted a gelateria. He needed a moment to collect his thoughts after the afternoon they'd had.

'Fancy an ice-cream?'

'Of course,' Ginny said. 'When in Rome.'

'Hazelnut is good, but the pistachio is the best,' Elisabetta chipped in.

'Pistachio it is then,' Ginny said.

'Coming right up,' Stephen said, glad to have a few moments to himself.

He'd been gone barely five minutes, balancing three ice-creams and was about to hand them over when he caught the tail end of their conversation.

'It's my job to try to stem the tide of art crime. And see the works restored to their rightful home,' Elisabetta said.

This was meant to be a casual meet and greet. He suspected it had been Ginny who had started on about work.

'Weren't the best part of the Romans' treasures made in Greece by Greek potters and vase painters? Their rightful home is there, surely?' Ginny said.

'The craftsmen were Greek, yes. But they were working on commissions for Roman patrons. And Greek vase-painters came to work here. They're Italian works of art which belong here. And we're trying to stop them being stolen and illegally exported.'

'Are you involved in protecting the cultural heritage of works disturbed by the extension of the Rome metro, too?'

What the hell's got into you?

'Not unless an actual crime has been committed. The archaeological team onsite do what they can to protect any works that get disturbed.'

'Isn't the act of putting a metro right next to the Colosseum an art crime?'

'I know what you're getting at, and I agree with you, but my job is to stop looting and theft. And we can't do that alone.'

Oh, oh, Stephen wondered what was coming next.

'We need the co-operation of auction houses, which at the moment we're not getting. There's still far too much work of disputed provenance being sold. We need people like you to look out for suspect artworks.'

Stephen didn't want to take sides, but it was Ginny who had gone on the attack. She deserved Elisabetta's icy response.

'Denham's isn't some dodgy, fly-by-night operation. We don't trade in suspect artworks, as you appear to suggest. Sorry, I have to go now, before I say anything I'll regret.'

Bit late for that now.

Ginny got up, picked up her gelato container and spoon, threw them into the nearest bin with more force than they needed, and walked off towards the apartment.

Mouthing 'sorry,' to Elisabetta, Stephen dashed off in pursuit. As he caught up, he could barely contain his fury.

'What was that about?'

'She practically accused me of trafficking in looted art.'

'Because you told her that the art she's spent her life's work trying to protect doesn't even belong here.'

'Couldn't you see when you took this damn job that this might happen? That your world and mine might get too close for comfort?'

'Of course I did. I even talked about it in my meeting with Reynolds. But as I was going to be in Italy and you were in London I thought that it might just work.'

Ginny twisted her fingers together.

Stephen sighed. 'This is about so much more than art, isn't it?' There was a long silence. 'What is it, do you think that's gone wrong between us?' There. He'd finally said it.

Ginny walked up to him, looking into his eyes.

'Nothing that wasn't there already,' she said, one fat

tear rolling down her right cheek. 'You only saw what you wanted to see.'

As they got back to the apartment, she said, 'I'm sorry, I have to go. I need to pack.' She disappeared into the bedroom and started to fling clothes into a suitcase.

'At least let me drive you.'

'No, I'll get a taxi. We can say goodbye here. Why drag yourself out to the airport? You'll only have to come back to an empty flat.'

'We're not leaving things like this. What if I come over next weekend?'

Ginny shook her head, whispering, 'No, I don't think so,' before quietly turning away and closing the door.

Maybe she'd seen through him—another promise he would have to break. There was practically no chance he'd get the time off.

'Your phone's here if you're looking for it,' he called out, in a clumsy attempt at civility. She'd left it plugged into one of the broken sockets. The battery had less than ten percent charge. Stephen unplugged it and moved it to the working socket. Just as he was about to put Ginny's mobile down, it buzzed. He couldn't help himself. He looked at the text.

Compliance are asking questions about provenance. We need a paper trail that looks like we tried, even if it is a work of fiction. Call me.

Ginny's phone was in his hand. Once a cop, always a cop. He heard the shower running.

The phone was locked.

What the hell was her PIN? She'd told him that if he couldn't be trusted to know it then nobody could. If he'd guessed it correctly, she'd used her date of birth in the first two numbers. With trembling fingers and a feeling of fore-boding, he keyed in 91 and came to an abrupt stop.

What had she said about symmetry? He added a 1 as the third digit. The last he would have to guess. It can't have been another 1. A 9 would make the number symmetrical. It was worth a shot.

Bingo. He was in.

He scrolled through her contacts. He didn't know the names, but most of them seemed to work for leading international galleries and museums. He had got as far as the letter L and was now at M. Under Mc, was none other than McCarthy, Michael. He was still listed as the contact at the Vatican Museums. Maybe his departure had been recent and the Vatican had kept it quiet.

Stephen heard the shower running as he reached up into a cupboard and started to rifle through a box he hadn't had time to unpack. He started to pull out wires and cables and spare flash drives. There it was. The card writer terminal. Next to it, the blank SIMs. He grabbed everything he needed and headed back to the sitting room.

Damn. She'd turned the water off already. He reckoned he had ten more minutes. Longer, if she needed to dry her hair.

He opened up the back of her phone, pulled out the SIM and placed it into the card writer terminal and plugged it in. He pressed copy.

Estimated time, fifteen minutes. She must have had a ton of data on there.

The door opened softly, and Ginny, wrapped in a towel came up behind him.

'You haven't seen my phone, have you?'

Shit.

'The socket you plugged it into wasn't working so I moved it. It's still charging. I won't let you leave it behind.' His tone was relaxed.

What am I doing?

'I just wanted to book an Uber, that's all.'

'I'll call a regular cab on mine. Uber isn't any cheaper here.'

'Thanks,' she said and turned to go back into the bedroom. She closed the door behind her and Stephen heard the sound of the hairdryer.

He got up and checked the download time left. Another ten minutes. He grabbed his phone and texted the cab company and booked it for twenty minutes. He needed to find a way to fill in time. He remembered the bottle of fizz in the fridge that he'd been planning to open the night Ginny arrived. He pulled it out and grabbed the wine glasses, hoping Ginny wouldn't mind that they weren't fancy champagne flutes.

The hairdryer had stopped now. Ginny would be putting on her make-up. He figured that would take five minutes. Then she'd need to get dressed. He popped the cork and poured two glasses.

Ginny, alerted by the sound walked into the kitchen. She looked at Stephen in surprise. Inside, he was quaking. He handed her a glass.

'Peace offering.' He avoided her gaze. She smiled back at him awkwardly. There was no going back.

'Cheers, I can drink it while I'm changing,' she said, with no enthusiasm. Turning her back on him, she took the glass back into the bedroom.

Stephen grabbed the phone. The data had fully down-loaded. He wrenched the SIM chip out of the reader and was putting it back into Ginny's phone, when she opened the door of the bedroom again, case in hand.

'Your phone's charged,' Stephen said, passing it and the charger back to her. The back of the phone wasn't clicked shut properly and to Stephen's alarm, the SIM fell out. 'Sorry,' he said, passing it to her. 'I must have knocked it.'

'Thanks. I'll fix it in the cab.'

They hugged briefly and that was it. As the taxi pulled up, the old Stephen would have grasped her hands in his, looked her in the eyes and told her that he wasn't giving up on her. He went in for another hug so that he didn't have to look at her and berated himself for being such a coward. Ginny gently released herself from his grasp and without turning to look back, walked out the door. As she got into the cab, he waved forlornly. After everything they'd been through, it had come to this. He turned sorrowfully and made his way slowly back to his empty, silent flat.

Naples, Italy

Geppo and Paolo were shooting pool in a sleazy bar late at night, the last two punters left. The barman was busy cleaning down the countertop, the ash from his cigarette about to fall at any moment. With a flick of a switch he stopped the pumping rock music dead. His cigarette ash fell onto the floor.

'We're closing in ten minutes. Hurry up and finish your game. I need to wash those glasses.'

Paolo downed his drink and called out to the barman.

'We're nearly done.'

The barman nodded. 'Make it quick,' he said, turning the music back up to full blast.

Paolo grabbed his cue, but stopped, just as he was about to take a shot.

'Hey Uncle.'

'Not again. You already told me Bill Gates wants to inject everyone with a microchip.' Geppo stifled a yawn.

'No. But you'll be sorry when the deep state takes over and you didn't listen to me,' Paolo said.

'Go on then, I'm all ears,' Geppo replied mechanically.

'Tony screwed us over. He died owing us money. And we act like losers. What if there is no new Tony and we never get paid?'

'That shit you read on the internet…doesn't tell you how the world works. Someone up the chain puts in an order. They need a Tony to get it delivered.'

Paolo leant over the green baize table, shooting the red ball into the pocket. He stood up, grinning.

'Why do we even need another Tony?'

'Because the only place we get to call the shots is here,' Geppo said, potting the wrong ball.

'If we were smart we could go straight to the top.'

'I was smart when I was your age. I even stuck my neck out. All I did was screw it up for the rest of the family, as you keep telling me. From now on I'll do what I'm told. You'll get yourself into all sorts of shit if you're not careful.'

'You think everyone's mafia,' Uncle.

'Tony protected us from all that.'

'Only so he could take his cut for doing bugger all.' Paolo slammed his cue down on the table so fiercely it bounced.

'Quit that will you. Or he'll definitely throw us out,' Geppo said, glancing at the barman who seemed to be in a world of his own, singing along tunelessly to Nirvana. Luckily he didn't notice. 'You ever thought about how come it's always just us that gets to go digging at night? They've warned off the others, that's why.'

'You're paranoid. One last shot and we're done, okay. And it'll be your turn to buy the drinks tomorrow night.'

Geppo was dismissive. 'Sure. Beginner's luck.'

'I'm reading a book. It says nobody makes money working for other people. Look at Berlusconi.'

'You want to be like him? I don't. Kid, you have to have customers. And we don't have any. Your business book got any answers for that?'

'I haven't got that far. You were the one who was mad when you found out that the top guy sold the prizes we dug up for a million dollars apiece.'

'And I'm still mad.' Geppo stopped mid-game and leaned on his pool cue. 'But that doesn't mean I'm going to run round trying to find who the top dog is. I don't want to know.'

'That's easy. He's a fancy art dealer with a gallery in Switzerland. His name was in the papers when he sold our stuff to that famous museum in America.'

'And you're going to ring him up and tell him what, exactly?'

'That we can save him thousands if we deal direct, but he has to pay us, say, 25% more. He'll still be making on the deal.'

'Well, son, let me know how you get on,' Geppo said, laying his cue down, grabbing his jacket and making towards the door.

'Tony made enough money off us to buy a beach house,' Paolo called after him.

As that sunk in, Geppo stopped and turned around to look at his nephew.

'You've got balls, I'll give you that,' he said, as he closed the door behind him.

* * *

Geneva, Switzerland

'Who is it, Maris?' Robert Hurst called out.

'Someone from Italy. Doesn't speak English. Keeps repeating a name, Antonio Sanzio.'

Robert Hurst got up from his chair as his wife held up the mobile phone and rolled her eyes.

'Pronto? Sono Robert Hurst.' There was a pause and what sounded like paper being shuffled.

'We have items for sale we found for Tony. Only Tony's dead, and we have nowhere to store them. If you want them, we can meet you.'

How the fuck had they got his number? Why hadn't Tony told him he had stuff on order?

'Okay, I'll try and sort this out,' Hurst said. He heard an argument going on at the other end in the background as the phone was passed from one to another.

'Try isn't good enough. Tony owes us money. And we have to pay the guys who work for us,' a younger-sounding man said.

'You'll get your money, I promise you. I just have to find a replacement for Tony,' Hurst said. To his astonishment, he heard a laugh down the phone.

'We don't want a go-between. We want to deal direct.'

Hurst could barely contain himself, but he held back. Now that Tony was dead, these lowlifes were the only ones who knew the exact location of the looting site. Until he'd been down there to see for himself, he had to humour them.

'Okay, let me think about it and we'll see if we can work something out,' Hurst said, the words sounding as though he meant them.

'You will?'

Hurst couldn't believe that the dumb fuck had fallen for it.

'Of course. You have an eye for antiquities.' Even a stupid person fell for flattery.

'I do?' The younger guy sounded surprised. There was whispering in the background and then arguing, as though the younger guy was describing what he'd just said.

'I'm the management guy. My uncle's the art expert.'

'Put him back on again.' He had these two clowns wrapped around his fingers. All he had to do was string them along.

'What's your name, sir?'

There was silence on the other end of the phone and an embarrassed laugh. He tried again.

'Geppo Corri.' And then another scuffle and a lot of whispering.

'Holy crap, Uncle. Now he knows who we are.'

'Be quiet Paolo. I can't hear the gentleman.'

'Signor Corri, thank you for all the treasures you've found.'

'At least someone appreciates me.'

There was more jostling and whispering. Hurst started to drum his fingers on a table. What were they doing now?

The younger one came on the line. 'We have two big ticket finds we'd like you to see,' Paolo began.

Hurst wasn't going to get excited until he knew what they were. 'Describe them to me.'

'One is identical to that large pot with all the drawing on it. And the other is a large head. A man with curly hair and a curly beard.' There was another Euphronios in that tomb and a warrior? He couldn't believe it.

'Send me photos and we'll talk.'

'Sending them now,' Paolo said, texting the photos.

'I'd have to see them of course. The head is intact and the krater is in three pieces. Is that right?'

'Correct and we want 20,000 euros for both. The same amount that you paid Tony.'

'10,000 for both and it's a deal,' Hurst said.

'Fifteen.'

'12,500 is my final offer.'

'Done. Cash on the day,' Paolo said.

'Be careful how you wrap them,' Hurst said.

'You'd better be careful how you transport them,' came the facetious reply. 'You break it. You buy it.'

Hurst counted to ten in his head to stop himself saying anything he'd regret.

'I'll travel to you. I'll meet you outside Naples Central Station. Just name the date and time.'

Chapter 15

Stephen had been up late going through Ginny's work emails including a long email chain that discussed items offered for auction by Robert Hurst, aka Tie Pin Man. He insisted on addressing Ginny as Darling. She must have loved that. When he wrote to her boss he was passive-aggressive. When he wrote to Ginny, he was boastful. He painted himself as someone of global standing.

Stephen felt sorry for anyone who had to plough through his pompous emails. They were full of obtuse references and jargon and he had a habit of giving nicknames instead of an official title, to the pieces he was trying to sell. It had to be deliberate. He must have learned his lesson from his run-in with the law back in 2000.

At 1.00 a.m. Stephen got a text from Renzo in Naples:

Corri rang a Robert Hurst. Offered him artefacts. They're meeting near the railway station in Naples at 4.00 p.m. the day after tomorrow.

So Hurst was meeting two small-time crooks? Whatever they had for sale must have been of sufficient interest to warrant Hurst travelling from, where did he live,

Switzerland, to Naples. Judging by the boastful name-dropping in Ginny's emails, he wasn't in the habit of mixing with types like Corri and his nephew.

Stephen took Sanzio's list of names and started to draw a mind map. He put the Fixer (Tony and beside that, deceased—vacancy) in the middle. And from that central point he drew an arrow down and scribbled Nighthawks (Geppo Corri and nephew). As far as he knew, there was still no sign of Sanzio's replacement. Sanzio had been able to chivvy the lowly nighthawks into doing his bidding and yet was able to command the respect of the kingpin at the top. Was that Hurst?

Tony had a sense of the bigger picture—he'd written this list in the first place. Maybe he'd done it to get more money out of his paymasters? Without him, the set-up was in danger of falling apart. And now Hurst was forced to deal with the tomb raiders himself.

What if Tony had got too big for his boots and someone higher up decided he needed to be taught a lesson. Then, in the act of giving Sanzio a warning by arranging for his car to be side-swiped on the motorway, the driver in the white Fiat had hit him too hard and given Sanzio such a fright it had resulted in the fatal crash?

Stephen didn't dispute that Sanzio was obese and had eaten a heavy lunch, nor that the cause of death had been a heart attack—but fatalities were rarely caused by one thing and were more often the result of a chain of unfortunate events.

One role in Sanzio's list that he hadn't yet been able to connect with the looting chain was the Sales Rep. In the snooty end of the art world, which Ginny inhabited, the word "sales," was replaced by the word "auction." And what were auction houses but fancy shopfronts where millions changed hands and it was all about money. Ginny had said her boss had put her name forward for her new job. What, Stephen wondered, did he want as payback? A friendly face in a major gallery with a massive acquisitions budget would grease the wheels, ensure there was a market for precious artworks.

If Stephen had played by the rules this would have been the perfect opportunity to recruit Ginny to help them bring down Hurst. But he'd well and truly blown it. It was bad enough that he got hold of the Hurst emails by illegal phone-hacking but to use his fiancée to do so was indefensible. Imagine if the press got hold of that information— he'd not only be vilified as a love rat but out of a job, if Elisabetta had anything to do with it.

And what if Ginny refused to help? She could argue the cost was too high—she'd be sacrificing her career to help bring down one of her former clients. And for what? Art looting was a victimless crime. Nobody was going to die from it. What scared him most was that Ginny herself might be a cog in the looting chain.

Stephen glanced at his watch. Another late night. He turned off his light and dreamt that Ginny and Elisabetta had found out about the stolen data. Ginny hadn't said anything: just shaken her head sorrowfully and walked out of his life forever. Elisabetta had him forcibly removed from work by security, where he'd literally been thrown out into the street. He woke up with a start at the persistent sound of the alarm.

* * *

'Renzo messaged me. Corti's meeting Robert Hurst in Naples tomorrow afternoon. I'll go down in the morning,' Stephen said.

Elisabetta looked up, surprised.

'I've left three messages for him and not had a reply to one. When you see him, ask him to return my calls.' Elisabetta seemed out of sorts.

'I will.' He deliberated whether or not to ask her what was up. But he needed her advice on what to do about Hurst first.

'If we see Hurst receive stolen goods, do we arrest him and Corri on the spot?'

'We need more evidence than one pot and a head. He could say it was a one-off when we're trying to prove that he's looting to order,' Elisabetta said. 'Get photos and follow Hurst.'

'Okay, will do. What's the score with Renzo?'

'I wish I knew. Why don't you go down this evening and meet up with him. Take him out for a drink.'

'Is everything okay?' Stephen asked.

'How do you feel he's fitting in?'

He was going to have to be careful how he answered this one.

'I think he's finding that we do things very differently up here.'

'That's the diplomatic answer. I get the feeling he had more autonomy down there.' Elisabetta said.

Stephen wasn't about to defend the guy and he wasn't going to make assumptions either. But he didn't say that to her.

She pushed on. 'I blame Alberti. He was the one who gave Renzo the choice to split his time between here and Naples.'

'I guess it's because his family is still there.'

'I don't want to come across as mean about his home life, and we do need him down there now and again, but I can't help feeling he's using it to his advantage.'

'Anything else I should know first?'

'Before he applied for the job he cultivated me. And it was only after he got it, I realised I'd been used,' Elisabetta said.

Stephen remembered that conversation he'd had with Vittorio when they'd first started working together in Naples. Vittorio couldn't wait for Renzo to leave so he'd be someone else's problem. He decided not to mention that to Elisabetta.

* * *

At Renzo's suggestion they had met in a bar-restaurant, tucked away in the back streets at the smarter end of town, near to Stephen's hotel.

'How are things?' Stephen asked.

Renzo looked at him.

'So so.'

Seeing an opportunity, Stephen waved to the barman.

'Another two beers, please.'

'I'm feeling the same way,' Stephen offered.

'You too? But you're not even married.'

'You didn't hear?'

'Nobody tells me anything,' Renzo said.

'I'm going to regret this,' Stephen said.

'Try me. Let's order some food when the waiter comes over.'

'Sure. I was getting married this summer until this job came up. And my girlfriend came to stay a couple of days ago and told me the wedding's off.'

'What?'

'And, oh, by the way don't think about getting back together as she's been head-hunted for a job in America and she's moving to Denver.'

'That's pretty bad.'

'And you?'

'It's going to come across as the biggest cliché in the world. My wife and kid left me.'

Stephen tried to keep a straight face, but because he'd been drinking, he couldn't help but agree. 'It does sound like a bit of a sob story.'

Just then the waiter came over with more drinks. 'You need the menu?'

Renzo shook his head and turned to Stephen.

'They do a great spaghetti vongole.'

Stephen nodded.

'Make that two.' As the waiter left, Renzo pulled out a photo of his baby daughter. 'That's Ava. Giulia's taken her away to go and live with her parents.'

Stephen felt bad. There was a kid involved. It wasn't something to joke about. He couldn't help but feel sorry for the guy.

Because he was drinking on an empty stomach and hadn't eaten anything since breakfast, he'd blurted out 'That's bad. But you can put things right can't you?'

'I hope so,' Renzo said.

'There's no turning back with what I've done,' Stephen said.

'What did you do that was so bad?'

'Ginny's job was always going to get in the way. I warned my boss that she works for a major auction house. They're big in antiquities.'

'Awkward,' Renzo said.

'Really. And I just can't let it go that she might be implicated in looting.'

'What makes you sure?'

'I'm not sure. Or I wasn't.' Stephen lowered his voice. 'Until I hacked her phone.'

'You did?'

Just then the waiter came over with two bowls of steaming clams over spaghetti. He hadn't noticed how hungry he was until the wafts of garlic butter reminded him. They fell upon their food.

'It was a heat of the moment thing. She was in the shower and a text came through about work. I just couldn't resist looking at it.' Stephen paused. 'We might not even see each other again. I didn't have anything to lose. Or so I thought. Apart from the fact that I don't have the guts to tell her what I did. If anyone finds out that evidence in the case came from my girlfriend's phone, I'll be on the first plane out.'

'Yeah you would.' It was Renzo's turn to laugh. 'And I thought you were Mr Nice Guy, too good to be true.'

'Let's forget we ever had this conversation,' Stephen said.

Renzo nodded, twirling spaghetti round his fork.

'Now that you know my situation, you couldn't lend me 400 euros could you, just until payday? It's so expensive running two households.'

What an opportunist.

Given all that Stephen had revealed, he could hardly say no, could he? Renzo definitely had the upper hand. Well it was too late now. He'd taken him into his confidence.

* * *

Franco had dimmed the lights in his studio so that the room was lit solely by an ultraviolet glow, as he moved his torch slowly over every inch of the painting of St Jerome.

'See the way the colour changes? If I shine the light here, on the subject, it's red, but when I move it here to the landscape, the rocks appear almost yellow.'

McCarthy peered closely. The conservator was right.

'And if you look where the lion is lifting his paw, you can see that the surface is uneven where the artist has been inconsistent with the layers of paint.'

'Why would that be?' McCarthy asked.

'That could be down to the technique, the type of paint used, or it could indicate that the canvas had been used before. I don't know until I have it x-rayed. Do you want me to go ahead? There will be a charge to have the equipment sent over,' Franco said.

McCarthy felt a mixture of excitement and fear that there could be another painting underneath St Jerome. He had enough money saved.

'Yes, go ahead.'

* * *

Stephen and Renzo watched as Corri and Paolo drew up in their van and parked illegally. Paolo, hands pushed deep into his pockets, seemed to have lost his swagger as he and Corri walked into Caffe Mexico on Piazza Garibaldi. It was one of a half dozen or so cafes in the piazza. Stephen and Renzo slipped into the one next door.

'When did you get hold of his phone?' Stephen asked, as Renzo passed him an earpiece that he put in his left ear. Renzo had the other earpiece in his right ear and tapped the table, pretending to drum along to music.

'I know the barman where he plays pool most nights with that idiot nephew. Corri has a habit of abandoning his phone on the table when he goes for a slash.'

Corri and Paolo took it in turns to speak. They heard a third, deeper voice.

'Gentlemen,' the man said.

Renzo whispered to Stephen, 'he's speaking Italian with a strong American accent.'

'We need a visual on him,' Stephen said. 'He's going to look a little different now to the police mugshot from 2000.'

'I'll go and buy cigarettes,' Renzo said, getting out of his seat, pulling up his hoodie over his head and walking out. Stephen watched him as he walked past the café window. Five minutes later, Renzo slipped back into the seat next to Stephen and showed him a blurry photo of Corri and Paolo with a well-preserved immaculately-dressed man in his eighties, who even seated had a straight up and down posture and appeared intimidating.

Stephen pulled out the police mugshot as well as a newspaper clipping of Hurst taken twenty years before and compared it with Renzo's. 'That's the same man,' Stephen said. Renzo nodded his head.

'We need to get something straight. I'd be more than happy to work with you. But things have changed,' Hurst said.

'What circumstances?' Paolo said.

'This is what you came for, isn't it?' Then the sound of paper rustling.

'Paying them off?' Stephen mouthed. Renzo nodded.

'It's all there,' Hurst said.

'What do we do with all the stuff we found for you?' Corri asked.

'I've paid you for the head and the krater as agreed. But hold onto everything else. I'll have the new Tony in place in a week. Maybe two. He'll go through everything you have. Then work out a fair price.'

'What's changed?' Paolo said.

'I'm not at liberty to disclose that,' Hurst said. Then there was the sound of a chair being pulled out.

'What do we do now?' said.

'I'll bring my vehicle round and we'll make the exchange,' Hurst said, 'After that, gentlemen, please don't contact me again. Have you got that?' It sounded like a threat. 'I'll see you in a minute.' Hurst's voice was more distant now, his footsteps fading.

'Bastard,' Paolo muttered.

'What if they both drive off?' Stephen said.

'Relax. They won't. We've got eyes on the two nighthawks and Hurst is hardly going to leave without his trophies, is he?' Renzo said.

Just then, a black Range Rover swung around the corner and parked next to Geppo Corri's van.

'Holy shit.'

'What is it?'

'It's the same vehicle that hit me in Geneva.'

'Deliberately?' Renzo said.

'It felt like it. Elisabetta passed it off as bad driving. We didn't get a proper visual on the driver. But it was the same make and model and had those distinctive reflective plates.'

Just then the boot of the Range Rover lifted up and Hurst wound down his window to say something to the waiting men.

Renzo fired off a series of photos.

Corri and Paolo opened the back doors of their van. Corri carried one box and placed it carefully in the boot of Hurst's vehicle and went back to help Paolo, who was lifting something heavier in what appeared to be the packaging for a microwave.

Hurst got out from the driver's seat and came around to inspect the boxes before awkwardly shaking both men's hands.

Stephen and Renzo got up simultaneously and walked

rapidly out of the coffee shop and into the street, Stephen talking into his walkie-talkie.

'Black Range Rover. Reflective plates. Tail him,' he said. As Hurst drove off a nondescript dark grey car pulled out after him.

'We'll follow you,' Stephen said as he and Renzo walked down the street and got into their waiting vehicle.

As they were driving along, the area became more exclusive.

'Where are we?' Stephen asked.

'Where the rich people live,' Renzo said.

Suddenly Hurst did a U-turn and headed straight for them.

'Shit,' he's seen us,' Stephen said, grabbing his radio. 'Hurst on the move, where are you?'

'I'm boxed in. A woman is dropping off her kids,' came the reply from the uniform police officer.

'We're going to lose him,' Stephen said. 'Where's he gone?'

Renzo shook his head. 'He outwitted us.'

* * *

Franco peered out on to the street, looking left, then right before he ushered McCarthy inside.

'You go ahead while I lock up.'

McCarthy wondered what had happened since he'd last seen him. He seemed flustered. Had someone tried to break in?

Franco pulled the door to the studio behind him and locked it. Once they'd settled themselves down in front of the painting, Franco turned to McCarthy. 'There was one more sample I took. It's a fragment of the background. Let me show you.'

The conservator's hands had always been small, but today they seemed tiny, McCarthy noticed, as he took out his finest scalpel and began to gently flick away the fragments of paint.

'You can keep them for further analysis,' Franco said, picking up the paint shavings with tweezers and popping them into a test tube which he carefully corked with a little rubber stopper. McCarthy got up and walked around the room. Franco had by now exposed a layer of paint the size of a euro cent. The paint underneath was in stark contrast to the layer on top—a lemon yellow that seemed to him to belong in an entirely different painting.

'It's been overpainted?' McCarthy asked. The little man took off his round glasses and rubbed his eyes.

'And recently, too.'

'St Jerome and the Lion is a fake?' McCarthy said in astonishment.

'Without a doubt. Rather a good one. The painter went to elaborate lengths to make it look like a Brunetti.'

McCarthy recalled the casual way Giuseppe had talked about the painting and had stressed that it was unsigned and from an artist's workshop without mentioning any particular artist.

'Shall we continue?' Franco asked. McCarthy nodded, trying outwardly to appear calm.

'I'm going to turn the lights off now so that we can see from the light of the UV torch,' Franco said. They were sitting in the dark, the only light the faint blue glow from the torch.

Staring back at McCarthy was the faintest trace of another scene. It seemed to be an interior. A woman appeared to be sitting down in front of what looked like a writing desk. The newly exposed lemon paint seemed to come from her dress. Across from her, standing, was another woman, holding something in her hand, a letter, perhaps?

But it was the black and white floor tiles that made McCarthy nearly leap out of his skin.

He locked eyes with Franco, who started to twitch.

'And you're sure it isn't a van Meegeren?' McCarthy asked.

'Of course I'm sure,' Franco snapped back. 'Van Meegeren may have fooled the Nazis, but they couldn't do the pigment analysis we can today. The natural ultramine in the yellow-green area is made from lapis lazuli. He would have had to have been using the synthetic alternative: it's been in use since the nineteenth century.'

'I didn't mean…'

'I know you didn't,' Franco interrupted. 'But it can't stay here. I don't want the responsibility,' the old man began.

'I understand. But I can't take it like that with the piece missing,' McCarthy said.

'Leave it with me. Once I'm finished, nobody will know it's anything but a Brunetti. I'll call you as soon as it's done. I didn't sleep at all last night.'

McCarthy felt the weight of responsibility hanging over him. Giuseppe had done this for a reason, McCarthy kept telling himself. He was using him as a conduit to make his peace with God. But just at that moment, McCarthy had unholy thoughts and wished, selfishly, that the patriarch had chosen another priest.

All McCarthy wanted to do was to slip quietly away to Mexico. Now he was responsible for a painting by the master of domestic quiet. Any discovery of a Vermeer would have been rare enough: he had barely thirty-five known works attributed to him. But this one was famous for another reason.

The Isabella Stewart Gardner had been the first museum McCarthy had taken Giuseppe to for his art history lessons. They had walked past The Concert, he was certain, but Giuseppe hadn't seemed that interested, preferring instead more dramatic pieces in the collection.

Walking home, McCarthy recalled that Giuseppe seemed agitated in his last moments on earth.

'I don't know what to do,' he had said. McCarthy had tried to reassure him, encouraging him to do what he believed was true in his heart. When he had told the old man it wasn't too late, he had been referring to confessing his sins. But Giuseppe in his morphine-induced fog had either misunderstood or was talking about something entirely different, unfinished business, perhaps. Then this: 'It's too late for me. They're safe, I can assure you.' McCarthy had thought at the time that the "they" he was referring to were loved ones, but what if it was in fact stolen paintings?

Joe already had his suspicions about why his father had gifted the artwork to McCarthy. What if he put two and two together before McCarthy had the chance to go to the authorities? Now Franco's life was in danger, and that was his fault too.

In hindsight, what was McCarthy thinking? That by teaching Giuseppe to appreciate beautiful art that he'd stop the torture and murder? That he could make him a better human being? If religion couldn't do that, then how could art? The problem wasn't Giuseppe's. It was his. Had his own love of art that transcended all else made him blind to the world around him?

All that he'd done by instructing Giuseppe on the rich and powerful art patrons of the Renaissance was to make him envious. Giuseppe must have imagined himself as a modern-day Medici. He had money, he wielded power.

What was missing was the art collection. If he couldn't afford to buy it, or it belonged to someone else, or if it just wasn't for sale, he could simply go and steal it.

For decades Giuseppe was the de facto leader of gangland Boston and nobody, not even the cops, could stop him. But as Giuseppe's physical strength began to fade away, he realised that soon he would be facing his maker, and he'd had a change of heart. By entrusting McCarthy, one of God's representatives on earth, with one of the stolen paintings, he hoped that McCarthy would do the job for him and go to the authorities. Giuseppe would be absolved of his sins and rest in peace.

Why had it taken McCarthy so long to grasp this? His life had been so entwined with that of the patriarch's that he had been blind to what Giuseppe was expecting him to do. But while McCarthy had followed his duty of care for the old man while he was still alive, all he wanted now was to put as much distance as he could between himself and the Russo family. It was time to pass the baton on.

Chapter 16

Rome, Italy

Stephen tried to piece together the connections between Robert Hurst, the Vatican and Michael McCarthy. Hurst had acquired a krater on the Vatican's behalf during McCarthy's directorship. Had McCarthy been for or against the acquisition? Not long after the krater went on display, McCarthy was fired. Was it a coincidence or were the two events connected?

Was Tony Sanzio aware of McCarthy? And could the priest be one of the nicknames in Sanzio's notes?

Stephen stopped to make himself a pot of espresso. Boston seemed to be where McCarthy had spent most of his career. Could there be something there? Was it worth combing through the parish records? There were 288 Catholic churches in Boston, but if he stuck to the Irish Catholic suburbs he'd have a better chance. Sure enough, by 9.00 p.m. he had a match in the parish of Allston.

To get any decent intel required boots on the ground:

going to mass, passing McCarthy's photo around among elderly parishioners who might remember him from thirty years ago. There was no way he could justify to Elisabetta a fact-finding mission to the USA to investigate a priest who could have bought looted items in Italy. He'd have to think of another way.

It was only when he had exhausted all his networks of former colleagues that it struck him. He might not have mates he could pull a favour from, but he did have a distant cousin on his mother's side, Cormac Hannigan, who he'd last seen when he was a teenager, but who was now Lieutenant Detective in the Boston Police Department.

Hannigan had been pleased to hear from him and assisted him in every way he could, but as McCarthy had a clean record there was nothing else he could do. Why didn't Stephen come over for a weekend, he'd suggested. Hannigan was a season ticket holder for the Red Sox and the Patriots, and the Sox were playing this coming weekend.

'That's too good an offer to turn down.' To hell with it, even if he didn't find anything on McCarthy, he'd have a weekend away to remember.

Hannigan laughed. 'Don't tell the rest of the clan, will you? Or they'll all be expecting major league baseball tickets when they come to visit.'

'You know, I was thinking when Ma finds out on the jungle telegraph that we're meeting up, I'll never hear the end of it.'

'Great. Let me know when you get in. The game's on Sunday.'

So that was that, he was going. If anyone asked, it was a weekend break to meet up with long-lost family. And if anything came of his McCarthy investigation, he'd try and recoup some of the costs from work later.

Just then his cover phone rang. 'Stephen Walsh.'

Stephen nearly jumped out of his skin.

'Michael McCarthy. I won't keep you.' He sounded agitated. 'I've changed my mind. I'd like to get a quote for insuring my artworks after all. I plan to break up the collection. Some will go into storage, some will be donated.'

There was none of McCarthy's usual hail fellow well met banter: something, or someone had clearly rattled his cage. The chance to see McCarthy's treasures on display was too great an offer to turn down.

'I'd be delighted to help. When would suit?'

'When can you get here?'

If only he'd waited a few more minutes before committing himself to his trip. But it was too late now.

'The earliest I can do is Monday afternoon, say around 2.00 p.m.?'

'I'll be here. I'll text you the address.'

'If I can get there any sooner, I'll call you, I promise.' He'd barely got the words out when McCarthy had hung up.

* * *

Boston, USA

Stephen's transit through Logan had been seamless and he was in a taxi forty-five minutes after the plane had arrived at the gate.

It was dusk by the time he got into downtown. The hotel was a dark brownstone, an old flatiron building on

Merrimac Street. From an angle it looked like a wedge of aged cheese. Dumping his stuff, he stashed his passport and valuables in the safe and headed downstairs to the bar. After a couple of beers and a bag of crisps, he was ready to hit the sack.

He walked into the room, threw his things down and drew the curtains, before switching on the TV.

Lieutenant Hannigan may not have been able to do anything to aid Stephen's investigation in his official capacity, but Cormac Hannigan, regular mass-goer, turned out to be a mine of information. He'd confirmed that McCarthy's old parish church was the one in Allston and prepared the ground with the story of a visiting relative from Ireland.

Flicking between Rachel Maddow on MSNBC and Anderson Cooper on CNN, he felt the wave of jet lag overcome him, especially when the pharmaceutical ads came on. When the earnest voice-over artist listed the potential lethal side-effects from taking a heavily promoted drug for a condition he'd never heard of, but now worried that he had, it was time to hit the shower and head for bed.

By nine the next morning he was on the Red Line subway train to Harvard Square. He walked down North Harvard Street across the Charles River. The corporate-style buildings of Harvard Business School gave way to a district noticeably shabbier, once he was away from the main thoroughfare. Two-storey clapboard houses seemed to have been divided into flats and many of the properties were separated by utilitarian chain-link fencing.

He walked down Brentwood Street. It took him a while to realise that the building he'd passed by was in fact St Augustine's. The honey-coloured stone made it look modern, but for America, it was probably old.

As Stephen walked in, he glanced at the congregation.

There were no more than a dozen parishioners on each side of the aisle. He sat down at the back so that he could observe the people there.

As he'd entered the church, he'd noticed a stone plaque and a dedication. He went over to it to read the inscription, mainly to kill time until the priest appeared:

St Augustine's is deeply grateful to the Russo family for the restoration and upkeep of this church.

If anyone asked, he was trying to track down his uncle, Michael McCarthy, last heard of as the parish priest in Allston. They hadn't heard from him in twenty years, and his sister was keen to get in touch.

A woman with kind eyes approached him.

'Is this your first visit?' she asked.

'It is, yes,' Stephen whispered.

'We're serving tea and coffee after the service, if you'd like to join us.'

Seeing this as his opportunity to quiz the parishioners about McCarthy, Stephen whispered his grateful thanks.

The woman held out her hand, 'Helen.'

'Stephen,' he whispered.

'I'll see you afterwards,' Helen said, as the priest swept in and began his blessing to the faithful.

Stephen looked around. From his vantage point at the last seat nearest the aisle, he had a clear view of the first few rows of the congregation. The front pew on the left caught his attention. He could see the backs of the heads of two burly men with military-style short hair. Between them was a willowy figure of a woman, dressed in black, her hair covered by a black veil. When the rest of the congregation knelt to pray, Stephen stayed seated. From his vantage point he got a clearer view of the trio at the front.

As soon as the priest had concluded the service, first

down the aisle was the ageing Jackie Kennedy lookalike, now with her veil lifted over her face, carrying herself with regal dignity. She was flanked on both sides by the two rent-a-thugs. She swept past in a cloud of designer perfume. She was frailer close-up and had thin arms and tiny wrists. Her fixed expression, staring straight ahead, seemed troubled.

Once the entourage had passed through, Stephen joined the throng and shuffled out after them. Once outside, the woman put on enormous dark sunglasses and was escorted to a black Cadillac with tinted windows.

'Ah, there you are.'

Stephen turned to look around. It was Helen, who escorted him over to the table where they were serving coffee and tea to the congregation. He took his cup and stood outside with the handful of remaining parishioners, enjoying the spring sunshine. The black Cadillac was still there with its engine idling. Stephen, with his back to the vehicle, passed the photo of McCarthy around.

'I'm not surprised your sister has lost touch with him. He hung around with *them*,' a parishioner said, glancing towards the limousine. 'Be careful.' She gave him a searching look before moving off to talk to someone else. As he slipped the photo back into his pocket, the limo glided away.

Stephen downed his coffee, gave his thanks to the volunteers manning the coffee stand and left. He'd arranged to meet Cormac Hannigan for lunch at an Irish pub close to Fenway Park before the Red Sox game that afternoon.

Hannigan had brought along a former colleague. 'This is Brendan Fitzgerald He worked the beat during Russo senior's time.'

'Pleased to meet you, Stephen,' he said, grabbing his

hand and nearly crushing his fingers. His accent was hybrid Kerry-Boston.

'You two go ahead. Me and Stephen can fill each other in with news about family over dinner this evening,' Hannigan said, winking at Stephen as he walked over to chat to a group of fellow Red Sox supporters.

As the Guinness flowed, Stephen passed McCarthy's photo over to Fitzgerald.

'I knew they went to the Catholic church in Allston and had paid for its restoration. I guess they thought that they'd bought the priest too. Me and the other Catholic cops, we avoided that church. We don't share communion with gangsters. I wouldn't know what the priest there looked like. Sorry.' Fitzgerald shook his head.

At least Stephen had the testimony of the parishioner. She'd been guarded, conscious of her surroundings, not wanting to say too much.

'I had to go to the house and take a statement from one of the sons after a traffic accident. Joe it was. I didn't think I'd get out of there alive. Russo was charm itself. Said if his boy had done something wrong he had to pay. That kid was a piece of work even then. As soon as his father was out of earshot, Joe threatened to have my hands cut off if the case ever went to court,' Fitzgerald said.

'And did it?'

He shook his head. 'The charges were dropped after I told my boss what had happened. He told me I was dumb to go there in the first place. That house, you should see it. It's like a museum. Full of beautiful stuff.'

'Russo senior, what was he like?' Stephen asked.

'More Don Corleone than Tony Soprano,' Fitzgerald said.

'Go on.'

'He acquired people and beautiful things. Maria, his wife…'

'The Jackie Kennedy lookalike? I saw her today, stepping out of a limo to go to mass.'

'That would be her, yes,'

'Go on,' Stephen said.

'Giuseppe collected people who were useful to him.'

'Cops?' Stephen asked.

'For sure. But not me. Guys who gambled in the clubs he controlled. Guys who couldn't pay their debts.'

'So what happened to these bent cops?'

'They were loyal to the old man up until the end. But they're all dead now, just like the old man,' Fitzgerald said, shaking his head.

'What happened?'

'Joe inherited his father's empire.'

'What sort of hold would the old man have had over the priest do you think?' Stephen asked.

'Blackmail, extortion, death threats to family members, that was Giuseppe's favourite MO.'

'McCarthy let slip he was given some artwork by a grateful parishioner. Doesn't seem like the kind of guy who could be easily bought.'

Fitzgerald shook his head. 'Because it's a power trip. Coercion, even. Or the priest got something out of it. But wherever he is, he'd better watch his back. He likely knows everything there is to know about that family. And he worked for the old man. Two unpardonable sins in Joe's eyes.'

'Thanks for the warning,' Stephen said. 'And I appreciate your time. Let me pay for this,' he said as the waiter brought them the bill.

While Stephen was paying at the bar, the supporters at the nearby table came over to talk to Fitzgerald. As they

made their way to the exit, there seemed so much cama-
raderie between the police officers and their former
colleagues that Stephen felt envious. Maybe he'd joined the
wrong police force.

'Let's go enjoy the game,' Hannigan said, slapping him
on the back.

* * *

Rome, Italy

Joe Russo sat in the back of a limousine with blacked-out
windows, going through the books with his accountant and
lawyer.

'What's this for?' He stabbed a chubby finger at a set of
expenses.

'That's the arrangement we have with the art dealer—
a 50:50 split,' the accountant said.

'Had,' Russo said. 'I don't care what Pop did, we're
doing it my way from now on. You got that.'

'Yes, sir.'

'Good.' How he loved making these fools squirm. 'We
get this Hurst guy in and explain we want a whole new
contract and that it's 70:30 from now on.'

'The current contract runs until the end of the year,'
the accountant said.

Joe interrupted. 'So what? New regime, new rules, Let's
call him up. Fix a meeting for Tuesday. Let's go and see the
priest,' Joe said, looking up across the square to
McCarthy's apartment.

* * *

An urgent knock made McCarthy jump. His first thought was that someone in the building was ill and was asking for help. He unlocked the door as quickly as he could. His face dropped when he saw the burly figure of Joe Russo and two of his associates. What were they doing unannounced and outside his apartment? McCarthy, gripped by fear, did his best to pull himself up straight. Joe's hair was slicked back, flattened against his head, making it look too large for his body. He left a trail of overpowering aftershave in his wake as he barged into the apartment.

'Mind if I have a look around?' Joe said as he pushed past McCarthy.

'To what do I owe the honour?' McCarthy said.

Joe didn't answer.

As they passed the hallway table, which had a ceramic bowl in the middle of it, crammed with keys, loose change and business cards, McCarthy noticed he'd left a pile of brochures about Mexico. He glanced back and saw a smirk on Joe's face.

'Pretty nice pad you got here, Father. You don't find it too busy with all this stuff?' Joe said, indicating with a nod to every inch of wall space, covered with a painting or a drawing. Joe's dislike of art had begun, McCarthy thought, when he had started to give Giuseppe an insight that art had meaning. With his father absorbed in a new interest, Joe began his attention-seeking behaviour. His triumph was causing his father maximum embarrassment, throwing that tantrum in the Stewart Gardner collection all those years ago.

At heart, McCarthy told himself, Joe was that same self-absorbed little boy. He had to concentrate on keeping his nerve and try to forget about the evil teenager and adult he'd become.

By then he and Joe had passed into the sitting room.

But worryingly his two acolytes were still lingering in the hallway. What had they seen that they shouldn't have?

Joe looked around the walls at the various artworks.

'I don't see the painting Pop gave you.'

Joe seemed obsessed. One more way to get one back on the old man. McCarthy held his nerve.

'It's being restored.'

'I spoke to the person Pop recommended. Interesting guy. Turns out he helped Pop with his art business. Quite a money-spinner. The one I knew nothing about,' Joe said, while staring at McCarthy.

Was Joe implying that McCarthy was in on Giuseppe's business dealings? It seemed he was.

'You know anything about that?'

McCarthy shook his head. 'I stopped advising your father about art years ago. I passed him on to a dealer who I knew by reputation. Robert Hurst.'

Joe beamed at him, which made McCarthy nervous.

'Di Lauro mentioned Hurst too. Someone else I'm going to be having a little chat with. Seeing as he now works for me.'

The one thing that Joe and his father had in common was that they assumed anyone was for sale.

'Di Lauro was disappointed he never got to restore that painting, especially after the old man recommended him,' Joe said.

McCarthy had to find a way to bat this one away.

'I used to work with a specialist who had worked on something very similar. I asked him.'

Joe Russo nodded.

'When you were working for the Pope? Hear it didn't work out so well for you.' Joe said with a knowing smile.

McCarthy stopped in his tracks. He flushed red with

embarrassment. How had Joe found out about that? It had been the most shameful episode of his life.

The doorbell ringing unexpectedly had brought it all back: two plainclothes officers from the Vatican police force turning up on his doorstep, pushing him aside, thrusting a search warrant in his face. They had an inventory and seized all the artworks he'd borrowed from the papal collection. Despite his protestations that these were works rotting in the storeroom, that they hadn't been displayed in more than twenty years, that he'd catalogued and which his predecessors didn't even know existed, he was forced to resign on the spot. But the worst blow of all had been that he was banned from his beloved Vatican Museums.

The official line was that he had resigned. McCarthy had always suspected that the Judas who reported him was Robert Hurst. He knew for sure it wasn't the conservator. But the look Joe had just given him was so smug and confident that it made him think. How did he know? What did he do? Bribe a lowly maintenance worker? Had he planted an insider in the museum waiting for him to put a foot wrong? McCarthy had been brought to his knees by the scandal. He mourned the loss of his job each and every day.

'Taking it all with you when you go? Like the rest of the stuff?' Joe said.

'I hope to, yes.'

'Let me know when you get the painting back. I'd like to see what it looks like when it's cleaned up.'

'Of course, I'll arrange to send you a photograph.'

Joe wasn't going to let this one go. He took one last glance around the apartment.

'If you need help moving out, let me know. I have a few contacts in the business.'

How typical of Joe to make his goodbyes an implied threat of eviction. He didn't need to worry. McCarthy couldn't wait to move out of the apartment.

'Thank you. I'll certainly call for help if I need it,' McCarthy said. Once Joe and his two associates had gone, he listened as they made their way down the stairs. He heard the front door of the building close and went to look out the window. They were walking away.

He went to find his phone and saw that it was lying on the hall table. That was funny. He didn't remember leaving it there. The ceramic bowl holding his keys and loose change had been moved. And the business cards seemed to have been rifled through. Franco's card was missing. And so was Stephen Connor's fake one. He'd put both their numbers in his phone. Why hadn't he thrown away the business cards? Stephen could look after himself, he was a cop, whereas Franco was utterly defenceless. He called him but the phone rang out before going to voicemail.

McCarthy sat down, his head in his hands and began to take short, sharp breaths. He grabbed his inhaler.

Chapter 17

Stephen thought about what Fitzgerald had said, as he boarded his flight back on Sunday night. He slipped into Rome early Monday morning and made his way to work. He'd had three missed calls from McCarthy on his cover phone, which brought on his anxiety. He was due at the apartment that afternoon. The messages McCarthy had left had been uncharacteristically abrupt: *call me urgently, we need to talk.*

Stephen struggled to keep his eyes open at work. Elisabetta had noticed.

'Rough weekend?'

'You could say that. Went away.'

'That's why I couldn't get hold of you. I knocked on your door on the off chance. Tried the phone too. I didn't leave a message: I heard it transfer to an overseas number.'

'It was a spur of the moment decision to go. A distant cousin's stag do.' That was enough. He'd covered his ass. He wasn't convinced Elisabetta believed him.

'Did I forget something,' Stephen asked, wondering why Elisabetta was keen to get hold of him.

'It was the briefing notes and paperwork for your meeting with Michael McCarthy. So that you sound like you know what you're doing when you're valuing his artworks. If you stick to the script you should be fine. Although it's better if you learn some of it off by heart so it won't sound too forced.'

Stephen felt guilty when he looked at all the material Elisabetta had prepared for him.

'It must have taken you all weekend. Saved me hours of time. Thanks.'

He grinned at her.

She shrugged in reply.

'Don't mention it.'

She'd covered everything and had every right to be pissed off with him. She put her head down and went back to work, carefully avoiding his gaze. Did she think he still wasn't up to the job? It was hard to tell.

'Forgot to ask you, how did it go with Renzo?' Elisabetta said, looking up from her desk.

Stephen looked around. He could see Renzo's desk in the next room. The chair was empty.

'It's alright he's not here. As usual.'

'His wife and kid left him. And he's got money problems. I lent him 400 euros,' Stephen said.

'You did? He asked me and Pasquale for the same. We're a small team. But he was foisted onto us. I'll have to talk to Alberti.' Elisabetta sighed. 'And it's a distraction from the job in hand.'

Elisabetta was hard to read but he got the sense that not only was she angry with Renzo, but with him too for being so unprepared for his meeting with McCarthy. If he screwed up, he'd let them both down. What was he thinking? That he could just get there and wing it?

He returned McCarthy's call, but there was no answer.

* * *

Rome, Italy

On the street, all was quiet as the modestly dressed man stepped out of an anonymous doorway. There was a clang as the bolts on the door pulled shut behind him. The scruffy exterior of the building gave no hint of the value of the artworks that were restored behind closed doors. McCarthy left Franco's with a rectangular parcel wrapped in black plastic, casually tucked under his arm. A passer-by glancing at him wouldn't give him or the building a second look.

McCarthy kept telling himself that in its present state, the painting was nothing more than a fake, pretending to be a Renaissance ensemble studio work. He resisted installing extra security measures—all that would do was alert Joe that he had something of value. Someone in his apartment block was spying on him, he felt sure. Who, he didn't know. His original plan of inviting Stephen around to his apartment, on the pretext of valuing his artworks, was to hand over the painting there and then.

But now, with Joe in Rome, everything changed. It was imperative that Franco be given police protection immediately. He was so agitated at the thought of the danger he'd put his friend in that he failed to hear the footsteps behind him. Someone grabbed him by the arm.

McCarthy was pushed down the alleyway, behind his apartment, away from public view. His attacker had a skinny wrist and was wearing a grey sweatshirt or a hoodie. But what McCarthy noticed most was his stale, unkept smell and that he was twitching.

'Bruno? Is that you? You don't have to do this. If it's money you want…'

'Shut the fuck up old man.'

As Bruno swung his fist, his pupils dilated, he could have been hitting a punchbag. McCarthy tried to shield his face and the painting, but the blow landed square on his jaw. He fell heavily onto the concrete. The painting landed on top of him.

Before he knew it, Bruno had snatched his wallet and the painting. He scurried away like a frightened rat.

As McCarthy tried to stem the blood from his forehead, his phone rang.

* * *

At last Stephen managed to get hold of McCarthy. He could hear scrabbling and laboured breathing.

Was he having an asthma attack?

'Are you having trouble breathing?'

'No.' McCarthy slurred his words. What little Stephen knew about the priest, being drunk at eleven in the morning wasn't his style.

'Where are you?' Stephen asked urgently.

'Piazza di Santa Maria, outside my…' McCarthy said, struggling to get the words out.

And that was when the phone went dead.

'It's McCarthy. Something's wrong. I have to go,' Stephen said calling out to Elisabetta as he ran out the door. McCarthy had been trying to finish his sentence. Was the missing word, 'apartment?' It was worth a shot.

He ran around the corner, into the small square, dodging a group of dawdling backpackers, while avoiding the badly parked vehicles protruding onto the pavements. He slowed down to a brisk walk as he neared a busy café.

He caught the chatter of patrons and the clink of cups, followed by the hum of traffic as he made his way towards Piazza di Santa Maria. He did a quick circuit of the square and tried each of the roads leading off it. No sign. He noted a number of alleyways that branched off, but it seemed odd that McCarthy would be on the wrong side of the street, away from his apartment.

Stephen scanned the exterior of the apartment building. He couldn't see a sign of any disturbance; the pots of geraniums were intact and freshly watered. He pressed the buzzer and waited. No answer. Then he tried the concierge. No reply there either. He saw a woman's face at a window, peering down at him. As soon as he glanced up, she withdrew. Then he heard the clank of the metal lift doors opening. A solidly built man in his seventies, keys clanking, peered around the front door.

'What do you want?'

'Carabinieri.' The door swung open.

'ID please,' the concierge said.

Stephen flashed his badge. 'And you are?'

'Sergio,' the man said, ushering Stephen in.

'Have you seen Monsignor Michael McCarthy today?' Stephen asked.

'Yes. Why do you ask?' Knowing other people's business was a perk of his job, Stephen supposed. He ignored the question.

'When?'

'This morning, about eight. He went for his usual walk.'

'Did you see him return?'

Sergio shook his head.

'How did he seem to you?'

The concierge shrugged. 'Like normal.'

'What did you talk about?'

'He said he didn't know how much longer he'd be in the apartment. He thought his landlord might want it back.'

'I need to take a look inside.'

Sergio hesitated, as though he was weighing up whether to comply.

'Come with me,' he said, pulling open the door of the little metal lift. There was barely room for one person, yet alone two.

'I'll meet you up there,' Stephen offered. He took the steps two at a time and met Sergio at the top. Jingling the keys, Sergio unlocked the heavy door to the apartment.

'I'll give you five minutes. No longer. He won't want you touching his stuff.'

The rooms had soaring ceilings, and each one was ornately decorated with heavy brocade curtains and dark, solid furniture. But what struck him was that every inch of wall in every space, apart from the modest, utilitarian kitchen, with its elderly electric stove, a small sink and tiny preparation area, was filled with shelving. Every shelf was either stacked with books or held an antiquity. He switched his phone to video and panned backwards and forwards as he walked from room to room.

He was in the sitting room, which had an enormous period fireplace. He peered through a set of panelled doors that led to a separate dining room, furnished with an opulent dining table and six chairs. The furnishings wouldn't have looked out of place in a bishop's palace. And indeed, no priest he knew from back home could ever dream of living like this, surrounded by books and expensive looking antiques. But McCarthy had been at the heart of the Holy See, in the inner circle of the Bishop of Rome and was unlike any priest Stephen had ever known. Even so, there was something that nagged at him.

No matter how high up you were in the church hierarchy, it would be hard to live like this without another means of support, surely? What that means was, Stephen was determined to find out.

As he walked into the dining room, the only clear space appeared to be the ceiling. The remaining walls had deep shelving, right the way up to the top. Some of them had been glassed in. Here, Stephen guessed, McCarthy kept his prized possessions: an array of figurines and sculptures. There was a portable wooden ladder parked in the corner of the room, the kind that you'd find in an old-fashioned library. He moved the ladder and climbed up. No sign of a disturbance up there, either. Just as he was putting the ladder back, he heard footsteps. He turned around to see Sergio staring at him.

'Everything appears to be in order,' Stephen said. 'Give me one more minute. One last room to check.'

As he walked into the book-lined study, he noticed the desktop computer was on. Light from the monitor bounced round the room through a series of reflections, scattering off a pair of beautiful glass lustres on the mantlepiece. Projected faintly on the glass doors of the bookcase was an image of what was on the computer display: a page open on eBay.

'He can't have gone far,' Stephen said. 'He's left his computer on.'

'Thought so.' Stephen detected a note of disappointment in Sergio's tone. 'Nothing to worry about. I won't tell him we were in here. It'll be our secret,' he said, looking expectantly to Stephen.

He has a damn nerve if he expects a tip. Stephen smiled and shook his head.

Sergio muttered to himself as he began to close the

door when all of a sudden they heard a commotion coming from the back of the building.

'Help, help. Call the police.'

Stephen and Sergio looked at each other.

'The widow who lives on the third floor. She walks her dogs in the courtyard at the back,' Sergio said, panting like an overweight Labrador as he lumbered towards the back of the building, with Stephen following behind. 'This way.'

They burst through the emergency exit that opened out onto a back alley where the bins were and there, sitting amongst the piled-up bags of rotting food was McCarthy, bleeding from a gash across his forehead.

An elderly woman, clutching the lead of her two pugs, was shaking.

'I was out with the dogs, and I found him like that.'

Stephen looked around and finding nothing suitable, unbuttoned his shirt, took it off and wrapped it around McCarthy's head.

'Get the first aid box, will you?' Sergio bustled about while Stephen sat down beside McCarthy, holding onto his shirt and calling the ambulance at the same time.

'There's no need, McCarthy said. 'I'm fine. It's just a gash.'

'It's alright, I've got this,' Stephen said as Sergio passed him the first aid kit.

Sergio turned his attention instead to the woman and her dogs. As he took her by the arm and tried to gently lead her away, she elbowed him.

'Don't patronise me.' Her angry tone set the pugs off barking at him.

'The police are here,' he said nodding in Stephen's direction.

The woman looked straight at Sergio.

'Him? He doesn't look old enough.' She gave Stephen a withering look.

He ignored her and knelt down to tend to McCarthy where he lay on the ground.

'I know who you are.' McCarthy said.

'I don't expect to be forgiven, but won't you tell me what happened?' Stephen asked gently.

'I walked into a door, that was all,' McCarthy said.

Sure. That's what every second victim of abuse from Rome to Roscommon would say.

Sergio took out his phone and busied himself taking photographs.

'What are you doing?' Stephen asked.

'What does it look like?' Sergio huffed.

'Like you're filming. So please stop.' Stephen said.

'It's a crime scene. That's what they do on TV.'

'Thanks, but it won't be necessary.'

'Suit yourself.'

McCarthy's right eye was so swollen, it looked like he could barely see out of it, but he acknowledged Stephen with a tilt of the head.

'Stay still. I think we both know what happened here,' Stephen said. 'How many were there?'

McCarthy, looking defeated, held up one finger.

'Did you recognise your attacker?'

McCarthy didn't answer.

Stephen tried again. 'What did they take?'

'My wallet,' McCarthy said.

'Anything else?'

McCarthy hesitated then opened his mouth to speak, but was drowned out by an ambulance siren.

Stephen stood up. As he did so, he felt a warm trickle of liquid flow from his shoe into his sock. And at the same time, noticed the distinct odour of ammonia. One of the pugs had peed on his foot. Their owner turned away and looked up as he glared at her. She turned to speak to Sergio.

'How do you know he's a police officer?'

'Who were you expecting, Inspector Montalbano?' Sergio said under his breath, as the woman turned to go inside, the incontinent pugs beside her.

While Stephen waited for the ambulance crew to attend to McCarthy, he walked away out of earshot and called Pasquale.

'Can you pull CCTV of the immediate area as per the GPS co-ordinates on my phone. Victim is male, Caucasian, early seventies and was unable to give me a description of his assailant.'

As Stephen walked back to where McCarthy was lying, the paramedics were insisting that his head wound was serious and he needed to go to Accident and Emergency.

'I'll come with you,' Stephen offered.

'There's really no need,' McCarthy said, brushing Stephen off.

'You don't know how long you're going to have to wait to be seen at the hospital. At least let me give you a lift home.'

'I appreciate the offer,' 'McCarthy said, his tone flat, indicating that he had no intention of taking Stephen up on it.

As soon as McCarthy was safely inside the ambulance, Stephen shot over to the cafe.

None of the regulars had seen anything out of the ordinary. The manager recalled some customers he didn't know, but they often had passing trade. Stephen uploaded the cafe's CCTV footage onto a memory stick. He wasn't hopeful.

Stephen puzzled over McCarthy's reluctance to cooperate. Did he recognise his attacker and had kept quiet? Statistics proved you were in far more danger from someone you knew than a stranger.

When Stephen's phone buzzed, he was surprised when he saw the text was from McCarthy.

Be careful. Your Stephen Walsh business card was stolen. They know about you.

Who was he talking about? Was this something to do with the robbery?

Back at the apartment building, Sergio sat at his desk and made a phone call.

'A cop came here looking for McCarthy. He's been mugged.'

'Mugged? What did they take?'

'Money, I suppose. Isn't that what they always want? I'm sending a photo of the cop to you now.'

Chapter 18

Bruno casually threw Michael McCarthy's emptied wallet into the Tiber as he loped across Ponte Principe towards the city. He touched the cash he had in the pocket of his hoodie. He was carrying McCarthy's dropped parcel, still in its black plastic wrapping. His skinny arms were no match for the heavy, oddly shaped package, which was beginning to weigh him down. He leant up against the bridge, tore open the packaging and peered in. He glanced at the brown heavy frame with a disappointed look.

He was about to dump it there beside the bridge, but must have thought better of it, as he slung it under his arm and carried on walking.

As he made his way down Via Acciaioli, taking in the various shops, he caught sight of a display board advertising payday loans and cash for goods.

He pushed opened the door and a buzzer rang. A man stood behind the counter, eyeing him up and down.

Bruno sauntered up, pulled the painting from its wrapping and plonked it on the desk.

'How much will you give me for this?'

The man put his glasses on and peered at St Jerome and the Lion.

'ID,' he said.

Bruno fished out McCarthy's driving licence from his wallet and handed it over.

The shopkeeper looked at the photograph of an older, grey-haired man and then at Bruno and laughed.

'Did you steal the painting off the guy whose wallet you pinched?'

Bruno shook his head.

'No. Give me 100 euros.'

The man looked at the frame and at the painting and then at Bruno.

The lease on the place ended next Friday. If he put it in the window, he could make a quick profit, so what the hell. The shopkeeper opened his cash register and handed over five twenty euro notes.

'Sign here,' he said, handing over a receipt.

Bruno signed an illegible scrawl and stuffed the money into his hoodie pocket, hiding his scarred wrists from the shopkeeper, before slinking out of the door and heading off into the city.

* * *

Elisabetta's phone rang. She glanced down at the caller ID and answered straight away.

'Hi,' Elisabetta said, mouthing 'sorry,' to Stephen as he watched her pace around her office, listening, nodding. It reminded him of his first day at work in Italy. Only this time, he understood most of what she was saying, despite talking at a hundred miles an hour.

As Elisabetta got off the phone, she was flushed with excitement.

'An old colleague who works in the office of the DNAA, the National Anti-Mafia and Corruption Prosecutor's office, just tipped me off about an anonymous call.'

Stephen wondered where this was headed.

'The caller reported comings and goings at odd times of day as well as large amounts of chemicals being unloaded from a lorry.'

'Not a spiteful neighbour wasting police time?' Stephen asked.

'They're treating this one seriously because of where it is,' Elisabetta said, pulling a map up on her laptop. 'It's in a wealthy neighbourhood. Trieste-Salaria, the embassy district. They think the call came from the New Zealand embassy, which backs onto the garden.'

'The chemicals could be for a swimming pool, maybe?' Stephen said.

'There's definitely a pool there. But the owner hasn't lived there for the past six months.'

'Do they know who owns it?'

Elisabetta shook her head. 'An anonymous offshore company registered in the Cayman Islands. Counterterrorism are investigating who the beneficial owner of the company actually is.'

'And counterterrorism are talking to us because?'

'They started watching the house and managed to get eyes on what they were unloading by hiding in the garden at night.'

'Which was?'

'Along with the chemicals and industrial quantities of bleach and other items which they were thinking might be used for bomb-making equipment, there were crates and crates of old pots and ceramics.'

'What?'

'I know, right. But you know what the best part is?'

Stephen shook his head.

Elisabetta slid her phone over.

'This vehicle is parked there six days a week. They ran the number plate and it belongs to Aniello di Lauro.'

'So that's where he went. It's di Lauro's house?'

'No, more like his place of work. Once they find out the name of the owner they can serve them with a search warrant. They want to mount a joint operation with us.'

'I guess we wait then.'

'We need to be ready to move once we get the go-ahead. And we're going to need Renzo, wherever the hell he is. He's gone walkabout again,' Elisabetta said, looking over at Renzo's empty desk. 'That's the third time this week. After you had a word with him, he seemed to get better. But now he's up to his old tricks.'

Stephen met her gaze and shook his head.

'Not in here, in case he's lurking,' she said. 'Let's get a coffee.'

'Okay.' Stephen grabbed his jacket off the back of his chair and followed Elisabetta out of the office door and down the stairs.

Stephen and Elisabetta sat opposite each other at a cafe table.

'If Renzo screws up, we'll get the blame.' Elisabetta sighed.

'It isn't just the divorce. The wife won't let him see their kid. If he has to go to court about access, it's bound to have an impact on him. Plus his money worries must be giving him sleepless nights. Especially when he's in debt to his colleagues.'

What Stephen couldn't tell Elisabetta was why he was so desperate to defend the guy. Or that he was willing to forgo the money he was owed. Stephen's debt to Renzo was far greater, the one person who knew his guilty secret about hacking Ginny's phone.

'I think he's the type who can keep home and work life separate,' Stephen lied.

'You'd better be right.'

'And as for the money he owes us. I'm not expecting to get that back.'

'I know you meant well. But as I keep stressing, we're too small a team to carry anyone.' Elisabetta said. 'And I was willing to make allowances for getting over a break-up.' She added sweetener to her coffee and stirred it in vigorously, before looking up. 'It's not like I haven't been there myself.'

This was the first time Elisabetta had dropped her guard and spoken about her personal life. Usually she was so private.

'You too?'

Apart from a brief head nod, she didn't so much as pause for breath.

'I took him aside as well,' Elisabetta said, glancing around. 'When I told him there was no hurry to pay me back, you know what he did?'

Stephen shook his head.

'He cried. A cop who's seen it all. Done it all. Reduced to tears over money. And you should have seen the way he walked out of that room. Head down, shoulders hunched.'

'I hadn't realised things had got that bad,' Stephen said. 'Another coffee?'

Elisabetta shook her head and pushed her espresso cup away.

'Renzo's giving me enough sleepless nights as it is. I won't sleep. The thing is,' she began, 'I know this is harsh…'

Alarmed, Stephen interrupted her before she could finish her sentence.

'I'll look out for him,' he said, although he couldn't help feeling that what Renzo really needed saving from was himself.

* * *

Michael McCarthy discharged himself from hospital, even though his doctor had insisted he be kept overnight for observation.

'Thank you for taking such good care of me. The painkillers you gave me have really helped. But if I stay here, I'll be up all night, worrying about the boy who attacked me.'

'You were knocked to the ground and you're thinking about your attacker?' The doctor shook her head.

'He's thirteen years old and an addict. That money he stole from me will have bought his next fix.' McCarthy said as he hobbled off. His only concession to his injuries was a taxi home.

Once the taxi dropped him off, he hurried upstairs to his apartment, left his things and was out the door. By then it was dark. The square outside his apartment took on a different, more sinister tone at night.

Two police officers were standing next to a huddled mass in a sleeping bag. It was Ernesto's usual sleeping place, but McCarthy couldn't see if it was him or not. He could hear someone ranting and raving.

McCarthy hurried over. 'Ernesto? What's wrong?'

'They want me to go to the shelter, but if I go I'll lose my spot,' Ernesto said.

The officers shook their heads. McCarthy heard one of them muttering as he walked off.

'We tried,' he said.

'Fuck off,' Ernesto shouted at the police officers. 'Sorry Father.'

McCarthy sighed. 'Have you seen Bruno tonight? It's really important I find him.'

'He was here half an hour ago. He was boasting about how he'd scored big time. He won't have gone far. He was already off his face.'

'Which direction did he go?'

Ernesto waved in the direction of the dome of St Peter's.

'I think he went to find Jesus,' he said as McCarthy headed off.

It didn't take long to find Bruno, sitting up against a fountain, legs sprawled, his head lolling from side to side. As McCarthy approached him, he looked up, his smile angelic in the moonlight.

'I bought so much gear,' Bruno said, his head lolling on one side and starting to drool, before passing out.

As McCarthy dialled 118 and gave the ambulance the address, Bruno fell in and out of consciousness. He laughed, cried and started hallucinating while McCarthy did his best to comfort him.

The paramedics did everything they could to keep Bruno alive. They took one look at McCarthy's still bruised face and black eye and shook their heads.

'He did that to you?'

'It's a long story.' McCarthy said, weary now. 'May I go with him?'

The senior paramedic shook her head.

'You need to get some rest,' she said, a concerned look on her face.

'He took something from me. And I'd quite like to get it back.'

'If he does recover, he won't remember a thing,' the paramedic said as she assisted her colleague loading Bruno into the ambulance. 'I don't think he's got too much grey matter left,' she said, as she climbed into the driver's seat and slammed the door.

As McCarthy watched the ambulance set off with Bruno on board, he prayed silently for the boy. He walked home, his mind churning about where to turn next.

* * *

The following morning, Stephen was walking to work when his phone rang. The caller ID flashed up as Michael McCarthy.

'Connor.'

'It's Michael McCarthy, but I expect you knew that. And I need your help.'

'Go on,' Stephen said, bracing himself for what was coming next.

'I wasn't straight with you when I told you I didn't know my attacker. I was scared your colleagues would pick him up and put him in youth detention.'

'The kid we picked up who we had to let go?' Stephen said, remembering the haunted look on the teenage addict's face but not his name.

'He took something from me and sold it to buy drugs. I need to get it back.'

'What did he take, Michael?'

'A gift from my former employer.'

Why wouldn't McCarthy say what the boy had stolen from him? Was he too afraid?

'The grateful parishioner?'

The silence on the other end spoke volumes.

'His son's in town and wants it back.'

There was more to this than McCarthy was letting on. If Joe Russo wanted something badly enough he'd get it. As he was talking, he got another call. It was Elisabetta.

'I have to take this other call, sorry Michael. I'll call you back,' Stephen said.

Elisabetta had rung off and texted him:

The Rome house belongs to Robert Hurst. All hands on deck for a 9 a.m. meeting. Find Renzo.

He called Renzo and got voicemail:

'Look mate, get your arse into the office now. Your job's on the line if you're a no-show.'

He was by the square in front of the office as he called McCarthy back. It went straight to voicemail.

'Give me a couple of days,' Stephen promised, knowing how lame that must have sounded. 'Lay low for a bit.' He felt guilty, letting McCarthy down like that, knowing that he was a sitting duck. Where was he going to go?

* * *

Stephen slipped into the operations room to find a group of officers he didn't recognise sprawled on the chairs. He sat down next to Elisabetta, just as Alberti took to the floor.

Alberti strutted up and down in front of a whiteboard, on which he'd scrawled the words: Operation Sunrise. While Alberti wasn't watching, Elisabetta slipped Stephen a one-word note: *Renzo?* Stephen glanced in her direction and nodded.

Alberti scrawled as he talked.

'The Alpha team is you seven from counterterrorism, plus one of ours, who will be raiding the Rome premises. Di Mascio, who have you allocated?'

'Bianconi,' Elisabetta said, shifting uncomfortably as

she glanced around the room. As if on cue, Renzo appeared and tried but failed to make himself invisible.

'Bianconi, there you are. I'm glad you could make it. Make yourself known to the rest of the Alpha team. If counterterrorism can make it on time, why can't you? And don't let the side down,' Alberti said, glaring at Renzo. 'Bravo, that's you, Connor and di Mascio,' he said, turning to Elisabetta and Stephen, 'Along with your Swiss colleagues.'

He waved to the video link, where the two Swiss officers were waiting patiently.

'The two raids will run at 0700 hours. I want you all back here at 1600 hours to run through the detail. Get to it. Bravo, I want you in Geneva tonight,' he said as he walked out. Stephen and Elisabetta looked at each other.

'I've got to chase up the search warrant,' Elisabetta said. 'You talk to the guys about the layout of Hurst's Geneva premises. We don't want any surprises.'

Stephen headed off back to his desk, avoiding Renzo who seemed keen to talk to him.

'Sorry, mate, not now. I've got work to do,' Stephen said, hurrying away.

Chapter 19

At 7.00 a.m. Stephen and one of the Swiss police officers stood outside the garages at the back of the ornate, nineteenth-century villa, while Elisabetta and the other officer rang the doorbell round the front.

'We're in,' Elisabetta said, talking to Stephen through his earpiece.

'Message received. Get the concierge to open up the garages and then lock them behind us, will you. I can hear shouting and an engine running,' Stephen said into his lapel radio mike.

As the garage door opened, Stephen and the police officer were confronted by grey smoke and an idling black Range Rover with an elderly woman at the wheel. A tall, grey-haired man was shouting into his phone, while feeding papers into a lit metal brazier.

'Nothing leads back to you,' Hurst said before abruptly cutting off his phone and slipping it into his pocket as he saw Stephen and the police officer, who had covered their mouths and noses from the stench of the smoke. The police officer ran over and stamped out the fire, pushing Hurst aside.

'I'll have you charged with assault,' Hurst said as he ran towards the Range Rover. 'Go, Maris, now,' he shouted.

The woman revved the engine and nearly ran Stephen and the officer down, before coming to a jerky stop as the gates of the garage remained firmly shut.

'Someone's in a hurry,' Stephen said as he walked over to the driver's side of the 4-WD. As he did so, he took in the registration. Italian reflective plates in a vehicle identical to the one that had tried to run him and Elisabetta down at the auction in Geneva. A blurry image from that day came back to him. Maybe it had been Maris Hurst behind the wheel. It was worth a shot.

'Wind your window down, please.' Maris Hurst glared at him but obeyed the instruction. 'That's the second time you've tried to run me and my colleague over,' Stephen said.

'I don't know what you're talking about,' Maris Hurst said, staring straight ahead.

'Oh, I think you do. Get the details will you,' Stephen said to the Swiss police officer standing by.

'Then follow me upstairs,' Stephen said. He spoke into his radio mike.

'I've found them. They were down here in the garage, about to leave.'

'What the hell?' Elisabetta was furious. 'Someone must have tipped them off.'

'Exactly. I'm bringing them back upstairs. Meet you up there.'

Stephen turned to the couple who were standing in front of him.

'Mr and Mrs Hurst.' Stephen flashed his badge at them. 'We'd like to ask you both a few questions. I think we best do this in your apartment. After you,' he said, pointing to the lift.

They reached the second floor and stepped out, where Elisabetta was waiting for them.

'This is my colleague di Mascio from the carabinieri in Rome.'

'We're investigating the illegal export of Italian cultural property. Given your expertise, we thought that you might be the person best placed to help us,' Elisabetta said.

'Has the carabinieri run out of Italians? Why are they sending an Irishman and an Australian?' Hurst asked, looking from Stephen to Elisabetta with contempt. 'I need to call my lawyers,' he said, taking out a phone, which Stephen noted was different to the one he'd been on when they'd caught him burning papers in the basement.

'Fine. We can wait,' Elisabetta said.

'I'll relieve you of your burner phone for now, Mr Hurst, while you make your call,' Stephen said. 'The one you were using earlier. It's in the right pocket of your jacket, in case you'd forgotten.'

Hurst fished out the phone and held it between two fingers, dangling it in the air as if he was holding a dead rat by the tail.

Stephen took it from him. 'Once you've spoken to your lawyers, we'll need that one as evidence as well as those belonging to your wife.' Hurst ignored him.

Elisabetta stepped forward, brandishing her search warrant.

'Before we search your premises, would you be so kind Mrs Hurst, to step aside so that I can conduct a body search.'

'Out here?' Maris Hurst said.

'It's the same routine procedure that you'd get at airport security,' Elisabetta said.

'When we travel we're taken to a private room along with all the other VIPs,' Maris Hurst said, tartly.

'Nothing to be alarmed about,' Elisabetta said as she patted Maris Hurst down.

'Is this your phone?'

'How dare you? Robert, do something.'

'Can you keep the noise down? I don't want the neighbours to hear,' Hurst said.

'Let us in, please,' Elisabetta said, dismissing Hurst's attempt at controlling the situation.

Robert Hurst, who was wearing a charcoal grey suit, a white shirt and a maroon bow tie, opened the door to the apartment. Stephen's jaw dropped. The exterior and entrance of the villa were ornately decorated with stonework, marble and wrought iron, but up here it looked like one vast, empty, gallery-style space, more like a warehouse than an apartment. As Hurst ushered them past a long and narrow sunroom, Stephen craned his neck to see that not only did the windows face Lake Geneva, but that at the back they opened up to a wide roof terrace. Next to that, a kitchen and living room with gleaming chrome appliances and a white granite countertop that looked like it had never been used. In the living area was a fireplace, but what struck Stephen most was that the art dealer's apartment was devoid of any artworks. There wasn't even one painting.

Robert Hurst watched as Stephen took in the view.

'Nothing can compete with that,' he said as if to satisfy Stephen's unspoken curiosity.

'We'll take a look around while we're waiting,' Elisabetta said.

Maris Hurst, who had by now regained her composure came and stood close to Elisabetta, towering over her.

'Yes, we do mind. What business do you have coming here questioning an eighty-two-year-old?'

She spoke in a similar American accent to Hurst.

'Maris, dear, it's a misunderstanding. Don't worry, I'll deal with it.'

'We know many prominent people in France and Italy,' said Maris Hurst, ignoring her husband.

'Do you?' Stephen said.

Robert Hurst's supercilious stare as he looked Stephen up and down brought out all the irrational fears he had tried his best to leave behind. Hurst looked at him as though he was a particularly unsavoury tradesman that he had been forced to do business with.

'And which part of Italy would you be from, again?' He said, addressing Stephen in a disapproving tone.

Don't react. He's trying to goad you.

Elisabetta cut in before he had the chance to reply.

'Once we start asking the questions Mr Hurst, you'll find out my colleague is from the part of Italy specialising in cultural crime.'

Stephen wanted to kick himself. Why was he still letting people like Hurst get to him?

'My husband has sold pieces to Madame Sarkosy and Signor Berlusconi. You should be careful.'

Stephen watched for Elisabetta's reaction to Maris Hurst's threat. She stood stock still, composed herself and smiled broadly.

'We'd prefer to do this with your co-operation,' Elisabetta said, taking out the search warrant again. 'As you'll see, it's been signed by a Swiss magistrate.'

Hurst turned his back, pretending not to have heard her or seen what was in her hand.

Elisabetta looked at her watch before turning to Stephen. 'We'd best make a start. Do you have the photos from Mr Hurst's meeting in Naples?'

Hurst glared at her as Stephen rifled through his paperwork and passed them over.

Turning to Maris Hurst, 'And does Mrs Sarkosy and Mr Berlusconi know these lowlifes too?' Elisabetta said, as she showed the photograph of Hurst passing a bulging envelope over to the tomb raiders.

Maris Hurst looked away.

'We'll deal with that meeting later. Can we turn our attention please to your gallery, Gallery d'Atlantide. This is a list of artworks you've sold. Recognise them?' Elisabetta opened up a folder of colour photographs of ancient Greek pottery and passed them over to Hurst. He cast a cursory glance at all them.

'I've sold thousands of pieces in my time. I can't be expected to remember every single one,' Hurst said.

'It must be difficult to keep track of where the artworks originated, I imagine?' Elisabetta said.

'When they're thousands of years old, yes,' Hurst snapped.

'I understand. This one here, for example. Do you recognise it?' Elisabetta said, passing over a photograph of a magnificently restored pottery wine container, one of those found with Antonio Sanzio's belongings.

'It's a black figure calyx krater, decorated by the Polos Painter. I sold it to the Oppenheim. Came from the collection of a wealthy Swiss industrialist,' Hurst said.

'Thank you. And this one?' Elisabetta presented Hurst with a photograph of an even larger pottery drinking vessel.

'That one went to the Chicago County.'

'And you got it from?' Elisabetta asked, raising her

trademark arched eyebrows.

'The Swiss businessman.'

'Anything else you'd like to tell me about?' Elisabetta said.

She'd certainly got the measure of Hurst, Stephen thought. Despite threatening them with his lawyer, Hurst was so arrogant that he couldn't resist the urge to show off, even though he ran the risk of incriminating himself.

Hurst pretended to ignore her and then appeared to change his mind.

'I do, as a matter of fact. There's another piece, decorated by the Polos Painter I'm especially proud of which I sold to the gallery at my alma mater.'

Elisabetta nodded, and her brows shot up.

'I think I have a picture of it somewhere. I just need to look in a drawer over there,' Hurst said.

It was something about his patronising tone, his moral superiority that had a familiar ring to it. It was a long shot.

'Which college Mr Hurst,' Stephen asked.

'Princeton, Ivy League,' Hurst boasted.

'And were you a member of any clubs while you were there?' Stephen asked. 'I have a nephew applying for Harvard. He tells me, if you want to get on, you need to join a fraternity.'

'I was as a matter of fact,' Hurst said. 'But I really don't see the relevance…Ah, here it is.' He pulled out a photo of himself at an official university ceremony, presenting the gallery with a Greek vase. But what stood out for Stephen was Hurst's tie pin. The Princeton photograph showed him wearing it again, a pin identical to the one in the photo taken at the Vatican Museums with Antonio Sanzio. Hurst had fallen right into his trap.

'Thank you. That's it for the moment. We need to search the apartment. You're welcome to stay. Or, if you'd prefer, my Swiss colleagues downstairs will look after you.' Maris Hurst put a hand to her collarbone in a defensive pose, where a double string of pearls swamped her bony neck. She was acting like this was a robbery and Elisabetta was about to rip them off her.

'If anything goes missing, we'll hold you responsible,' Maris Hurst said.

'They'll be in evidence bags with a full inventory,' Elisabetta said, beaming. 'Including your phone, please.' Maris Hurst's face was so tight, presumably from one facelift too many, that she couldn't even manage a frown, before reluctantly handing over her phone.

'Robert, I want a coffee,' she said as she grabbed her bag.

Her husband seemed reluctant to leave.

'One more thing, Mr Hurst. The Swiss businessman. Are you still in contact with him?' Elisabetta said, still smiling.

'Try Dignitas. They were the last people to see him,' Hurst turned abruptly and strode out, slamming the door in the faces of the group of officers waiting to assist with the search.

'How convenient,' Stephen said, copying the photo Hurst showed them onto his phone.

Elisabetta opened the front door and ushered the officers inside.

'We'll take a room each. Connor will search the couple's bedroom, I'll do the living room. You others can take the rest. If we have to pull the place apart, we will,' Elisabetta said.

'Even if we do find Hurst's Princeton fraternity tie pin, I wouldn't put it past him to deny that he's the other man in the photograph.'

Stephen hurried down the hallway.

The austerity of the rest of the apartment continued in the Hurst's bedroom. There were white walls, white bedding and pale cabinetry. The bed, actually two beds side by side, appeared to tilt, with storage underneath. Stephen lifted the mattresses and peered in. He ran his hands in the gap and felt something hard and flat. He pulled out what appeared to be a bound manuscript. He stood there, rifling through the pages, stopping to skim read.

I began my collecting career after touring the archaeological sites of Turkey, Greece, and Italy. These cash-starved countries were displaying these once magnificent works in a pitiful state: exposed to the elements and at the mercy of uncontrolled looters. I began to wonder if there wasn't a better way to restore these items to their original condition and at the same time to allow as many people as possible to see them. Of one thing I was entirely convinced—only the most dedicated art lovers would bother travelling all the way from America to visit these poor run-down regions to see this art. Finding good quality accommodation is impossible. I devised a plan that if Americans couldn't come to Greece, then Greece would have to go to America.

'I've found something,' Stephen called out. He heard the sound of footsteps as Elisabetta poked her head around the door.

'What is it?'

'Hurst's unpublished autobiography. Here, read this,' he said, passing it to Elisabetta, who scanned the page.

'Let's see what he has to say about it when he comes back,' she said.

'You find anything?'

'The bank statements and the accounts from the gallery are missing. There's an old-fashioned Rolodex with names and numbers in it, which I've bagged.

Stephen was confronted by a vast walk-in wardrobe which he still had to search.

'Here. Let me help. I'll take this side, and you can concentrate on his stuff,' Elisabetta said. She worked quickly, pulling all the clothes back from the rails, patting each item and checking each drawer.

'I want to know about his network of companies, where they're based and how they operated. Find out if they're holding companies or a nested series of shell companies, and whether any of them are based in safe havens like Lichtenstein, Monaco or the Cayman Islands.'

'Where would Hurst be likely to store tie pins?' Stephen asked.

'That's easy,' Elisabetta said, looking round. 'Somewhere handy, so he can boast to everyone he meets about his Princeton connections. They're probably in one of those boxes,' she said, pointing. Sure enough, there was Hurst's fraternity tie pin, sitting in a display case. He picked it up with his gloves and put it into the evidence bag.

As soon as they were done, Stephen phoned the police officers who were with the Hursts.

'You can fetch them from the coffee shop.'

When they re-appeared, Elisabetta took Robert Hurst aside.

'Any chance we could talk to you about your autobiography, Mr Hurst?'

'Autobiography? Dear, don't take any notice of that, it's fiction,' Hurst said.

'And there was me thinking I'd find it in non-fiction in

the library,' Stephen said. 'You won't mind if we take it away?'

'Can you find me a publisher while you're about it?' Hurst seemed to be enjoying himself. Maybe he'd have something to say about the tie-pin, which Stephen retrieved from the evidence bag.

'I couldn't help noticing your distinct fraternity tie-pin. How many students belonged to your fraternity in your year, can you remember?'

Hurst stared at Stephen.

'What has this got to do with your investigation?' Hurst said.

Stephen pressed on. 'I'm guessing around thirty for each year.'

'That would be correct. It's an elite club,' Hurst said, puffing himself up.

'No more than a few hundred living members left then?'

'If you say so.'

'There's a photograph I'd like you to look at.' Stephen grabbed his evidence file and pulled out the photograph of Tony Sanzio and the man with the tie-pin taken at the Vatican beside the Euphronios krater. 'Do you recognise this man?'

Hurst shook his head and looked with disapproval.

'You think that I'd mix with someone who looked like that?'

'If you look here, reflected in the shine of the krater, is a tie pin. Identical to your Princeton fraternity one.'

'We have the same tie pin. So what?'

Elisabetta and Stephen looked at each other.

'You first,' Stephen said in a low voice.

'I'm not so sure the Vatican would agree with you, Mr Hurst,' Elisabetta said. Before he had the chance to answer, she pushed on. 'I take it you're not denying you sold them the calyx krater you see in this photograph?'

'Yes, and?' Hurst said. 'I can't be expected to remember every single piece I've ever sold off the top of my head,' he added. It was clearly a phrase he'd practised.

'Here's a photograph of that same storage vessel, only unrestored and with earth on it, Mr Hurst. All the proof the Vatican would need that it was looted. I haven't got around to dropping that bombshell, yet by the way.'

'You don't have a shred of actual evidence, though do you Ms di Mascio? These are merely photographs of vases. I mean, this one with the dirt on it could be any one of a dozen kraters. There's nothing that ties it to the one in the Vatican. Or indeed that I was involved. All you have is theory and coincidence. No judge is going to convict an innocent man on those grounds.'

Elisabetta shook her head and smiled. 'No they're not,' she said, as an incoming text message buzzed on her phone. 'Excuse me for a moment, Mr Hurst, will you.' Elisabetta glanced down at the message.

'Let's just say our investigation is ongoing Mr Hurst. And I'd like you to answer further questions that I have, relating to the way you structure the companies you own. We could do this back in Rome this afternoon. You have a house there, don't you?'

'I hire someone else to look after that sort of thing,' Hurst said. 'And I don't own any property in Rome,' Hurst said.

'No, but an off-shore company you control does. Your home there is currently being raided by my colleagues. But I think you already knew that, didn't you?' Elisabetta said, looking straight at Hurst.

Hurst ignored her.

'Suit yourself. We can do it here, if you prefer. I've seen

some transactions where one company sold a piece at auction, and then another purchased it. On paper, they appear to be independent entities, but when I traced these transactions they led back to one holding company, which you own.'

At this point, Hurst started singing.

'My gallant crew, good morning.'

Stephen recognised the lyrics immediately. 'H.M.S. Pinafore. My grandmother adored Gilbert and Sullivan.'

Elisabetta looked startled but pressed on.

'That's alright Mr Hurst, I'll be speaking to your accountant if you would give me the details,' Elisabetta said.

'I hope you're all quite well,' Robert Hurst sang, in a rich baritone, which took Stephen by surprise.

'I am in reasonable health, and happy

To meet you all once more.'

Elisabetta beckoned Stephen over and asked him to step outside with her.

'Here, look.' She showed him the text message from Renzo which had a succession of photographs attached.

Aniello di Lauro taken in for questioning. Seems to be running a massive factory, cleaning up old and broken pots in an underground swimming pool.

Stephen grinned. 'Do you want to tell him or shall I?'

'Let's see how long he keeps up this pretending to be crazy routine when we tell him this,' Elisabetta, pushing back her hair in exasperation. As they walked back into the room, Hurst, who had obviously been saving up the chorus, bellowed,

'I am the Captain of the Pinafore.'

He broke off, turning to the two bemused police officers.

'And you two are meant to reply with, "And a right

good captain, too!" The two officers stood as still as sentries.

'Thank you, Mr Hurst. We've enjoyed the impromptu concert. We'll be needing to speak to you again,' Elisabetta said. 'And as I said, it would be better if we did this in Italy.'

Maris Hurst who had been listening, angrily fidgeting beside her husband, burst in, 'Leave him alone. He's done nothing wrong.'

'That's not what my colleagues in Rome have said. Here's the inventory of all the items they found on site. And that search warrant. We can provide your lawyers with all the paperwork. They can contact me at this address,' Elisabetta said, handing over her contact details. 'Now we've got to go,' Elisabetta said.

Stephen watched Hurst's face as the colour drained from it. He grabbed the back of a chair and sat down with as much grace and dignity as he could muster.

'You're free to travel anywhere within Switzerland and the Schengen area.' Stephen waved their passports at the couple, before passing them to the two Swiss police officers. 'But don't try going further afield, you'll be stopped at immigration control,' he said as his parting shot.

Stephen and Elisabetta walked out of the apartment. As they got into the lift, they heard Maris Hurst's parting shot. 'It's disgraceful.'

'Those two are a piece of work, aren't they?' Stephen said.

Elisabetta rolled her eyes. 'You said it. They tell so many lies, they don't know what the truth is any more.'

Stephen turned to her. 'It must be exhausting to keep up that routine. I can't help feeling that Hurst is acting. Pretending to be someone he isn't.'

'You might be right, but I don't see how that's going to

help us solve this case. Let's see what Corri and his nephew have to say for themselves,' Elisabetta said. She looked at her watch. 'The Naples flight leaves at two.'

* * *

Naples, Italy

In an interview room, Paolo and Corri, with a court-appointed lawyer, were seated across from Stephen and Elisabetta.

'For the purposes of the tape, interview with Geppo Corri and Paolo Giorgino resumed at 1800 hours,' Stephen said.

'Evidence sheet 167, transcript of the phone call with Robert Hurst. The section highlighted claims that the alleged middleman Antonio Sanzio, deceased, owed you money. Then over the page, here's where you offer looted antiquities to Hurst,' Elisabetta said.

Corri's lawyer, an eager young woman in her first job, went to interrupt. Elisabetta carried on before she had a chance to do so. '168 a series of photographs, all date stamped, taken at your meeting with Robert Hurst. Here he's handing over a large envelope and, in the others, you're unloading the items you offered to sell him and putting them into the back of his vehicle.'

'They're home appliances. He asked us to get them and he paid cash. That's a microwave box and that one's for a slow cooker,' Paolo said, smirking.

Elisabetta ignored him.

'169, is a signed witness statement from the Somali asylum seekers, who Corri employed illegally. They were hired to dig tombs and retrieve artefacts. It's all here.'

Corri looked uncomfortable but Paolo stared straight ahead.

'Tell us everything you know about Hurst and we'll keep you out of jail,' Stephen said.

'How it worked with Tony, all the tombs you raided, where and when,' Elisabetta added.

'What's the difference between being killed in jail or outside of it. They'll still come after us.' Paolo said, shrugging.

'Tell us who they are so we can help you,' Stephen offered.

'Give us a minute, will you,' the lawyer said.

Stephen and Elisabetta stepped outside the interview room.

'Do you think they'll go for it?'

'I don't think they have a choice,' Elisabetta said as the lawyer opened the door.

'We're ready to talk.'

Corri and Paolo looked at each other.

'You first, Uncle.'

'Hurst is mafia,' Corri began.

'Why do you say that?' Elisabetta said.

Corri squirmed in his seat. He looked at Paolo who shook his head and rolled his eyes. Corri turned his back on his nephew.

'At every tomb we found, we had the place to ourselves. Everyone else kept away.'

'Why is that, do you think?' Stephen asked.

'Because someone didn't want them there.'

'How did they do that do you think?' Stephen asked.

'Threaten them or their families, beat them up, that kind of thing. It has to be someone powerful to do that,' Corri said.

'Have you ever been the victim of an intimidation

campaign?' Elisabetta asked.

Corri glanced around the room.

'Don't, Uncle.' Paolo warned.

Corri hesitated before answering. 'How did you know that?'

'It's my job. You spoke up when that bridge collapsed, correct?'

'Look where it got me.'

'The building inspectors who signed off on it knew about the cheap concrete. They were too afraid to report it. You, on the other hand…'

'I did it for him,' Corri said, indicating Paolo.

'If you help us, we'll help you get back on your feet,' Elisabetta's face softened as Corri wiped tears from his eyes.

'Did Robert Hurst, who you have said is mafia, ever bring anyone to one of the sites you were looting.'

'We weren't looting. We were excavating,' Paolo said.

'Okay, my mistake,' Elisabetta said tartly. 'I'll ask you again. Did Hurst bring anyone to the site that you hadn't met before?'

'Hurst didn't. We'd never met him before we got in touch with him. Tony did,' Corri said.

'You mean Antonio Sanzio?' Stephen said. 'And for the tape can you tell us who he was?'

'Fat Tony was the one who paid us, gave us our instructions, took our stuff and then sold it on,' Paolo said.

'He brought an elderly American man down once,' Corri said.

'Do you remember what he looked like?'

Corri nodded.

'We'll take a break while we get photos to show you.' The others nodded.

'Interview terminated at 18.42' Stephen said.

Chapter 20

Rome, Italy

As Joe's men burst into his apartment, McCarthy was glad about one thing. He'd got rid of much of his furniture and household items in case Joe decided he wanted the apartment and evicted him without warning. And at least his artworks were safe. He'd been so spooked by Joe's last unannounced visit that he'd packed up all his antiquities and shipped them off to the retreat in Mexico, in the hope that he'd be able to follow them there soon. He'd told Sergio he was craving a simpler life and had donated all the remaining works to various galleries. Of course, he'd kept back the one votive he couldn't bear to part with.

McCarthy stood back as Joe's goons pulled curtains from their rails, ripped up floorboards and turned his study upside down. It would take days to sift through the debris and put it right again.

One of Joe's thugs was talking into his earpiece as though he was giving a running commentary. As soon as he pulled the earpiece out, Joe was caught mid-rant. 'Find it,' he said. McCarthy's stomach tightened in a knot. He looked away, pretending he hadn't heard, but Joe's man must have been watching his every move, as he gave him a tight little smile.

'Sorry boss,' the thug said, turning his back on McCarthy. 'We made a mess of your new apartment.' He nodded, listening to the reply. 'The boss wanted me to show you this,' Joe's henchman said, passing the phone over to McCarthy.

It was a set of photographs, each one more horrific than the other. Franco was tied to a chair, with a gag in his mouth, in what was once his studio. There were pots of paint upturned on the floor, as well as brushes and all the specialised equipment he'd been hoping to sell before he retired, in a hundred pieces. In the second photo, Franco was hooded. And the third, his face was reduced to a pulp.

'The boss wants to speak to you,' he said.

'When we came to see you I asked about the painting and you told me it was being restored. We paid the restorer a little visit,' Joe said.

Where was Franco now? McCarthy wanted nothing more than to be done with this abject cruelty.

'I'm going to ask you again. Where's the painting Pop gave you?'

McCarthy had run out of options.

'It was stolen by a thirteen-year-old drug addict.'

'Where's the kid now?' Joe asked. 'And don't tell me he's living on the streets, because I can round up every drugged-up teenager on every street corner in Rome and offer them money to tell me which of their mates is missing. So let's get this over with now.'

'He's lying in ICU, in a coma. Half his brain is missing.

If he ever does wake up, he won't even know his own name,' McCarthy said.

'Which hospital?'

'Gemelli.'

'Good,' Joe said. 'We're getting somewhere. Pass me back will you.'

McCarthy went to give the phone to Joe's man, who snatched it from him, before talking to Joe. He was trying to have two conversations at the same time.

'What's the kid's name?' Joe's man said to McCarthy.

'Bruno.'

'What do you want us to do?' McCarthy didn't hear Joe's response. The two men left abruptly without a word. The irony didn't escape him that they left him to tidy up one unholy mess.

* * *

Stephen had barely slept in the past forty-eight hours. Now it was the turn of the team of specialists to sift through the evidence. Their case against Hurst was a strong one. But even though he was the brains behind the looting, he couldn't have been acting alone: their job was far from over.

They were due to sit down with a forensic accountant tomorrow to try to unravel the web of offshore companies and trace the money flowing in and out of numbered bank accounts.

As he was hurrying home to snatch a few hours sleep his phone went. It was McCarthy. He berated himself.

'Connor here. I'm so sorry. I meant to call you.' He'd sounded sincere, he knew that, but still, it was a poor excuse. Stephen could barely bring himself to ask. 'Has something happened?'

'Joe's men came back.'

'Did they hurt you?' Stephen said.

'No, but they beat up a frail old man.'

'What's the connection?' Stephen asked, hoping he hadn't sounded too inquisitorial.

'Franco had been restoring a painting for me. When he couldn't produce it, they hooded him, tied him up and trashed his studio. He told them that I'd already picked it up. But it didn't stop them.'

Joe's men beat up an old, defenceless man who they knew didn't have what they wanted, just so they could demonstrate to McCarthy what they were capable of?

Stephen hesitated. 'And Franco. Is he going to make it?'

'He's severely traumatised. He was due to retire this week, after sixty years in the business. There was even a little party planned.'

'Joe used Franco to intimidate you. But they left you alone.'

'That's just it. They didn't lay a finger on me, even when I said I didn't have it,' McCarthy said, sounding weary. 'In the end, I told them the truth. I didn't have a choice.'

What was McCarthy not telling him?

'They've given me until the end of the week to produce it.'

'It was the gift given to you by the grateful parishioner?'

McCarthy started to wheeze.

Stephen jumped back to the last conversation he'd had with him after the robbery. Bruno hadn't just stolen money off McCarthy—he'd been stupid enough to steal something which Giuseppe had given McCarthy and which Joe wanted back.

'It wasn't just your wallet Bruno mugged you for, was it?'

'If he'd known it was a painting he'd have left it. He just picked it up and ran.'

'Where's Bruno now? And what did he do with it?'

'Sold it to buy drugs. He's in a coma in ICU.'

'Which hospital?' Stephen grabbed his things and prepared to race out the door. 'And remind me of the kid's surname.'

'Bruno Bianca. He's in Gemelli.'

Stephen did a search on his phone for the address as he jogged along.

'And Joe's men know this?'

'I only told them because I know he might never wake up,' McCarthy said, sadly.

'We'll give him police protection. And nobody will be allowed to breathe a word about his recovery to anyone. Not even relatives.'

'He doesn't have any. He was abandoned as a baby. Nobody wanted him. Been in and out of care homes ever since,' McCarthy said, his voice cracking up under the strain.

McCarthy was as vulnerable as the kid.

'I'll speak to a colleague to sort out a safe house for you,' he said. Renzo owned him one. He could do it.

'I'm too old to be constantly on the move, always looking over my shoulder.'

'We'll do everything we can to stop Joe harassing you.'

'You concentrate on Bruno. I'm moving out. Joe wants the apartment back,' McCarthy said. His breath was uneven and he started gasping. 'I'm sorry, excuse me a moment.' Stephen heard the sound of McCarthy puffing on his asthma inhaler.

He was planning to move out? He hadn't mentioned that before.

'I'll call you once I've seen to Bruno. Before I forget, send me the details of the painting will you? I'll talk to you soon,' he said, hanging up.

* * *

Stephen was directed to the High Dependency Unit, where Bruno had been moved. The ward manager was professional and polite, but he got the impression that she wasn't particularly happy that he had showed up in *her* hospital. There was an air of calm and order. It felt as though the unit was shut off from the outside world, a cocoon where all that mattered was the patient.

'As you'll see, he isn't allowed any visitors. Not even from the carabinieri,' she said, looking him up and down.

'I'm not here to disturb him. I'm here about his security.'

'Lieutenant Connor, if anyone did turn up here waiting for him to recover, they'd have a long wait. He can't breathe unassisted and will need oxygen for the rest of his life. And we have perfectly adequate security here at night.'

She wasn't budging.

'Let me call my department and see what we can come up with,' Stephen said.

'As you wish,' the ward manager said. 'You can sit in my office while I do my rounds. If you need me, I'll be at the nurses' station,' she said, with a nod. He watched her walk off down the long corridor, the sound of her shoes receding into the distance.

He called Renzo. No answer. 'Ring me as soon as you get this, will you. It's urgent.' Then he tried Elisabetta.

'Joe sent the heavy mob. They beat up an elderly man

who was working on one of McCarthy's paintings. Now they have that junkie kid we picked up in their sights.'

'What's the kid done now?' Elisabetta said.

'Stole the painting, then went and bought drugs with the proceeds and overdosed. I'm at the hospital where he's in a coma. And the moment he wakes up, Joe's men will be round here like a shot.'

'Whatever you need, Stephen. I'll square it with Alberti.'

'We should be able to manage with two officers. The ward manager stressed that their night security team is up to the job. It's McCarthy I'm worried about,' Stephen said.

'Get Renzo on it. He might be able to persuade him.'

'I tried but he hasn't got back to me.'

'What's he playing at?' Elisabetta said. 'McCarthy can stay in a hotel for the night and we can sort out protection for him tomorrow. I'll kill Renzo when I see him.'

'Not if I get to him first,' Stephen said.

He called McCarthy, who was slow to pick up.

'I'm still at the hospital. They've moved Bruno out of ICU. I'll be done here in twenty minutes. I could meet you. We want to put you in a hotel for the night while we put measures in place to keep Joe away from you,' Stephen said.

There was silence at the other end.

'Don't come here,' McCarthy said eventually. 'Joe knows who you are.'

McCarthy seemed to have little regard for his own life. It was always others he wanted to protect first. He tried another tack.

'We can work out where Bruno went, who he might have met. The painting can't be far away,' Stephen offered. 'What am I looking for?'

'A Renaissance scene of St Jerome removing a thorn

from a lion's paw. It's around seventy by seventy centimetres with a heavy frame.'

Stephen jotted this down.

'Can you send me a photo?' He was matter of fact, taking down notes when McCarthy cleared his throat.

'Should something happen to me and you do find it, don't judge a book by its cover. It's what's on the inside that counts,' he said, before hanging up.

Stephen sat up. Whatever did he mean? Just then, the ward manager came back into her office, glaring at him, as though he'd outstayed his welcome.

* * *

On his way home after leaving the hospital, it struck him that McCarthy might have been referring to himself, when he'd made that reference to judging by appearances. What had McCarthy done? Did he know something about Joe that made him a target?

He looked at his watch and counted back six hours. It was still office hours in Boston. Cormac Hannigan might still be at work. He scrolled through his contacts list.

'Stephen, good to hear from you. I was about to call you.' Hannigan's tone was warm, welcoming in fact. 'Planning a return trip to Boston?'

'I wish. Joe Russo is in Rome and he seems to have McCarthy in his sights. Why would a priest fall foul of a mafia boss? Unless he was an informer.'

'We're wondering that here too. I couldn't tell you in front of Fitzgerald, when you came to visit but we got an anonymous tip-off about the death of Joe's brother. I've been working on the cold case. We've been wanting to talk to McCarthy for months now, pleading with him to come back here to go over his statement. But he won't. He'll only talk on the condition I come to him. He's terrified that the moment he lands in Boston, Joe will find out,' Hannigan said. 'I'm planning to fly over to Rome to interview him in the next day or two.'

'Whatever support you need, I'm here,' Stephen said. 'Let me take you out for a beer, at least.'

'I'd like that. Be in touch.'

Sleep evaded him that night. Why was McCarthy being so cagey? Had Russo senior used the painting to hide some dirt about his youngest son? Or was there a message hidden in the painting itself?

McCarthy's theory that Bruno didn't know what it was he'd stolen seemed likely, especially if he was high at the time. From his memory of him, the kid's arms were like twigs. Bruno was a flight animal, motivated by fear, desperate to get his next fix. He must have offloaded the painting for cash to buy drugs. But who in his list of street dealer contacts would be interested in a painting?

And then it hit him. The hoodie who knocked over McCarthy after their lunch got into a black four-wheel-drive, which could have been Hurst's. Then the kid has to go and bite the hand that fed his drug habit, by stealing the painting from under Joe's nose. No wonder they couldn't wait for him to wake up. Stephen drew a two-kilometre circle around McCarthy's apartment and vowed to cover every street and every building, even if he had to do it on his own.

Chapter 21

At 8.30 a.m. the next morning, on via Acciaioli, the shop-keeper at Flog It! was busy slapping stickers in his shop window:

Everything Must Go, Last Chance Sale, It's a Steal!

He was calling it quits because he was up for a lease renewal and his greedy landlord had doubled the rent. When he'd try to haggle with him the guy wasn't interested.

'I can get Ferragamo and Chanel, in here, you know. Businesses prepared to pay a market rent.'

The shopkeeper had laughed in his face.

'You'd better get rid of the rats in the basement first. Otherwise they'll chew through every handbag in the shop and wash them down with perfume.'

It had been a busy week. All that was left were a few items, including the stupid painting he'd bought off that kid, which he now regretted. Still, the frame alone was worth more than a hundred euros, if only he could have persuaded someone to buy it.

On his last day, he loaded up his van and headed home.

'Can you find a place in the house for this,' he offered, showing his wife the painting of St Jerome.

She shook her head.

'Why would I want a holy picture on my wall? All that priest could do when we got married was stare at my stomach.'

'You were up the duff.'

'Well who's fault was that? Why don't you offer that painting as a prize for the tombola? Then the old ladies won't nag you for money for the restoration of the church fresco again.'

'Okay, why not,' the shopkeeper said, glad to get rid of the painting. If the kid had nicked it, and he was certain that he had, there'd be no comeback.

* * *

Boston, USA

Joe Russo opened the front door quietly, not wanting to wake the sleeping household. He yawned. He'd managed some shut eye on the flight from Rome, but he was glad to be home. He was about to take a shower when he saw light shining from underneath a bedroom door.

'Good morning, sweetie,' he called as he pushed the door open gently. An angel with dark wavy hair and long eyelashes was sitting at her desk, busy with her crayons. He loved the way her little face scrunched up when she was concentrating and the way the curls around her face made her look like that actress in the movie about the little girl who fell off her horse.

'Daddy.' Mollie came running up with her gap-toothed smile and hugged him. He picked her up and swung her round.

'I did a picture for you,' Mollie said.

'Do you want to show me?' The little girl nodded her head vigorously as Joe lowered her to the floor. She took his hand and led him over to her desk.

'Let's take a look,' Joe said.

Mollie picked up the drawing she'd been working on and handed it to her father.

'It's not finished,' she said solemnly.

Expecting to see the latest Disney princess, Joe stopped and stared. His kid had done this?

A man, standing on the left of the picture was dressed in a black wide-brimmed hat and a black cloak. Round his neck was a white collar, that reminded Joe of those cones that the dog had to wear when it came back from the vet. To the right of the man was a seated woman, wearing a long ugly black dress and another dog cone around her neck.

'They have this kind of stuff in school books these days?' he said, shaking his head. 'Things sure have changed since I was a kid.'

'No Daddy. It's a picture of a picture,' Mollie said, shaking her head.

'That's great honey. It's a cute drawing. It looks like something from way back when.'

Mollie shrugged. 'I dunno.'

'Shall we show Mommy?'

'Okay, Daddy.'

A woman's voice called from downstairs.

'Anyone ready for pancakes?'

'Me,' Mollie called back.

'Let's go,' Joe said, taking Mollie's hand. As they made

their way down the stairs, the little girl jumped onto each step.

* * *

As they were finishing up breakfast, Joe turned to Mollie.

'You go play, honey, while me and Mommy plan what we're going to do today.'

Mollie swung round on her bar stool and got down from the breakfast bar and skipped out the door. As soon as she'd gone, Joe pulled out her drawing.

'You seen this,' he said turning to Carmela.

She took a cursory glance at it.

'Aww. Cute.'

'Notice anything?'

Carmela leaned over and took another look. 'It's a kid's drawing. Kids have wild imaginations at that age.'

'Because it looks kind of old to me. Who dresses like that now?'

'They went on a school trip to the Museum of Fine Arts and she drew what they saw.' Carmela turned the paper around. 'I think it's the Pilgrim Fathers on the Mayflower.'

'I hadn't thought of that. I'll take it back up to her.' Joe kissed Carmela on the forehead, grabbed the picture and took it upstairs where Mollie was still drawing.

She was using crayons to draw a ship, with what looked like a wooden mast. She put the brown crayon down and picked up a grey one and started to fill in grey circles above it.

'We saw a ship like that down in the harbour. You remember what they're called?'

Mollie squirmed in her seat. 'Tea Party ship?'

'Yep, that's right. Did you go with school?'

'Yes, Daddy. And to the museum.'

'You saw a picture of a ship?'

Mollie nodded vigorously. 'Of course.'

'Where?' Joe asked.

Mollie looked at him like he was stupid. 'In the cave, silly.' The kid certainly did have an active imagination. Maybe when she said the word "cave," she'd meant museum?

'Does anyone else know about the cave?'

Mollie shook her head, got up from her drawing and went over to Joe for a hug.

'Grandpa did,' she whispered. 'I miss him, daddy.'

'I miss him too, honey. Maybe we could go look in the cave together. Is it in Grandpa's house?'

Mollie shook her head vigorously.

'Nope. Not there. And Grandpa said nobody was allowed in except me.'

'Hmm, okay. It can't be too far away. How about a game of I-Spy and if I guess I can stand outside while you go in?'

'Yes,' Mollie said emphatically.

Joe smiled indulgently.

'You have to close your eyes and count to ten and come and find me,' Mollie said. And in a fit of giggles, she rushed out of the room. Joe heard her soft footsteps fade away.

What had the old bastard been up to, creating some kind of hiding place in his son's house, behind his back?

'Five, four, three, two one. Coming. Ready or not,' he said. He walked first into the family bathroom. No luck in there. Then he glanced into Carmela's dressing room. The door to the walk-in closet was ajar. He peeked in. Mollie liked to hide among her mother's shoes and dresses, but she wasn't there today.

He came back onto the landing and tried the next room, a guest bedroom, one they hardly ever used. He listened. A high-pitch giggle came from somewhere inside the wall.

'Am I cold, am I warm, or am I hot, Mollie?' he called.

'I think you're warm, Daddy,' came the reply. Joe opened the closet door. It was half-full, clothes and shoes neatly stacked. Nothing stood out. Yet, Mollie was nowhere to be seen. His bare feet trod on something sharp. He winced, then bent down to retrieve the item and picked up a pink hair clip. As he was bending down, he saw that the clothes had been pushed aside at the back of the closet. On his knees now he shuffled over to take a closer look. He ran his hands along the back of the wall and traced the outline of a door, the height and size to allow a six-year-old child to crawl through.

He thought back to all the times Grandpa had offered to babysit while he and Carmela went out on the town. The cunning piece of shit must have been working on it for years.

'I'm coming to get you,' Joe called. 'Can you open the door for Daddy?'

There was a scuffle and then a beaming Mollie appeared at the tiny doorway. Joe would have to lie on his front just to peer inside.

'See Daddy, Grandpa said he made a special kid size door. And he said, you'd never fit in there.' Mollie couldn't stop giggling.

'Can you stand aside for me honey so that I can see what's in there?'

'Sure.'

Joe lay on his front, his shirt rucked up and heaved himself as close to the doorway as he dared. It would be just his luck to get stuck. He fumbled in his pocket for his phone, raised his arm and lifted his head as he shone the torch app into the room. Inside, it was round like a cave. It reminded Joe of the houses in that film where that hobbit kid goes in search of a ring.

The room was stuffed with paintings, all in old frames. So was the old man's house, but they were on the walls, not hidden away in a secret cave in his son's house.

Joe had hated his trips to those museums and galleries the old man had dragged him and Luca to, but right now he wished he'd paid more attention. What the hell were these paintings? He'd need help to find out.

'Mollie, I want you to do something for Daddy. I want you to take his phone and take a picture of all the pictures. You know how to do that?'

'Of course I do.'

Mollie stuck her hand out and Joe passed her the phone. She walked around the room and when the flash went off the room lit up.

'Can I put the light on Daddy?' Mollie chirped up.

'There's a light switch?' Joe said.

'Yep,' Mollie said as the room lit up.

Now he could see better, the painting Mollie had copied, which was much larger in real life, was partly visible. He felt proud. She'd done a pretty good job at capturing the wooden ship at sea. The painting had been signed. There was a capital letter R followed by e, m then the letter b. The remaining letters he couldn't quite make out.

Mollie walked over to her father and handed him the camera back. 'Can I go back and play now?'

'Of course you can, honey,' Joe said. 'When you've finished playing, come find Daddy in his office. He's got work to do. One last look at the ship, then we'll close the cave.'

Joe stared at the sailing ship again. He hated boats and just looking at the sea made him feel seasick. The old man had been the same. The only thing he'd been interested in was rubbing out his rivals and keeping the feds off his back, until that priest came along and got him seriously into art.

Joe took his phone out and scrolled through the photos Mollie had taken of the paintings. He opened the photo of the ship and enlarged the signature. What had the old man said when the priest was praying over him?

That he didn't know what to do. And then his yes-man had said that he must do what he believed was right. Joe had got bored listening in by then but had pricked up his ears when the old man had said, "they're safe."

Not any more they aren't, Pop, when one of them turns out to be a freakin' Rembrandt. Even your numbskull of a younger son has heard of that dude.

* * *

Joe was in his office, late at night when his Italian burner phone rang. He glanced down. It was the snitch.

'What do you have for me?'

While they talked, Joe typed 'missing Rembrandt' into a search engine.

'It's about the priest.'

'That loser?' Joe sneered.

'A cop from Boston PD flew over to talk to him. They met at cop HQ.'

'What the fuck?'

'It's a cold case they've reopened. New evidence.'

'Which cop?' Joe said.

'Cormac Hannigan.'

Whatever the priest had heard or seen, the Boston PD

thought it was important enough to fly all the way over to Italy to speak to him. It could only be to do with something he or the old man had done.

'That priest,' he exclaimed. 'He's nothing but trouble,' he said before hanging up and calling the duo he'd sent round to intimidate McCarthy.

'Don't let the priest out of your sight.' Joe said. 'He's been blabbing to the Feds.'

'Okay boss. Did you want us to lean on him again about the painting?'

'I told you to wake that kid, didn't I?'

'Yes boss. I'll do it straight away.'

Still bristling with anger, Joe put his phone away. He'd deal with McCarthy and Hannigan later.

Looking back at the search results, he clicked through the top link and found himself staring at the FBI's Most Wanted list. He sat there for a moment, dumbstruck. He couldn't see beyond the words "five-million-dollar reward." He read on. "…for information leading directly to the recovery of the artwork in good condition." Thirteen paintings stolen from the Isabella Stewart Gardner museum in Boston, the night after St Paddy's day.

He'd been a teenager when the thieves had struck. They'd laughed at the timing—the city full of revellers weaving their way home, too drunk to notice that the world's biggest art heist was taking place right under their noses.

And his old man did this? Joe's grudging admiration soon turned sour. He wouldn't have put it past him to have worked out that by the time the FBI found out, he'd be dead. Using his own son's house as a secret dumping ground for stolen paintings meant it would be Joe who got the blame. He could argue that he'd been too young to pull off a heist like that, but it wouldn't matter. They'd just say he had to be involved. All the evidence would point to him. As far as his old man was concerned, it was the perfect crime.

On top of it all, Pop had used his own grand-daughter to get revenge on Joe. The innocent little girl had kept it a secret all this time. All Joe had to do was to get her to keep it a little longer.

Yet Pop's devious plan was dependent on one thing— that the FBI did find out. But that meant he'd told someone, and that someone could only be the priest. He can't have told him in confession—priests had some strict rule where you had to keep schtum. But if his father had said something afterwards when they were chatting, that was fair game. That last visit, Pop was so far gone he went and died on the spot, right in the middle of the Last Rites.

Now the priest was talking to the Boston PD. What about? Had Pop managed to sneak some kind of message across? Joe needed to find out before he made a decision. He dialled his police informer.

'Find out what cold case Cormac Hannigan is working on. I want to know what new evidence they've found.'

So far, only three people knew about the cave. One of them was dead, and the other was Mollie. Even if the old man had told the priest about the existence of the stolen paintings, he wouldn't have risked telling him where they were hidden.

Had his father found out that he and Luca were together down at the river when his brother slipped and fell? Had he hidden the paintings in Joe's house as payback for Luca's death?

Two could play at that game. All he had to do was find a way of levelling the score. He'd do it by setting up an elaborate sting. Five million dollars to be paid into an untraceable offshore account in exchange for a Get Out of Jail Free card when the paintings were returned.

He scrolled through his phone and looked at the photographs of the stolen paintings and counted them off one by one. Eleven, that couldn't be right. There were meant to be thirteen. The five million was for the recovery of all the paintings. He counted again. Damn it, he'd have to find a way of drilling into the cave as Mollie called it, so he could see if she'd missed any. And he'd have to do that when she and Carmela were out of the house.

* * *

The next morning Mollie was beaming as Joe was driving along.

'I can't wait for school, Daddy.'

'That's cute honey. What's happening today?' He smiled into the driver's mirror and glanced back at her. There she was as proud as punch, sitting up in her little kid seat.

'Show and Tell.'

'What did you bring?' Joe asked.

'A picture with ponies Daddy. Can I have a pony?'

'We'll see. It must be a very little picture if it fits in your backpack,' Joe said, changing the subject.

'It's a kid picture,' Mollie said.

Joe slowed to a stop and opened the car door as he parked on double yellow lines outside the school. He unclipped Mollie's car seat and she wriggled out, grabbing her pink backpack, hoisting it on her shoulders before he could help.

'I can do it.'

'Alright honey, see you tonight. Mommy will pick you

up. Daddy has to go to work,' Joe called out, before driving off.

He was getting better at the school run. When she first started there, he'd worried that his rivals would find out that Mollie was his daughter and try to kidnap her. He got a lump in his throat just thinking about that.

Chapter 22

The school desks were angled in a U-shape for Show and Tell. Mollie's teacher, Miss Arnott, a young woman in her twenties clapped her hands.

'Thank you, Amelia. You can go back to your desk. Mollie, would you like to come up and tell us all about your Show and Tell?'

Mollie blushed. 'Yes Miss Arnott.'

On Mollie's desk was a package wrapped in tissue paper, about the size of Miss Arnott's hand. She unwrapped her painting and walked up to the front and beamed at her classmates.

'Hold up your picture so that everyone can see and off you go.'

'This is from the cave that my grandpa made. I like it because it's small but has ponies in it. I like ponies. Is that enough Miss Arnott?'

Lisa Arnott could scarcely believe what she was seeing. The "pony picture" was a watercolour, no bigger than a postcard, depicting racehorses and their jockeys lining up for the start of a race, surrounded by a crowd dressed in frock coats and top hats. The detail was extraordinary. And what stood out was that the artist had chosen to depict the horses and the crowds with their backs to the viewer, to give the effect of the subjects on the move, disappearing into the distance. The painting brought back memories of that trip to Europe, that she'd scrimped and saved for in a desperate attempt to turn her Master of Fine Art into a career. It was painful to think how unworldly she'd been, pinning her hopes on a job at the end of it. Yet no gallery would offer her one. Why would they, when they had the pick of eager, rich kids, who would work for nothing?

'Thank you, Mollie,' she said as she got up to usher the child back to her seat, and to get a closer view of the painting. 'If you leave your picture here on the front table we'll have everyone up with theirs and put them on display.' She pulled out her phone and took a photo of Mollie's picture while the next child walked up to the front of the class to say his piece.

At recess, instead of heading for the staff room, Lisa stayed behind in the classroom and took her phone out to look at Mollie's picture. Fortunately she wasn't on schoolyard duty and had already prepared her lesson plans for the day.

She ruled out Stubbs and other British artists from the eighteenth century who painted prized animals for the wealthy. Mollie's picture was more urban: a day at the races, in a big city, perhaps, with racegoers and jockeys alike sharing their excitement. She'd seen those sepia and orange tones before. Then it struck her. It was in Paris at the Musee d'Orsay, the home of Impressionism. She scrolled through her phone. And sure enough, there were many similar scenes in paintings by Degas. But had he really painted something that tiny?

Lisa looked at her watch. The bell was about to ring

and soon the keen ones would be trooping back into the classroom. She walked up to the Show and Tell display table and quickly took a measurement. The painting was just four inches by six inches.

She'd give it one last shot. She typed in the search bar for the smallest watercolour of horses and jockeys painted by Degas. And what popped up stopped her in her tracks: "La Sortie Du Pesage (Leaving the Paddock), once stored in cabinets in the Short Gallery, shows two horses and their jockeys lining up for the start of a race, surrounded by a crowd. It is one of five Degas works on paper stolen from the Isabella Stewart Gardner Museum, and the most highly valued among them."

It could be a print, or even a forgery. One thing Lisa knew about Degas was that he had the misfortune to be one of the most frequently forged artists of all time. The rational approach was to find a way to keep the Show and Tell display there, while she got to the bottom of the mystery. She tried to push away a niggling thought; what should she do if, after all her investigations, the painting turned out to be genuine? And what would she do if she came face to face with Mollie's father?

Carmela hadn't been feeling well and cancelled her yoga class, so Joe hadn't managed to get back into the cave that day. Instead he'd been working hard, putting pressure on his Boston PD informer.

A witness had come forward claiming to have seen Luca's death all those years ago. He said he'd been running under the Eliot bridge on the Boston side of the Charles late at night and was by the woods when he saw two men pushing each other by the water's edge. He heard a splash and cries for help. The witness claimed he'd had to run all the way to the Harvard campus to find a security guard to call 911 but had been too traumatised to give a statement to police at the time. That had been enough for a judge to give the Boston PD authority to re-open the case. Add that to McCarthy's testimony, and Joe had a serious problem.

He called Rome. It went straight to voicemail. 'It's time,' he said. All that was left was to find the Boston witness. Joe was so busy thinking about what he'd do, when he found out who it was, that he was late to pick up Mollie. What if someone found out, came to collect her and they convinced the school to hand her over? He narrowly missed slamming into the truck in front at the thought.

His cold sweat didn't let up until he got there to find her waiting patiently for him. He'd felt so bad that when she'd talked non-stop, he hadn't had the heart to interrupt her. When they got home, he'd fixed her a snack of fruit and then snuck a cookie onto her plate while her mom wasn't looking.

'Honey, did you put all the photos of the paintings in the cave on my phone?' Joe asked. 'I counted eleven.'

Mollie stood in front of her father, playing with her hair. She rested her index finger on her chin and frowned.

'No, there's one more.'

'You forgot it? Can you go back into the cave and photograph that one for Daddy?'

Mollie squirmed, embarrassed. 'I took it out of the cave. And put it in my schoolbag ready for Show and Tell.'

Joe stopped in his tracks.

'Your schoolbag? How did that fit a painting?'

Mollie stared at her father.

'I told you I had a picture. A kid sized one, remember? Did I do something wrong?'

'No honey, you didn't do anything bad. You showed it to Miss What's Her Name, the other kids and then what?'

Mollie giggled. 'Miss Arnott not What's Her Name. Miss Arnott said we could have our Show and Tells up until Friday. I'll draw it for you if you like.'

'Daddy would love that. Now you run along and get your crayons,' Joe said.

'Okay.' Mollie skipped out the room.

With his little girl out the way, Joe pulled up the FBI website once again. He typed in "smallest painting stolen" and sure enough, up popped "a tiny watercolour measuring four inches by six inches." He held up his palm. He could fit the damn thing in his hand.

He looked at it closely. The kid had been right. It was a pony picture, but one that had the potential to make him five million dollars richer.

Mollie had slipped back into his office and was quietly drawing. Joe had calmed down now. If he called the school and made a fuss, it would alert them that something was up with that picture. If Mollie was allowed to bring it home on Friday as planned nobody would be any the wiser. All he had to do was to be sure he was the one who collected her from school. Then he would have twelve paintings. But there was a problem. He was as far away from five million dollars as he'd ever been. He desperately needed to find one more.

* * *

Rome, Italy

A male nurse, dressed in scrubs, walked down a corridor and slipped through a door marked Disposal Room. He opened a plastic bin marked flammable, pulled a lighter from his pocket, and held it until it lit a paper hospital gown. He opened the door, quietly checking the coast was clear before walking out.

As he approached the nurses' station, the smoke alarm sounded. The nurse on duty called out,

'Did you smell smoke on your way past? I think it's coming from the disposal room.'

'No. Could be a spider that crawled in there and set it off.'

The duty nurse walked off, calling out behind her.

'You're probably right. Better go and check, though.'

With the duty nurse out of the way, the male nurse checked each room one by one, before walking towards an annexe where the more serious cases were kept.

A cop stood outside one particular door. The male nurse hurried towards the police officer, shouting over the ringing of the fire alarm.

'You need to get out of here'.

The cop looked at Bruno through the glass in the door. 'What about him?' he said.

'I'll look after him, you call the fire department,' the nurse said, urgently.

The cop left his station and ran down the corridor as the male nurse pulled the door into Bruno's room open.

Bruno was lying on his back, his left wrist connected to an arterial line. Another IV line was connected to his groin. His breathing was smooth and rhythmic.

The nurse pulled on gloves, then slipped a prepared syringe with a long, thin needle full of clear liquid out of a box and laid it down.

He pulled back the sheet and examined Bruno's torso. He was a bag of bones and his ribs stuck out. The nurse counted to the fourth intercostal space and pulled the cap off the syringe. He slid the plunger back and with his other hand felt for the gap between the ribs in one smooth motion, before plunging the needle in.

The nurse looked at his watch and counted. Never had thirty seconds gone by so slowly. A minute in and still nothing. He double-checked the syringe. It was empty. Then, Bruno began to shake. He sat up suddenly, eyes wide open.

'What did you do with the painting you stole off the priest, kid?'

Bruno flapped his mouth open and closed in rapid succession, like a goldfish out of water. 'You remember, don't you?' Bruno nodded his head vigorously up and down as he began to convulse.

The alarms rang out on all the machinery he was connected to.

'Shit,' the nurse said, as he fled.

Chapter 23

Rome, Italy

Michael McCarthy walked around his apartment for the last time. He picked up his two suitcases and walked them slowly downstairs.

Sergio was sitting in his office. He looked up.

McCarthy passed his keys over.

'These are for Signor Russo. And this will be collected, ' he said, passing a letter addressed to Stephen Connor.

Sergio looked at the letter and then at McCarthy and back at the letter.

'The policeman?' Sergio asked.

'And if he doesn't come to pick it up, there's his phone number.' Sergio took the letter and propped it up on his desk. 'Could you call him on this number and let him know it's here.'

Sergio was behaving just as McCarthy hoped he would. He would have opened the letter and be on the phone informing on him in less time than it took him to get out the door.

'And here's something for your trouble,' McCarthy said, passing him a hundred euro note. Sergio nearly fell off his chair.

'No need to thank me,' McCarthy said as he left.

He patted his breast pocket again. He felt his passport pressing against his chest, as well as the printout of his e-ticket. Pickpockets were everywhere in the city. You couldn't be too careful. He'd need to be on the train to Fiumicino at 5.30 p.m. latest, for an 8.30 p.m. departure, but if he hurried, he could fit in a few of his favourite monuments as a fitting farewell to Rome.

He had a yearning to sneak back into the Vatican, but it was a risk. One last lingering look at the Pieta was his dearest wish. But what if security recognised him? He imagined himself frog marched out by the Swiss Guards, in front of all those tourists. He fought back the tears at the thought of all the artworks he'd never get to see again. All because of Robert Hurst. The hurt and shame he had felt came flooding back. It could only have been Hurst who had betrayed him to the Vatican authorities. Hurst had been incensed when asked to produce a more detailed provenance for the Euphronios krater.

Once McCarthy had left, Hurst acquired the piece for the Vatican and they put it on display in pride of place. Franco had recently told him that the krater, which had arrived with such fanfare, had been removed from display without warning. All that was left was the empty plinth, with a note that it had been taken away for restoration. Yet when Franco had asked his colleagues if they'd seen it, nobody had laid eyes on it. It was time to alert Stephen Connor and his colleagues at the carabinieri art unit.

He deliberated whether to send Connor a text or to

drop a note to him at work. The letter addressed to him at the apartment was for Joe's benefit. He could send a text, but that would just encourage Connor to call. Besides, he'd turned his phone off and was planning to dump it soon. No, he'd drop a note to him. His writing paper and envelopes were at the top of his carry-on luggage. But first, he needed to offload his suitcases.

He struggled up the steps to St Pietro in Vincoli. The resident priest had agreed to store his bags for the day as mass wasn't until six that evening. As he waited for him to appear, McCarthy slipped the little votive, which he'd been carrying close to his chest, inside the suitcase.

The priest appeared and grasped his hand as he greeted him warmly. 'Let me help you with those,' he said, looking down at the cases. 'I'll leave them in the confessional booth nearest the altar on the left-hand side.'

'Thank you. I'll be back in plenty of time before mass, I promise. I just need to catch my breath for a moment.'

'Of course, take your time.'

McCarthy opened his carry-on bag and pulled out his writing materials. He wrote a quick note, sealed it up and addressed the envelope to Stephen Connor, before shoving it into his jacket pocket. He picked up the carry-on bag and hurried over to the confessional where the rest of his things were and left it there.

It would take him twenty minutes to walk to Connor's office at Palazzo Sant'Ignazio. And with that, McCarthy hurried off, determined to make the most of his last day in the city he'd made his home for over a quarter of a century.

He'd miss the smell of traffic fumes mingled with the heady scent of pine and plane trees. But Mexico, he imagined, would be filled with fragrant citrus blossom and jasmine. For the first time in many years, Michael McCarthy dared to dream.

* * *

Boston, USA

It hadn't occurred to Joe until now that the old man must have known that the five-million-dollar reward was for the return of all the paintings.

How could he have missed it when the answer was staring him in the face? The old bastard had given the priest a painting, the one that he said needed restoring.

Joe pulled over to the side of the road, got out his phone and Googled the missing paintings again and compared them to the ones on his phone. He didn't know what was so damn special about the missing one, but it had been done by some famous Dutch guy. A guy and two girls inside a house. One was playing the piano or something. But the painting Pop had given the priest was of an old guy in a robe with a lion. Not the same picture at all.

He picked up his phone and pressed the number for his contact in Italy. It went straight to voicemail.

'Call me, will you. That kid's got to tell us what he did with that painting. If you can't wake him up, I will,' Joe threatened as he hung up.

* * *

Rome, Italy

. . .

Over at Our Lady of Miracles, a crowd was gathered in front of the church, where a fundraising tombola was taking place.

The Master of Ceremonies, whose day job was to sell fruit and vegetables in the market in Campo di Fiori, was pacing up and down, microphone in hand, clearly relishing his chance to shine. A group of onlookers moved forward, curious to see what was on offer.

'Roll up, roll up, ladies and gentlemen. Every ticket wins a prize. Come on, don't be shy.' In front of him was a display table set with a cheerful gingham tablecloth, on top of which sat bottles of homemade wine, jars of honey, fresh jams, a basket of assorted vegetables and a hamper with biscuits and cakes. There were soft toys and knitted baby clothes, but pride of place went to the painting of St Jerome and the Lion.

'We have something special today for one lucky winner. A beautiful painting of St Jerome gently removing the thorn from the lion's paw. St Jerome, as you know was a son of Aquileia. And the lion became his faithful companion. So what better subject to hang on your wall than the story of one of our favourite saints.'

A couple in their seventies stepped up, the woman waiting while the MC rolled the tombola in a dramatic flourish. The woman put her hand in to draw out a ticket. She turned to her husband. 'I really want the hamper.'

'Your number please,' the MC asked.

'428.'

'Drumroll please. You are the lucky winner of today's star prize—this beautiful painting. Congratulations.' There was a burst of applause followed by an awkward silence as the woman's face fell. She shifted uncomfortably from foot to foot, then looked to her husband for guidance.

'Thanks,' he said gruffly and picked up the painting. She followed him forlornly, muttering.

* * *

As he made his way back after his day's sightseeing, McCarthy no longer felt alone. He didn't know exactly where he'd noticed another presence that day. Perhaps it had been at Bramante's Tempietto, the little temple which had been the prototype for St Peter's and was said by historians to have been built upon the exact spot where St Peter was crucified. Was it St Peter himself who was looking over his shoulder? McCarthy couldn't be sure.

It was a fair hike back. The nearest metro was at least a kilometre away, and by the time he got there, the hills of Rome were illuminated with an ethereal light, and McCarthy couldn't bring himself to plunge into the dark depths of the metro.

The presence he'd felt at the temple was still with him, only this time it manifested itself in a more earthly way. A shadow here, a footstep there. Out in the open felt safer than in the bowels of the earth. McCarthy regretted slipping the little votive into the suitcase, instead of keeping it in his pocket. It had kept him safe for all these years.

He was short of breath by the time he walked up the steep steps of the Oppian Hill. He looked around. The sun had gone behind a cloud, and the magical reflections had disappeared. It was time to head for the airport.

Once back inside St Pietro in Vincoli, he moved down past the pews where elderly women, too frail to kneel were sitting, their heads bowed in prayer. Amongst them knelt one solitary man. As he headed for the last confessional booth, McCarthy saw that his suitcases were there just as the priest had promised. He was running ten minutes ahead of schedule. He'd rather be early than late for the metro to Termini and on to the airport train.

A small tour group with their French-speaking guide gathered around the church's star attraction, the tomb of Pope Julius II. Julius II was not unlike McCarthy's former benefactor. Julius's original grand design, which was destined for St Peter's, included forty statues by Michelangelo, the most celebrated sculptor of all time. Giuseppe Russo too surrounded himself with priceless works of art. Except, they hadn't belonged to him.

Once Julius II and Giuseppe Russo died, their successors wasted no time in relegating them to history. Leo X cast Julius out into a minor church in Rome and Joe, who had boasted he was building a mausoleum to honour his father in Boston's finest Catholic cemetery, had failed to commission so much as a drawing. The old man lay forgotten in a makeshift grave, only mourned by Maria, Joe's mother.

The seated figure of Moses gazed down sternly upon him in judgement for his sins. As he reflected upon Michelangelo's masterpiece, he realised it was too late to wish he'd never become involved with Giuseppe Russo. All he could do was ask for forgiveness. As McCarthy knelt for a moment in silent prayer, to his embarrassment, his phone began to ring. He can't have turned it off properly. It was Stephen Connor. God came first. Connor would have to wait. He switched the phone off.

* * *

'Come on, pick up,' Stephen muttered. He slammed his phone on his desk just as Elisabetta walked in and handed Stephen a letter. 'This just came for you.'

'Thanks.' He put the letter on top of his inbox and swivelled his chair round to face her.

'You okay?'

Stephen shook his head.

'It's McCarthy. I can't get hold of him. Here,' he said, 'this just came through.' He showed Elisabetta a message he'd just received from Cormac Hannigan in Boston.

The star witness in the same cold case McCarthy gave evidence just had his car blown up. He wasn't in it. McCarthy could be next. I've called homicide. They say he's gone missing. Anything you can do?

'You two know each other?' Elisabetta asked.

'He was the officer who flew over to interview McCarthy, who happens to be a distant relation of mine. Irish people are like Italians. They're everywhere.'

'Ah, okay. The stag weekend in America. I wondered why he'd got in touch.'

'If I don't find McCarthy, someone else is going to get there first.'

'You want me to come?' Elisabetta said.

'This is my doing. I don't want to involve you.'

'I'm here for back-up if you need it,' Elisabetta said.

'Thanks,' Stephen said, grabbing his jacket and rushing out the door.

As he approached the piazza where McCarthy lived, Stephen glanced up. The windows were open, and there was a cleaning company's van parked outside. He pressed the intercom to the apartment. Maybe someone saw him go?

'Anyone home,' he called. The front door was ajar. As he pushed it open and walked inside and up the flight of steps, his phone rang. It was the ward manager from Gemelli.

'Bruno Bianca passed away,' she said.

'Did something happen?'

'I can't tell you the circumstances until the results of the post-mortem and the toxicology report has come through. I'm sorry,' she said, her tone, regretful. 'I'll keep you posted,' she said, before hanging up.

A post-mortem, he could understand, but a toxicology report? That kid must have taken so many drugs in his young life that his body must have had a high tolerance for them. Had his condition deteriorated gradually or had he died suddenly? Or had he developed an infection? And when he did finally find McCarthy, how was he going to break the news?

'Hello,' he called. A cleaner, mop in hand answered the door. Behind her, McCarthy's apartment was bare.

'Gone,' she said and then shut the door. Stephen went to the top floor and started knocking on doors. There was no answer. He carried on, making his way gradually down until he reached McCarthy's floor. A man of around seventy peered around his door and beckoned him over.

'He's popular today. Has something happened?'

Not yet. 'Someone else beat me to it?'

The guy nodded.

'I assumed he was plain-clothes. Flashed one of those IDs that look like a passport.'

Stephen held up his ID for the man to study. 'Like this?'

'Same. He was wearing a leather jacket with a shirt and tie. Dark chinos. Or maybe jeans. But it was the way he rattled off his questions, like you're doing now. He was practised at it.'

'When you showed up, I thought it was him again. He looks a bit like you. But your accents are different. He's from the south.'

'Thanks, you've been very helpful.' Stephen turned to

leave. 'Just one more thing. Did McCarthy say where he was going?' Stephen asked.

'No, but he was carrying a couple of suitcases,' the man said. 'I didn't say that to the guy who was here earlier. There was something about him.'

By his calculation, out of the many thousands of his fellow officers there would be a fair few who wore leather jackets with a shirt and tie and came from the south. But how many of those would be keeping tabs on McCarthy?

Stephen returned to McCarthy's apartment, this time flashing his police badge. The cleaner was at once afraid.

'I know nothing,' she said beseechingly.

'It's okay I'm not from immigration,' Stephen said, trying to reassure her. He guessed she may have fled Syria or Afghanistan. 'I want to search the rubbish. Paper recycling.'

She invited him into the apartment and showed him four rubbish sacks, two which contained paper. He started sifting through the contents until he found what he was looking for. An itinerary. Just as he pulled the paper out of the bin and read that Michael McCarthy was due to catch a plane from Fiumicino in three hours, he called Elisabetta.

'McCarthy's leaving the country. Can we get a geoloca-tion on his phone? I want to make sure he's alright.'

'Send his number over and I'll do it,' Elisabetta said. 'Call you straight back.'

As Stephen waited, there was a knock on the door. Stephen opened it. It was Sergio, the annoying concierge. He was holding an envelope.

'I think this is what you're looking for,' he said.

Had he been listening outside the apartment the whole time? Stephen took the envelope addressed to him and turned it over. By the way it peeled open, he guessed Sergio had already read it.

Stephen imagined McCarthy's voice, reading the letter aloud:

Dear Stephen,

By the time you read this note, I will have safely returned to Ireland to retire to a little house by the sea. The next time you are in Wexford, be sure to look me up.

Stephen flung the letter aside. I might not know you well, Michael McCarthy, but I know enough that this is entirely out of character. And unless that itinerary was another red herring, Mexico was one hell of a detour from Ireland.

He ran down the stairs to hail a cab. McCarthy must have been still in town, or at the airport. Just as a cab stopped for him, his phone rang. It was Elisabetta.

'I've tracked his phone. It's in Monti, right near the Metro on Via Cavour. On the steps leading up to the church of St Pietro in Vincoli.'

'On my way,' Stephen said, instructing the cab driver. As the cab sped through the streets, Stephen read the rest of the letter:

Despite both of us harbouring secrets, I value your friendship and I'm glad to have met you.

Yours, Michael McCarthy.

Perhaps it was Moses's disapproval he felt or his earlier experience that day at the site of St Peter's crucifixion, but as he walked back to the confessional to collect his suitcases, he realised that there was one last thing he had to do. Or rather, that Moses, who had gathered the Ten Commandments, had guided him to do. He opened one of the suitcases, took out the votive and left it there in the confessional, without so much as a backward glance.

As he walked out of the church, suitcases in hand, he brushed past the gaggle of French tourists, now gathered around the exit. One of the tourists jostled him and spoke in a low voice.

'Joe wants his painting back. Tell us where it is, or we'll finish off the art restorer.'

'Tell Joe it's too late for that. Killing Franco won't get it back.' It was as though the weight of the world had lifted from his shoulders. The words of the Second Commandment rang in his head. "Thou shalt have no graven images."

McCarthy felt a sharp pain in his arm, like a sting. He tried to brush it off. A wasp, perhaps? Whatever it was he would attend to it later. He didn't want to let it spoil the moment.

As he tripped over the top step, he dropped his suitcases. On and on he tumbled, rolling down the steep steps until he came to rest almost at the intersection with Via Cavour.

* * *

The ambulance, heralded by its klaxon-like siren, drew up and two paramedics ran towards the small crowd who had gathered around. Stephen ran towards them. Had he got there too late? As he got closer, Stephen saw that McCarthy had his eyes open and appeared to be breathing. When he saw Stephen, he reached out to take his hand and clasped it.

'I lied to you, I felt bad about that,' Stephen said.

'Don't be. In the line of duty and all that. I got my own back,' McCarthy said, squeezing Stephen's hand.

'I didn't fall for it,' Stephen said. 'Sure, it would be great to go home to Ireland for the summer. But I imagined you there in the winter, pining for galleries, restaurants and the anonymity of the city.' The life was seeping out of McCarthy, Stephen could see, but he was desperate to keep him alive, to find out who had driven him out of his home in such a hurry.

'This is my fault. I failed you…' Stephen said, his eyes filled with tears.

'No. You saved me. And Bruno.'

Stephen shook his head.

'I couldn't even do that.'

McCarthy looked up.

'He's gone?'

Stephen nodded.

'He was living on borrowed time,' McCarthy said. 'It's not your fault.'

McCarthy's forgiveness brought a lump to his throat.

'I wish I'd known you were going away. I'd have come to say goodbye.'

'I wanted to go back home. But he said he'd find me there if I did.'

'Who, Michael? Joe Russo?' Just then McCarthy's eyes cleared momentarily, and he pulled himself up to rest on one elbow, and in a voice sounding years younger, the voice he must have used saying mass, he pronounced.

'Find good understanding in the sight of God and man.' From the dusty recesses of his schooldays, Stephen recognised the saying from the Book of Proverbs.

Then McCarthy relaxed back to the ground, whispering 'I wanted you to have something to remember me by.'

Stephen looked at McCarthy's eyes as they clouded over again.

'Don't leave me. Tell me what it is,' Stephen said urgently.

McCarthy struggled to breathe. 'I left it at your office.' In the halfway house between life and death, McCarthy held the palm of his left hand aloft and with his right mimed picking up an imaginary pen.

That note that he thought was some circular and had left in his in-tray for later was from McCarthy?

'You are that man,' he breathed, the punchline of the phrase Stephen recalled from Proverbs. In the short time they had known each other, McCarthy had seemed secretive and pre-occupied. Now he sought good understanding.

The ambulance crew were running now, a stretcher and drips at the ready. But before they could manoeuvre their way through the crowd, Stephen felt McCarthy's grip loosen, and his hand fall away. The daily rhythm of Rome began to stir again. He stood back as the medics busied themselves, just another onlooker. He called Elisabetta.

'McCarthy's dead,' Stephen said. 'Murdered in broad daylight. His killer will be long gone.'

'I'm on my way. Someone must have seen something,' Elisabetta said.

For the next twenty-four hours, conspiracy theories would be flying from bar to restaurant about the priest's dramatic death, Stephen reflected. Then they would go back to their usual topics—railing against the government, moaning about immigration and the cost of living. How hard it is to be a good man in evil times, he heard himself say, not knowing if it was himself or McCarthy he was thinking of.

Chapter 24

Rome, Italy

Stephen was at the wheel as he and Elisabetta drove through the thinning traffic. The clock on the dashboard read 10.00 p.m. As he pulled up outside Elisabetta's apartment, she turned to him.

'I'm making pasta. Want some?'

What else did he have to do? Go home to an empty flat to eat a takeaway pizza and mourn the loss of his friend? McCarthy's murder was so raw that he couldn't bear to deal with it yet.

McCarthy's note was a sad confession. As they'd thought, he'd been forced out of the job he loved at the Vatican Museums because he suspected that the Euphronios krater, acquired by Robert Hurst, who he'd employed, was most likely looted. Hurst never could provide a paper trail. The board was so besotted with the krater that they were willing to overlook Hurst's shortcomings and took his word that it had been owned by a wealthy collector.

"Hurst came to my home for a meeting, He must have spotted and photographed Vatican property in my apartment. Three days later the Vatican police arrived with a search warrant, seized the artworks and presented me with my letter of dismissal."

McCarthy was murdered before they'd had a chance to take a sworn statement from him and even this written confession to Stephen wouldn't stand up in court. Despite it being a frustrating day, he and Elisabetta were confident they had enough evidence to bring a case against Hurst for looting, even without McCarthy. But they were still some way off pinning any financial crimes against him.

'I can knock out a bowl of spaghetti in the time it would take you to drive home,' Elisabetta continued.

'Sorry, was thinking about today. You had me at pasta.'

'Come on,' Elisabetta said. 'I'll make a start if you can grab the wine. There's a late-night grocer back there. We passed it on the way. You might just catch them.'

Stephen parked up and headed off on foot towards the shops. As he did so, his phone rang. It was Tariq. 'Steve, Cara's been in touch.' He paused. 'It's you she wants.'

Stephen felt a jolt through his body. What did he mean? She still had the power to unsettle him, even after all this time. Tariq wasn't making any sense.

'What's happened?'

'I get this parcel in the post, and it contains a memory stick and a snarky note:

Do us a favour. Give this to the Old Bill, will you?

P.S. Bet that window in your office is as dirty as the day I left.

'No-one does pithy, quite like Cara, do they? Where was it sent from?'

'Indonesia.'

'Can you download the contents of the memory stick and send them through?'

'Already done that. I've sent the instructions to open the file by separate cover.'

Stephen groaned.

'It's been a while since we did this.' Tariq chuckled.

'I'm on another job right now,' Stephen said, as he passed two bottles of red wine across the counter of the grocery shop. 'Be on to it late tonight or first thing tomorrow.'

'Okay,' Tariq said, a note of disappointment in his voice before hanging up.

As Stephen finished paying and grabbed his purchases, the shop assistant grinned at him. 'Working, eh? Have a good night,' he said.

Stephen nodded sheepishly at the innuendo. But there was no denying he was having dinner a deux with a colleague, at her invitation. As he walked back to Elisabetta's his mind was churning. Whatever Cara had uncovered, it couldn't have come at a worse time. He was in danger of spreading himself too thinly. He still had to crack the Hurst case.

He looked at his watch. He'd been gone ten minutes.

'Sorry,' he said, as Elisabetta opened the door. 'It was busy.'

'No problem, I just have to throw in the pasta,' she said, deftly chopping a shallot and parsley, then zesting a lemon.

'Can I do anything?' Stephen said.

'Open the wine, will you,' Elisabetta said, eyes shining, as she passed Stephen the corkscrew.

'Watch me make a hash of this,' he said, flipping open the knife and cutting the thin metal seal covering the cork.

He managed to pull it off without cutting his finger as he usually did. The cork came out easily.

'Once you've done that, you can grate the parmesan,' she said, passing over a wedge of cheese.

She drained the pasta and tossed it with the vegetables and brought it to the table.

'Linguine con limone, I hope you like it.' Stephen poured two glasses of ruby coloured wine from the bottle of Velletri. They clinked glasses.

'Saluti,' they both said at once.

'It's a novelty having someone to eat with,' Stephen said.

'Cooking for one sucks. I always make too much and end up eating it for days on end,' Elisabetta said. 'I still haven't got used to the single life.' She reached out her hand across the table. He reciprocated. Theirs was a companionable silence.

He wanted to ask her how long it had been and what had happened, but thought better of it. Why bring up painful memories?

'Did you always want to be a cop?'

'I wanted to be an investigative journalist.'

'Why didn't you?'

'My uncle got killed by the mafia for doing exactly that. He was following up on a story about art theft. He got lured into a trap.'

Stephen recalled Elisabetta's reaction when he'd played the tape of Geppo Corri and she'd pinpointed his accent.

'In Naples?'

'The same housing estate where you met Corri.'

'You don't have to,' Stephen began.

'I know I don't. But I trust you.'

You wouldn't if you knew what I'd done.

'What happened?'

'There was a showdown. Because he was the one who went in armed with nothing more than pen and paper and a passion for the truth, he got killed, while the cops fired back and got away,' Elisabetta said.

'I'm sorry.' It sounded so trite.

Elisabetta's eyes misted up.

'So yes, I'm the cop secretly hoping to avenge the death of her beloved *zio* who was killed by the mob. Think you can handle it?'

Yes, he could handle it, Stephen thought, as he leaned back in his chair and folded his arms. She was single and now he supposed, so was he.

'We had the mafia in Ireland too when I was growing up. Or a version of it. As well as Irish nationalism. And because it's a small place and everyone knows your business, before even you do, it's easy to get up the nose of the wrong sort. A prominent political activist warned me off. He didn't want me being a police officer in his patch. So I left.' He held Elisabetta's gaze as she instinctively reached for his hand once again. He gave it back. 'I know I won't be driving home, but we might regret this.'

'Coffee?'

'I'd like that.'

Elisabetta got up to make espresso and Stephen walked around the apartment and into the kitchen. She touched him on the shoulder. He wanted to pull her towards him. He took her hand in his and then let it go.

'It's not that I'm not tempted. But,' he said gazing into her eyes. 'Ginny and I aren't good right now. And I don't know if we'll ever be able to fix it.'

'No, it isn't that.'

What was it then? Stephen shook his head, grabbed his coffee and downed it in one go.

'I'd better go. I'll leave the keys with you. You can pick

me up in the morning,' he said as he made his way to the door. 'Goodnight.' The cool night air refreshed him as he started walking home, reflecting on what Elisabetta had said. He wished he'd told her the truth.

Stephen had gone barely another fifty metres before his phone rang.

'I'm sorry, I shouldn't have confronted you like that,' Elisabetta said.

He heard the clack of boots on pavement and turned around. She was walking towards him, arms outstretched. Stephen fell into her spontaneous embrace. There was a warmth between them, an understanding he hadn't felt before. As Elisabetta let go of him, her fingers brushed his. He reached for her hand.

'I'll walk with you for a bit,' she said.

'Then I'll feel obliged to do the same. We could be doing this all night,' Stephen said, his face a broad smile.

'Won't you tell me what happened to you?'

Elisabetta had been the first to let down her guard. She trusted him. Now she was asking him to reciprocate.

'Some time ago I was forced to make a split-second decision. And I worry I got it wrong.'

Elisabetta nodded. 'And it keeps you awake at night, wondering what you'd have done differently if you knew then what you know now?'

Finally, he'd found someone who knew what that felt like. No one he'd met in civilian life had ever been put in that situation. Here he was with an ally, a friend, someone at last who understood.

'I had the chance to protect Cara, my environmental-ist…friend to do the right thing. In the few seconds I had, all I could think about was that if I went with her, we'd always be fugitives, two wanted people on the run.'

'Like Bonny and Clyde?'

'Except that we'd been set up. If I'd run, they would have used that as an admission of guilt, and let the real culprits get away scot free. I put her on a plane and gave her money to flee. I thought the best thing for me to do would be to stay behind and fight to prove Cara's innocence, even though I knew she had a bounty on her head and they'd go after her. Now every tabloid calls her an eco-terrorist.'

'Your girlfriend knew about this?'

'That's the crazy part. Ginny was there. She was the other reason I chose to stay.'

They walked along in an easy silence as Stephen felt the weight of the past two years lifting from his shoulders. 'When it was all over, I came up against the oil company. They'd spent a fortune on a PR campaign to discredit her. There was an independent inquiry into the refinery explosion. It proved that the protestors didn't cause the accident, but the PR company disputed the findings. They carried on putting out stories naming Cara. And there wasn't a damn thing I could do. It was trial by tabloid. I feel so damn guilty I didn't do right by her.'

Elisabetta stopped and faced Stephen.

'You did everything you could. You're a good man, Stephen Connor. Never forget that.'

They stood there for a few moments, neither wanting to be the first to leave.

'It's late,' Stephen said. 'And we've got one hell of a day ahead of us. Thanks for listening.'

Elisabetta patted his arm.

'You're right. See you tomorrow,' she said and walked away.

* * *

It was one o'clock in the morning by the time Stephen managed to work through the files Tariq had sent him, most of which were about Greg Palmer and his tangled network of companies. One line Cara had highlighted leapt up off the page. Palmer had set up an office in the USA, bankrolled by a company controlled by none other than Boston gangster, Joe Russo.

Tariq, he saw was still online.

'I knew you'd still be up,' Stephen said.

'You took your time.'

Where the hell did she get this stuff?'

'I like to think she learned from the best,' Tariq said, proudly.

'Don't tell me any more. The truth is I think she learned her trade from the eco-warrior cult she was holed up with Down Under.'

'Can you use it?' Tariq asked.

Stephen leaned back on his chair. Palmer funded by the proceeds of organised crime. He could certainly tip the FBI off. It would be up to them to carry out their own investigation.

'Just taking all this in Tariq.'

'No hurry. I thought you'd like it. You'll keep her name out of it won't you?'

'She's clever enough to have made sure nothing can be traced back,' Stephen said.

'That's a relief. I was worried they'd go after her,' Tariq said.

'I know I was the one who played devil's advocate when the Australian police found her stuff. And I'm sorry. I didn't want you to get your hopes up again and the trail run cold, that was all.'

'I'm not cleaning that office window until she comes back. I keep looking at the screen grab you took of her at the disaster relief site. Always looking out in case someone recognises her.' Tariq sighed. 'Please, Steve, find a way of shutting down Palmer. He's the one who forced her to live like this. He's kept up the hate stories, spreading lies, accusing her of terrorism. She's not safe until that man is behind bars.'

'I'll do everything I can. Now can I get some sleep? I've got a big day tomorrow.'

'Yes, sorry. Bye mate.'

Once Tariq hung up, Stephen's mind was racing. He looked at the clock again. It was four o'clock when he turned out the light.

The alarm went off at seven. He stumbled out of bed and groggily made his way into the kitchen, running the cold-water tap. He filled a glass, opened a tube of soluble vitamin tablets and dropped one into the water, eyes fixed on the effervescence.

* * *

Stephen had been going over the Hurst evidence all morning. With the nighthawks' testimony, they'd been able to understand how the looting operated and were able to name a number of key players in the chain. Geppo Corri had identified Russo senior as the American who had paid a visit to their looting site, but they still needed proof that Hurst wasn't operating alone.

Stephen took out his mind map drawing with the list of nicknames Tony Sanzio had given to his various associates. Only this time he drew it as a hierarchy, starting with the bottom rung. At the bottom of the food chain were the Nighthawks (Geppo Corri and nephew). He drew an arrow up and wrote the Fixer (Tony Sanzio). As the middleman, Sanzio was uniquely placed. He got the nighthawks to do his bidding but reported to the next person up in the chain of command.

Tony had that person as the Great Gatsby. And then it came to him.

He called out to Elisabetta. 'What do you know about the Great Gatsby?'

'Is this another crossword clue?' Elisabetta said, crossly. 'If so, you aren't busy enough.'

'All I know is the movie with Leonardo di Caprio,' Stephen said.

'It's about a guy who came from nothing who becomes rich,' Elisabetta said. 'Why are you asking?'

'It was something you said about the Hursts when we raided their apartment that got me thinking,' Stephen said.

'You were the one who said they were acting,' Elisabetta said.

'It was about their grip on reality, that they didn't know what the truth was any more. And that would fit. Hurst is the master of invention. The whole Ivy League thing. Maybe he was an outsider, from a humble background who got to Princeton on a scholarship. And that's why he has to keep up his routine. Tony Sanzio would have had no idea how astute he was giving Hurst the nickname the Great Gatsby in his diagram.'

'Let me take another look,' Elisabetta said.

'What about these middle-ranking four here: the Lawyer, the Sales Rep, the Guardian, the Accountant. Is Sanzio being literal or ironic?' Elisabetta said.

'That I don't know and I still haven't managed to pinpoint a name for any of them yet,' Stephen said. 'Their role was to enable the boss at the top to function, which much to Hurst's dismay isn't him, because he doesn't have the money, never has had. Hurst is forced to work for Don

Corleone, at the top of the food chain, who must have been Giuseppe Russo.'

Elisabetta got up from her desk. 'Not much is making sense to me this morning, but I'm willing to hear you out,' she said, grinning. 'More coffee?'

'See this,' Stephen said, pointing to the scribbled balance sheet he'd written of Hurst's income and expenditure.

Elisabetta walked round to his desk, grabbed a chair and sat down next to him.

'There's the villa in Rome, the apartment in Geneva, a house in Cape Cod and a summer residence in the French Riviera. How many people would he have to employ to run four properties?'

'Eight minimum, more if you include maintenance workers, gardeners and so on,' Elisabetta said.

'Then there's the business. He buys looted artworks, pays the bare minimum and onsells for a big profit. But there's people to pay off: the middleman, the looters, a team to clean up the antiquities, assistants, a driver. How is he doing all that on his own?'

'His wife could be loaded.'

'She'd have to be heiress rich.'

'So what are you thinking?' Elisabetta asked.

'Or, it has to be someone else's money in those offshore accounts. Hurst gets to use their cash to acquire big ticket items,' Stephen said.

'What else is going through those accounts? Money laundering?'

'On a major scale. He's got a business partner who cleans his money through the art business. Could be drugs, could be guns, could be anything.'

'Hurst wouldn't care where the cash came from, as long as his ego was massaged. He can boast how well he's doing when the reality is, he isn't doing nearly so well as he pretends he is.'

'Who is it?'

'Somebody who likes art.'

'What's the connection with McCarthy?'

'This is where I'm struggling. Hurst is from Boston and McCarthy spent years there. They likely knew each other, moved in the same circles, met at gallery openings, that kind of thing,' Stephen guessed.

'Are you thinking Hurst knew Giuseppe Russo? Did McCarthy introduce them?'

'McCarthy isn't here to answer, but if we assume he did, it would have been mutually beneficial. McCarthy could leave for his job in Rome with a clear conscience if those two hit it off.'

'Say Russo senior and Hurst decide to go into business together, setting up a looting operation in Italy which benefits them both. Do you think McCarthy knew, or suspected?' Elisabetta asked.

'I think he was paid off by Russo in gifts of artworks and was too afraid to ask where they came from. He must have figured out that they were tainted. That a gangster like Russo was never going to play by the rules,' Stephen said.

'And by then he was in way too deep. McCarthy must have thought he was safe at the Vatican, but he'd made a serious error of judgement when he hired Hurst,' Elisabetta said.

'By way of a thank you, Hurst then goes and betrays him. All McCarthy had in life was the church and the job he loved. How humiliated he must have felt to have to tell everyone he met he'd retired, when he was forced out. McCarthy was reported to the Vatican Museums. That someone had photographic proof he had Vatican artworks at home. Look.'

Stephen showed Elisabetta an email from Hurst inviting himself round to McCarthy's place.

'And according to your contact, McCarthy had never in all the time he'd been at the Vatican, invited a colleague to his home. They'd always met in galleries or restaurants.'

'Talk about ruthless, McCarthy must have been furious.'

'That's what I thought. He was off work, recovering from a fall and Hurst takes advantage, giving an ultimatum that he must have his budget signed off,' Stephen said. 'McCarthy had no choice but to meet at his apartment.'

'That was on the fifteenth. And when was he fired?' Elisabetta asked.

'Three days later when the Vatican police came and knocked on his door with a search warrant, seized the artworks and presented him with his letter of dismissal. It can't have been a coincidence.'

'Then Hurst goes on a buying spree. He acquires expensive, glamorous items for the Vatican. Some of them he already owned—they'd been looted to order. Some he buys with laundered money. With McCarthy out of the way, nobody was querying their provenance. Except he slips up. He allows Tony Sanzio his photo opportunity in front of the looted krater. And is betrayed by his own reflection in the picture.'

'Exactly. When Russo senior died, Joe took over the looting business. McCarthy knew far too much about the family secrets. He was becoming a liability for Joe.' Stephen said

'And the revival of the cold case into Joe's brother's death was the last straw. He must have found out that McCarthy was talking to Boston PD.'

Just then, a call came in on Stephen's phone. He ignored it.

'But nobody knew he was here. Even our colleagues wouldn't have known. We made sure of that,' Elisabetta continued. 'Aren't you going to answer that?'

Stephen shook his head. 'That's what I can't work out either. They could have bugged McCarthy's phone. Then they could have tracked him here.'

'But that doesn't explain how they knew that he was here to talk to Hannigan. He could have been here reporting a burglary or a stolen car,' Elisabetta said. 'And they wouldn't have known that Hannigan was working on a cold case. That takes someone pretty skilled at intercepts.'

'A person or persons unknown working for Joe Russo. Whoever betrayed him had inside knowledge,' Stephen said.

Elisabetta glanced up. 'In here?'

Stephen shrugged. 'It's a possibility.' He was non-committal. He didn't want to alienate her, and he knew there was no point in throwing around accusations without evidence. He checked his messages while he was making his mind up about what to do next.

'Holy shit,' he said. Elisabetta looked up.

'Listen to this,' Stephen said as he played the message:

"Bruno Bianca died of cardiac arrest. The autopsy report concluded that there were sufficient amounts of a non-prescribed stimulant to alert homicide."

'I need to let Hannigan know about Bruno as well as McCarthy. Want to be in on the call?' Elisabetta nodded.

Now that she had mentioned the possibility that there was a mole, Stephen felt a growing sense of certainty that there was. He couldn't stop thinking about the one person he'd never got along with in the Rome office, and who had never hidden his dislike for him from the start. But before he tackled that problem, he needed to call Boston.

Cormac Hannigan picked up the phone after the first ring.

'Stephen. I'm so sorry I didn't have the chance to call you when I was in Rome. I flew in and out the same day.'

'I understand. I'm with my colleague Elisabetta di Mascio. I'm calling about McCarthy. Mind if I put you on speaker?'

'Go ahead. What's happened to him?' Hannigan sounded tense.

'His luck ran out. They got him.' He hated putting Hannigan on the spot like this and berated himself for not telling him straight after it had happened.

'Because of giving evidence into his brother's death?'

'No, we don't think so. McCarthy wasn't a witness was he?' Stephen said.

'Correct. And I'm grateful you called me. After that news we're going to have to do everything we can to keep our star witness alive.'

'We're working on an antiquities looting case that has networks across Europe as well as the United States. We believe Russo senior was the boss and that Joe has inherited the business,' Elisabetta said.

'Are the FBI involved?' Hannigan asked.

'Not yet. Got to square it with my boss here first,' Elisabetta said.

'Alberti?' Stephen mouthed. Elisabetta nodded.

'I've got a contact in the FBI you can talk to if you need to,' Hannigan said.

'Thanks,' Stephen said. He looked at Elisabetta and whispered, 'can I tell him?' She nodded.

'We think McCarthy was murdered because of a

painting Giuseppe Russo had given him as a gift. But McCarthy no longer had it.'

'Where is it?' Hannigan asked.

'Nobody knows. The junkie kid who stole it is dead as well,' Stephen said.

'Overdose?' Hannigan said.

'If it was, he didn't administer it himself. The kid was in hospital with an armed guard on the door.'

'Stephen, you really need to give my contact a call,' Hannigan said.

Chapter 25

Boston, USA

Lisa Arnott thought carefully before taking her concerns to the school principal. She investigated whether Mollie's painting had been the work of Tom Keating, the British art forger. But no matter how clever Keating had been at painting in the style of the artists he tried to pass off as his own, (one of which was Degas), he couldn't possibly have forged this one. He'd died six years before the Stewart Gardner theft.

The principal tried to shut her down, refusing to entertain the possibility that a valuable painting had been brought into her school. She laughed off Lisa's art history credentials and challenged her to prove that the little painting was not in fact a reproduction. Lisa patiently tried to explain that it would be extremely difficult to forge a work that tiny, but her boss wasn't having a bar of it. And when Lisa had asked if she could contact the FBI, as they had the painting listed as missing on their database, her boss went ballistic.

'Mollie's father would be over here like a shot, demanding its return if that painting was real.'

Far from supporting and protecting her staff member, her boss seemed intent on exposing her to the wrath of Joe Russo.

'Under no circumstances am I going to have law enforcement come to the school and scaring the children,' her boss continued. The principal seemed to have conveniently forgotten their annual open day with both the Boston Fire Department and the Boston PD. The children got to see round the fire trucks and play with plastic handcuffs and wouldn't stop talking about their experience for weeks.

Feeling anxious and alone, Lisa backed away, wrapping herself around the tiny watercolour, like a cat protecting her kitten.

She sat down in the empty classroom and tried to figure out what to do next. The longer she waited, the greater the danger she was in. Sooner or later, Mollie's father would find out about the missing picture. If her principal wasn't going to help her, who was?

The cop who had talked to the students at open day seemed friendly and approachable and not bad looking either. She had his contact details on her phone. He had a Scottish name, she recalled as she scrolled through her phone. Ciaran? No, it was Cormac and he was Irish.

She listened out for the principal's red sports car firing up and watched as the remaining teachers drifted out towards the car park on their way home, before carefully wrapping the tiny painting in tissue paper and popping it into her handbag. Then she picked up her phone.

'Lieutenant Hannigan? It's Lisa Arnott from Middle

Park School.' It took a while for him to remember her. 'Yes that one,' she said.

Unlike her principal, Hannigan had taken her seriously. She counted the minutes until he arrived in a plain-clothes car. They sat in the car as the rain began to fall and together they hatched a plan.

After they finished, Hannigan turned to Lisa.

'And you're sure about this?'

'I've thought it through,' Lisa said.

'Even if it turns out that the painting is a copy, everyone will know it was you who went to the cops,' Hannigan said.

'When you say everyone, you mean people out there who could make my life very unpleasant?'

'The very same.'

'I studied art and now I've seen that painting I can't unsee it. And I have a strong feeling that it's real. And you can't put a price on that...'

'Before you go to the FBI, there's a police officer in Italy who would be interested to hear about your painting. Do you mind if I give him a call?'

'Sure.' Lisa said.

Hannigan mouthed, 'Voicemail,' before leaving his message: 'Stephen, it's Cormac. I wanted to give you a heads up. A painting belonging to Joe Russo has been brought to my attention by a member of the public and we're on our way to the FBI to get it authenticated. Call you later.'

Lisa got out of Hannigan's car and got into her own. As she drove her car out of the school car park she checked in her rearview mirror. Hannigan waited for two other cars to go by before he pulled out into the street and followed her.

Instead of her usual route home, Lisa took a detour

over the Mystic river to Chelsea and the headquarters of the FBI. Hannigan waited as she got out of her car and was about to enter the building. She gave him a wave and he drove off.

As soon as she gave her name, two officers appeared and escorted her to an interview room. She repeated the story that Hannigan had outlined, only this time, telling the officers that the child who brought the painting to school was Joe Russo's daughter.

'If it turns out that the painting is genuine and the evidence you have provided leads to arrests and conviction of criminals, your personal safety will have been seriously compromised,' one of the officers said.

'I am aware of that, yes. I regard this as my civic duty,' Lisa said.

'And if we go ahead, you understand that you won't be able to return to your job, or your apartment or your old life for the foreseeable future. Are you prepared for that?'

Lisa paused 'I am,' she answered. 'But I have a cat at home.'

'We'll take care of the cat,' the FBI officer said.

'Do you mean you'll find him a good home?'

The two officers looked at each other. One shook his head at his colleague.

'Yes, I will personally see to it that your cat is adopted by an animal lover,' said the officer who seemed to be the senior of the two.

Lisa hesitated.

'Now, may we have the picture,' he asked.

Why hadn't she thought about Smudge before deciding to do this? If anything happened to that cat, she'd never forgive herself.

There was no way out now. She reached into her purse, pulled out the painting and passed it over.

The Lisa Arnott who had walked into the FBI office in Chelsea was never seen again. At the back of the building a woman who looked vaguely like her was bundled into a waiting vehicle with blacked out windows and was driven to a safe house. Out the front, a police officer, dressed in Lisa's clothes with a hood pulled over her face, drove off in Lisa's car.

* * *

It was just before magic hour as a group of armed Boston PD officers drew up in a leafy neighbourhood of large detached houses. It was so quiet on the wide streets that every footstep was audible. The sound of unfamiliar vehicles woke one dog, who started barking, before it was joined by two others.

Cormac Hannigan watched as a convoy of five armoured vehicles with blacked out windows pulled up alongside the PD vehicles. One of his officers challenged the driver of the lead vehicle. Hannigan caught snatches of their heated discussion, as it rapidly escalated to risk being loud enough to take away any advantage of surprise they might have had. He ran over towards the altercation.

Spotting Hannigan's badge, the officer in the vehicle flashed his FBI credentials. 'Stand your officers down,' he ordered. 'We're here for Russo and you're in our way.'

Hannigan shook his head. 'No sir. We're here for a felony. Why didn't you tell us you were going to make your move today? If we stand here any longer, Russo will have slipped out the back. Let's roll together.'

There was a mad scramble as plain-clothes FBI agents and the Boston PD surged forward and circled the Russo compound. Hannigan and the FBI lead beckoned the security guard who was cowering in the gatehouse.

'We have a warrant. Open up,' Hannigan said.

The security guard pressed a button, the gates to the property swung open and Hannigan and a group of agents and police walked briskly to the main entrance. Lights went on in the house and there was the sound of fumbling and swearing as Joe Russo opened his front door to see his house surrounded by cops.

'What the fuck?' He looked from the uniformed cops to the plain-clothes detectives.

Cormac Hannigan glanced at the FBI officer before stepping forward. 'Joe Russo…'

'Wait a minute, will you,' Joe said, before turning towards the stairs and yelling,

'Honey, can you call my attorney and PR will you? Tell them to get their asses down here fast.'

Carmela Russo swept down the stairs, bathrobe wrapped tightly around her. 'What's going on? You're upsetting my family.'

Joe turned back to Hannigan and said belligerently, 'You were saying?'

'Joe Russo, I am arresting you on suspicion of the murder of Luca Russo. You have the right to remain silent. Anything you say can be used against you in court. You have the right to talk to a lawyer for advice before we ask you any questions.'

'My attorney's on his way.'

Hannigan ignored Joe and pressed on, reading out the rest of the Miranda rights before Joe interrupted him again.

'What do you mean, if I cannot afford a lawyer? Joe stood back and laughed. 'I could hire OJ Simpson's entire legal team if I wanted.'

Hannigan stood firm at this interruption. 'If you

decide to answer questions now without a lawyer present, you have the right to stop answering at any time.'

As Joe shrugged, Hannigan stepped back and a plain-clothes FBI agent took his place.

'Joe Russo, you are under arrest on suspicion of theft from the Isabella Stewart Gardner museum.'

'Are you shitting me?' Joe said, shaking his head.

* * *

London, England

Greg Palmer was in London when he got the call from Boston.

'Our house is surrounded by cops. You've got to help him,' a tearful Carmela Russo said.

'Which cops?'

'FBI and the Boston PD.'

'You called his lawyer?' Palmer said.

'He's on his way. When can you get here?'

How was he going to break the news to her that he was in London? Joe would be furious.

'Carmela, listen to me. I'm out of town. And as soon as I can finish up here, I'll be back in Boston. Can I speak to Joe?' Palmer said, secretly hoping that Russo was already in custody.

'No, you can't. The Boston PD have him cuffed and are bundling him into a van. And the FBI are swarming all over the house looking for paintings they say Joe stole. They're making my six-year-old daughter help them. Can you write a story about that?' Carmela said.

Palmer was so busy on the phone that he barely glanced up as a waiter escorted a woman to a table, directly opposite from the sprawling sofa where he was seated.

* * *

You're meeting Palmer, right?

What the hell? Ginny hadn't recognised the email address or the sender.

Who wants to know?

Keep him in place long enough and I can guarantee he'll get what he deserves.

Who the hell are you?

I have enough dirt to get that man put away till his teeth fall out, but you need to play your part.

Charming. She'd thought for a moment that it might have been Stephen but this wasn't his style.

Why now?

The bastard has spent the past few years trying to have me killed. Life on the run doesn't come with high-speed internet.

Still the same spiky Cara, even after all this time.

Do me a favour and record your conversation will you? It's not for the cops, it's so I can have the pleasure of hearing him slag me off. I know he won't be able to resist boasting about me.

As she walked up the steps of one of the most exclusive private members' clubs in London, Ginny couldn't help but reflect that it was a far cry from when Greg Palmer had plucked her from the string of willing assistants, anxious to learn from the king of spin himself.

This time, he had called her. What was his agenda? As usual, he hadn't bothered to reply when she'd asked him what he wanted to discuss. She put that one down to his controlling personality. Two could play at that game. She chose to turn up late.

As she was shown to her table, Ginny spied him glued to his phone, despite the club's etiquette on mobiles.

Only when the waiter approached him did he look up, then made his way towards her, greeting her effusively, kissing her on both cheeks.

'Ginny darling. I hear a celebration is in order.' He waved over to the wine waiter who came hurrying over. 'A bottle of Krug, please.'

Ginny stiffened.

'You know already? The ink's barely dry on the contract.'

'I'd heard the rumours,' he said, glancing up and down, taking in her appearance. She hated the way he did that. Inwardly, she gritted her teeth. 'I knew they were going after you.'

Ginny was wide-eyed.

'Don't look so shocked. I shouldn't be telling you this, but they called me. And, naturally, I sang your praises.'

Now he wanted something from her in return.

'You're looking fabulous by the way. I'm sure you'll take America by storm.'

There was an awkward silence. God, this was excruciating.

'And how is the home life with… the detective.'

It could have been worse. The last time they'd all been together, Palmer had referred to Stephen as "the cop."

'We've split up. That's why I'm back. We're divvying up the contents of the flat.' She hadn't come here to talk about her love life.

'I'm sorry. But he did give the impression he was uncomfortable in your world.'

Ginny had forgotten how blunt Palmer could be. He'd made no secret that he despised Stephen and regarded him as a loser. Even though they weren't together anymore, she wasn't going to let Palmer trash Stephen's reputation.

'He's an honourable man, in a difficult job.'

'Of course, he is.'

Platitudes again.

'I won't keep you. I'm sure you're busy. Let's talk again when I get my feet under the table,' Ginny said. She knew he wanted something. Maybe now he'd come out and say it.

'But you've barely touched your champagne,' he said, feigning hurt. She'd long ago seen through the way he liked to control every situation, only this time she was playing him.

As she was getting up, Palmer looked at her.

'You know the Australian police found that crazy missing terrorist's belongings, don't you?' He could barely disguise his smirk.

I've got news for you, mate, Ginny thought. She just hoped that her phone, tucked inside her handbag on record, was picking all of this up.

'I was very sorry. Nobody deserves to die alone in the desert. It sounded as though she got lost and disoriented and ran out of water.' As she spoke, Ginny realised the suffering must have been real, even if the dying part wasn't.

'She'd been on the run for two years. We thought we'd got her but she got away. Her luck ran out that was all.'

'It was you who wanted her out the way,' Ginny said. 'Not the police.'

'The police let us down. I'll never understand why your ex let her go like that. She was a wanted terrorist.'

'You know as well as I do what happened to the real perpetrator. They wanted a scapegoat, and Cara was it, thanks to your spin.'

'Even I find some of the jobs I have to do distasteful. But as I said to you when you came to me looking for a job, corporate PR isn't for the faint-hearted.

Ginny had to fight back every instinct to get up and leave.

'I have a little proposition for you,' Palmer said.

She shifted her weight in her seat but forced a smile.

'I'm setting up an office in the States. I'd like to have the gallery on board as my first major client. Art instead of oil.'

So that was it. He was looking for work. Well, she'd learnt how to spin from him, hadn't she?

'I'll put it to the board,' she said. 'Shall I order us another bottle?'

Palmer raised an eyebrow. 'Not your usual style, Ginny. Why not? We could retire to my suite and have a bottle sent up there.'

The thought of going up to Palmer's room made her want to puke. How much longer was she going to have to keep up this charade? As she was thinking up a way to keep him at the table, two men, not dressed for a private members' club, came striding towards Palmer, who raised his voice in protest. Was it money he owed them? Or a deal gone sour, she wondered. She backed away to pick up her coat from the cloakroom, still disturbed by what he'd told her. Had there been a massive cover-up? A plot to silence Cara that Palmer had known about?

Ginny's hands were trembling as she dialled Stephen's number. No answer. Was he blocking her calls? She texted him instead.

This isn't about us.

She wrote, then deleted, *It's more important than that,* before continuing:

All that press stuff about Cara disappearing in Australia was a pack of lies. I heard it from the king of spin himself. Call me. I leave London tomorrow morning.

As she put her phone away, she heard a commotion behind her.

'Mr Palmer, we're arresting you on suspicion of profiting from organised criminal activity.'

Palmer stood there, swinging backwards and forwards on his heels, raging so loudly against the perceived injustice that the rest of the caution was a blur.

'What organised criminal activity? You mean that unpaid speeding fine?' Palmer said.

'Mr Palmer, all you have to do is come quietly.' Ginny turned around to see Palmer in handcuffs being firmly escorted down the steps.

'There's a mistake. Ask her. She used to work for me. Ginny, tell them who I am,' Palmer said. Ginny swung around to face the police officers.

'The scum of the earth, that's who you are.'

Ginny passed her card to one of the officers. 'Here's my number. I'd be glad to give a character reference.' Ginny paused. 'For the prosecution.'

She had a lightness in her step as she set off down the street, gloating, while Greg Palmer was manhandled into a waiting police car.

* * *

Boston, USA

Mollie was showing the child liaison officer her drawings when a diminutive female FBI agent walked into the playroom. She mouthed to her colleague. 'I need to ask her a few questions.' The officer nodded.

The FBI agent crouched down next to the little girl. 'Mollie, honey, we're looking for some pictures like the ones in your drawings and we've searched the house and can't find them.'

Mollie put her head on one side as though she was asking an unformed question.

'You're not in trouble,' the agent said.

Mollie stared down her drawing. She sat there solemnly for a few seconds and then lifted her eyes and pointed upwards towards the ceiling.

'We searched up there,' the officer said.

'He'll be mad if I tell,' Mollie said.

'Give us a moment, will you,' the child liaison officer said, motioning to the FBI agent to step out the door.

'Your daddy's going to have to come with us today. I don't know how long he'll be away. It's not your fault. Never forget that, okay? Shall we go help the other lady?'

Mollie nodded, taking the officer by the hand. She walked down the corridor, FBI officers following. She took them into the guest room and went straight inside the spacious walk-in closet.

'You pull it back like this,' Mollie said, indicating a kid-sized cupboard door.

The FBI officer spoke into her radio. 'Boss you'd better come up here.'

A disembodied voice replied. 'What have you found?'

As the cupboard door swung open, the officer replied, 'The gateway to Narnia,' before getting on her hands and knees and following Mollie inside. She struggled to squeeze into the crawl space.

'Guys,' she warned. 'Don't follow me. You'll get stuck.'

Once inside the officer looked around before cautiously easing herself up into a little attic.

'I'm sending the kid back,' she said, speaking into her radio. 'Thank you, Mollie. I'll keep everything safe here.'

As Mollie disappeared, the FBI officer saw that the

attic had been set up as a playroom come storeroom. There was even a light switch, which she flicked on. A bronze eagle and an ancient Chinese vase sat on a shelf, seemingly put there out of harm's way. Paintings were leaning against the walls. She took a closer look at them, then stood back open-mouthed, before fumbling for her radio.

'I have two Rembrandts: A Lady and Gentlemen in Black and A Storm on the Sea of Galilee. Then a tiny Rembrandt etching, what looks like a Manet, but don't quote me on that. And four Degas works on paper.'

'Jesus Christ,' came the muffled response from the other side of the wall.

'I'm looking right at him.'

* * *

Joe Russo stood in front of the judge. She had flecks of grey in her hair and dark circles under her eyes, but with an immaculate French manicure. She looked Joe in the eyes.

'Mr Russo, you have been charged with murder, which is a major felony, which does not allow me to permit bail. You will be held without bail until the case comes to trial.'

'Your honour, a word,' Joe's attorney said.

The judge looked up at him. 'You have thirty seconds,' she said, before admiring her nails.

'The defendant has a home, a family. He's not a flight risk,' the attorney pleaded.

'Even if I did have discretion here, and I do not, I disagree with you. I think he poses a real risk of not returning on future court dates. And in the light of the defendant's previous criminal history, the nature of the charges and the chance of a lengthy incarceration, I have refused bail. Time's up. Take him down to the cells.' The judge looked down at her papers, signed them and waved the defence attorney away with her hand.

'Next case, please,' she said.

As Joe was being led away, he turned around to his attorney and mouthed, 'you're fired!'

* * *

Rome, Italy

'Wow,' Elisabetta said. 'Take a look at this. That call you got from Hannigan about that other Russo painting?'

'What about it? Stephen got up and walked over to Elisabetta's desk.'

An alert on her computer had flashed up: Attention all Police Jurisdictions:

The Federal Bureau of Investigation (FBI) would like to announce, subject to formal authentication, that all but one of the stolen paintings from the Isabella Stewart Gardner heist have been recovered. A suspect is in custody.

'There's no mention here of the antiquities ring that we tipped them off about,' Elisabetta said.

'Why do you think that is?'

'This is the biggest art theft of all time. And the FBI just solved it. That's going to be in every newspaper and all over social media.'

'Joe Russo pulled off the Stewart Gardner heist? He wouldn't know the difference between a Tintoretto and a tennis girl poster.'

'I doubt he did it alone. And there's one more they still have to find,' Elisabetta said.

'Which is?'

'The Concert by Vermeer. You couldn't even put a price on it when it was hanging in the gallery. Now it's going to be the stuff of legend—like Leonardo's Salvator Mundi,' Elisabetta said.

'What happened to that one?'

'It depends on which conspiracy theory you believe. On a super-yacht; in a Swiss vault; maybe it's a fake, or it's been abducted by aliens. Anyway, here's a photo of The Concert, just in case you happen to trip over it in the street,' she said, with a grin.

'Right.' Stephen laughed, casting a cursory glance at it. 'I haven't even been able to find that studio painting the junkie kid stole off McCarthy.'

'Did we ever get a photo of it?'

'I asked McCarthy. He never sent it.'

'What happened to his phone?' Elisabetta said.

'It went to homicide. They've got it for evidence in case his killer is ever found. Fat chance of that,' Stephen said, a note of resignation in his voice.

'Let's see if we can get permission to search it. Then at least we know what we're looking for.'

'I wrote down the subject matter. St Jerome and the Lion by Brunetti.'

'It's a common enough iconography. Still worth a few hundred euros though.'

'I'll go over there today.' He filed the information away for later and got back to what he was doing, trying to work out who the hell in the department was the mole working for Joe Russo.

His phone rang. 'Connor.'

'Stephen, it's Cormac. We've arrested Joe Russo on suspicion of murder of his brother, Luca. He's been remanded in custody.'

'He won't like that.'

'Murder isn't the only charge he's facing right now,' Hannigan said.

'We saw the FBI press release. We guessed it had to be Joe, after you alerted us to that painting you were about to hand over,' Stephen said.

'That turned out to be a stolen Degas.'

'That was some find.'

'It was a member of the public who spotted it.'

'Brave of them. Thanks for the tip-offs and keeping us in the loop,' Stephen said.

'Likewise. And if the FBI ever decide to acknowledge your help in the case and invite you over, you know where I am.'

As Hannigan rang off, Stephen turned to Elisabetta. 'What do you think?'

'Antiquities trafficking isn't even going to get a look in,' Elisabetta said.

'All the same, Joe's going to go to prison for a very long time.'

'Don't count on it. He's got the money to hire the best lawyers. They're bound to do a plea bargain. That's how the system works over there,' Elisabetta said. 'We just have to hope they can tack on the money laundering as well. If not, Hurst will walk.'

'You're kidding?' Stephen said.

Elisabetta shook her head. 'I'm not. Hurst is an old man. They don't like to lock up the elderly here. Not unless he's a mafia boss who's been implicated in murder.'

'We did our best. We brought him to justice. We aren't responsible for the sentence,' Stephen said, a note of bitter disappointment in his voice. You win some, you lose some, he thought. That left just one major job to do. He was determined to find that mole who had ratted on McCarthy and got him murdered.

Chapter 26

Stephen went over to homicide the next morning and spoke to the desk sergeant.

'I'm looking for the memory stick with the data from Case Number 4572.'

The desk sergeant looked up. 'Give me a minute,' he said, searching on his computer.

'One of your lot picked it up,' the sergeant said. 'Checked out to the art unit yesterday.'

'Who signed for it?'

'Hang on. I'll look. Pasquale Romani.'

'What the hell? But that's not the only copy is it? You've still got the SIM.'

'We should have. But I'd need to check with the evidence room. Can't you get the information you need from your colleague?'

Colleague? Judas, more like.

If the SIM had gone along with the memory stick, he would have no choice but to tackle Pasquale head on.

'I'll try that first. But let me know if you still have it or not, won't you?'

'Of course we'll have it. Who do you think we are? The Keystone Cops?'

'Thanks,' Stephen muttered, as he fled, running down the steps and out onto the street. He punched the last number dialled on his phone.

'Di Mascio,' Elisabetta said.

'Ask Alberti if he knows why Pasquale has gone off-piste on our case, will you?'

'What the hell?'

Stephen jogged along. 'Pasquale checked out the memory stick containing all the evidence from McCarthy's phone. He may have taken the SIM as well. And Homicide didn't back up.'

'*Madonna.*'

* * *

A group of nervous looking men ranging in age from seventeen to seventy, and a woman in her forties, sat in a semi-circle, with the facilitator facing them. Next to him was a portable whiteboard and marker pens.

'Renzo, how's this week been for you?'

Renzo glanced at the others and then down at his hands.

'It's got better. My wife's agreed to give me another chance. She's going to move up here. It's partly for financial reasons. We were trying to run two house-holds. And money was so tight that I went back to gambling.'

'Thanks Renzo. I just want to take up your point about using debt as a reason to gamble. Anyone else had that experience?' Three in the group raised their hands.

The facilitator got up and picked up a pen.

'What are some of the tools you have in your toolbox

to overcome the negative thinking that enabled your gambling?'

As Renzo sat there, listening to the facilitator droning on, his phone, which was on silent, lit up.

Destroy the evidence.

He put the phone in his pocket and got up.

'Sorry, got to go,' he muttered.

The facilitator nodded and Renzo walked out of the room, shoulders hunched.

* * *

Renzo pushed open the door to his one-bedroom apartment. He was greeted with suitcases in a disorderly pile.

'How did it go?' Giulia asked.

'Good. They're happy with my progress. I told them about you.' Renzo smiled down at her.

'I'm proud of what you're doing.'

'It's for us.'

'I know and I'm grateful,' she said, pushing the hair out of her eyes.

'She asleep?' Renzo asked, changing the subject.

'Out like a light. Tired from all that travelling.'

'Listen,' Renzo said. 'Something's come up. I've been called back in.'

Giulia's face fell. 'But I only just got here.'

'One of the guys has called in sick. I promise I'll make it up to you.'

Giulia eyed Renzo suspiciously.

'What?' he said, aggressively.

'Nothing,' she said wearily. 'I'm shattered. I just hope I've made the right decision.'

Renzo turned his back on her and strode out the door.

* * *

Elisabetta and Stephen were waiting outside Pasquale's apartment in an unmarked car. Elisabetta was behind the wheel.

'Here he comes,' Stephen said.

'He won't be able to get far if he's on foot.' Elisabetta said.

'Tuck in behind this parked car, will you. See that van up ahead, it's pulling up. He's getting in. Checking the plate, now,' Stephen said, punching in the numbers. 'Registered to a fruit and veg wholesale company.'

The van pulled out and drove off.

'Go, go, go,' Stephen said urgently.

'Why would you need a van that size to pick up one person?' Elisabetta said.

'Because there might be more on board. We're going to have to call Alberti at home,' Stephen said. They looked at each other.

'And we need Renzo on this. Give him a call,' Elisabetta said. The phone rang out.

'Try him at home.'

'Someone's answering. I'll put it on speaker,' Stephen said.

'Why are you calling at this time of night?' Giulia said, crossly. 'I've only just got the baby off to sleep.'

'We're so sorry to call you, Giulia. I just needed to ask Renzo a quick question. It's Elisabetta from work.'

'Ask him yourself. He left for work ten minutes ago. Or call him on his work phone,' Giulia said, putting the phone down.

'It wouldn't be the first time a man lied to his partner telling her that he's got to work,' Elisabetta said, concentrating on the road ahead.

'True. But where the hell is he?'

'It's Pasquale who we need to talk to first. He signed out the memory stick,' Elisabetta said.

'How do we know that Alberti didn't ask him to do it? We'd look pretty stupid if we ring him up and he tells us where to get off,' Stephen said.

'Maybe Pasquale's gone for a night out.'

'You know as well as I do that guy is a loner. If you can get him out at all, after one drink he's looking at his watch.'

'True.'

'And how many stag nights call for a bullet-proof vehicle to drive around in?'

Alberti was furious. 'What do you mean Pasquale has gone rogue? Your evidence better be watertight, di Mascio. Or else you'll be back in uniform walking the beat.'

They were by now, four, maybe five vehicles behind the van and back in Marconi, not far from the abandoned warehouse, that Hurst had used for cleaning up the looted antiquities.

'They're turning off,' Stephen said.

'We'll have to follow them on foot,' Elisabetta said. 'They'll see us.'

'We're not doing this on our own are we?' Stephen said.

'If we need reinforcements we'll send for them. But for now, yes. I'd prefer it if there were three of us. When I see Renzo again…' She broke off. 'You ready?'

Stephen nodded.

'Let's do it. I'll take the loading dock at the back. You take the front entrance.'

* * *

In amongst the shadows of the gloomy warehouse, Stephen's eyes adjusted to the poor light. He could make out a man on his knees on the floor with his hands tied behind his back.

Someone, he couldn't quite see, had a gun to his head.

'We told you that if you were followed this would happen,' said a thick-set man.

Shit. The hostage was Pasquale. It was a set up.

He texted Elisabetta.

Call backup. They've got Pasquale.

She texted back.

On my way.

'They'll know it was me who signed out the memory stick.'

'Hand it over then.'

Pasquale tried to wriggle his hands, but the cable ties were cutting into his wrists.

'Here,' he said indicating the pocket in his shirt.

The thick-set thug reached in and pulled out a memory stick and two phones. He threw the memory stick on the floor and smashed it into two with his boot, crushing it with his heel as he ripped open the phones and took out the SIM chips and proceeded to destroy those.

Stephen heard a floorboard creak behind him. He swung round. Elisabetta had her fingers to her lips as she crouched down beside him.

'How many?' She whispered.

Stephen held up three fingers, Elisabetta two, pointing to the front entrance.

Five against their two.

The three standing guards left two others, who were going backwards and forwards to the loading bay.

'What's in the van?' Elisabetta mouthed.

Stephen was about to reply, when Renzo stepped out of the shadows.

'You took your time,' Stephen said.

Renzo grinned sheepishly. 'Sorry about that.'

'Reckon we can take them out?'

Renzo nodded. 'Let's do it.'

Elisabetta stepped forward and in that split second, Stephen felt the cold hard steel of a muzzle on the back of his head. He made the gesture of a loaded gun, to try to warn Elisabetta.

'You couldn't even wait for the cavalry, could you?' Renzo said in a flat tone, pulling out a pair of handcuffs. He clipped one set of cuffs round Elisabetta's wrist and the other around Stephen's. 'Let's see how inseparable you really are,' Renzo said as he frog-marched him and Elisabetta into the area where the thug was guarding Pasquale. 'Look what I found lurking in the shadows,' Renzo said.

'You don't have to do this Renzo,' Elisabetta said.

In response he swung round and slapped her across the face.

She was motionless, poised even as she took the blow without complaint. She tilted her head towards Stephen and as if on cue he took up where she'd started.

'And there was me blaming Pasquale. I thought that he was the one protecting Hurst when it was you all along. And that white Fiat that was resprayed. That belong to you by any chance?' Stephen said. Renzo ignored him. 'Tony Sanzio might have died from a heart attack, but it sure didn't help you trying to run him off the road. What did he do?'

'Shut the fuck up, Scotland Yard,' Renzo said.

'You're going to kill us both anyway, so you may as well hear me out. McCarthy would have got away but for you. I hold you responsible for his murder.'

'We'll kill that one first,' Renzo said.

But before Renzo could draw breath, Elisabetta had swung round with all her body weight and dealt Renzo a karate kick that sent him crashing to the floor.

'The keys,' Elisabetta scrabbled on the ground. As Stephen reached into Renzo's pocket there was a shot followed by another. Pasquale lay bleeding.

'Lousy shot,' Elisabetta whispered, leaping up as soon as Stephen had unlocked the cuffs. Renzo, still concussed, lurched to his feet and reached for his gun, aiming once again at Elisabetta. She was behind a pillar as she returned fire. She moved forward slowly, covered by Stephen. He took a deep breath, then raised his pistol at arm's length, sighted carefully along the barrel, and fired a single shot just above ground level. A short, sharp cry of pain came from the other side of the space.

For a moment nothing happened, then Stephen ducked as another gun fired, but the shot was wild, straight into the roof. It pinged on a metal brace between the steel pillars as it fell back to earth followed by an eerie silence.

Elisabetta signalled to Stephen. A piece of canvas strung up between two pillars was flapping near an open window. Stephen saw a shadow then just at that moment the canvas rippled and fell, and two ski-masked bandits stood back to back. They didn't even aim, just squeezed their triggers. In an instant, the place was ablaze with star-like flashes, rat-a-tat-a-tat-ing around the vast space.

Then in amongst the confusion there was a hiss and a loud bang as the air was filled with smoke and a team of six armed response officers ran forwards shouting.

'Armed police. Put down your weapons.'

'Call an ambulance. Man down. He's bleeding out.' Stephen shouted.

There was the sound of running as Renzo's accomplices, one on each side, tried to run the injured man towards the rear of the building.

'Which way are they headed?' Elisabetta said running after them.

'Back entrance.' Stephen said, right behind her.

'You and you, cover the front,' Elisabetta ordered to two of the armed officers. 'You others, come with us.'

'Let's try cutting them off,' Stephen called.

There was a burst of gunfire as Renzo and his team fired indiscriminately. The two armed officers returned fire. First one gangster fell, then the other, till the only one left was Renzo, dragging his injured leg towards the exit. Stephen brought him down, shooting him in the other leg as Elisabetta kicked the gun from his grasp.

'That's the last time I recommend anyone for promotion,' she said.

'You're going to go down a long time for this,' Stephen said.

'You're not so perfect either, Scotland Yard. You tell her what you did?' Renzo said indicating Elisabetta, who was standing over him, her weapon aimed steadily at his groin.

Stephen turned away, embarrassed.

'Thought not,' Renzo said.

'That should give you time enough in prison to earn that money you owe us,' Elisabetta said.

Chapter 27

Rome, Italy

It was Stephen's last day in the carabinieri office. He and Elisabetta had warned Alberti that as a result of the case against Hurst, they believed that the Euphronios krater displayed in the Vatican had been looted. Alberti had prevaricated, arguing that as the case hadn't even come to trial, it was premature to approach them.

'And if it's no longer on display, what's the problem?' Alberti said.

'Everything indicates the Vatican krater was stolen. It's evidence,' Elisabetta had argued.

'We can't afford to get on the wrong side of the Vatican, di Mascio. You of all people should know that,' Alberti replied. 'And you know how slowly these things go in court.'

Walking out of Alberti's office, Stephen shook his head feeling slightly deflated.

'That went well. Meanwhile, where have they hidden the missing krater?' Stephen asked.

'Quietly spirited away to the Freeport in Geneva, along some anonymous corridor, hidden in a warehouse strongroom like hundreds of other priceless works of art, never to be seen again,' Elisabetta said.

Stephen's shoulders slumped.

'Hey, none of that. We did what we could. And even if Hurst never spends a day in prison, we'll have won,' she said.

'I have something to tell you,' Stephen began.

'Is this to do with Renzo?' Elisabetta asked.

'Yes and no. I was desperate for evidence to bring Hurst down. And I...I'm ashamed at what I did,' Stephen said.

Elisabetta looked thoughtful, as though she was weighing up what to say.

'You heard him. We can't afford to get on the wrong side of the Church. If the case ever gets to court we'll deal with it then,' Elisabetta said, looking Stephen in the eye. 'In the line of duty and all that.'

She was letting him off the hook?

'Come on, let's finish up working with the artist on the St Jerome composite,' Elisabetta said.

'You're right. I'm just not used to leaving a job that's incomplete, that's all. And the McCarthy painting. That's another piece of unfinished business. And so is this.' Stephen drew out his organisational diagram.

'You're not still going on about that are you?'

'I am actually.' Stephen wrote McCarthy's name beside the word the Guardian.

Elisabetta raised an eyebrow.

'The Guardian, metaphorically, as in God's representative on earth and literally, of that missing painting.'

'Fair enough. But Tony Sanzio wouldn't have known about the painting,' Elisabetta said.

'It doesn't matter. It's my interpretation of it,' Stephen said, before closing his notebook and putting it away.

'Just because you're going back to London doesn't mean we'll stop looking. The painting's got to be out there somewhere,' Elisabetta said.

Alberti had laid on a buffet and some drinks. There were awkward speeches and conversation that carefully avoided any reference to one of their own in jail awaiting trial.

'Thanks once again, Scotland Yard,' Alberti had said. Stephen cringed and saw Elisabetta do the same at the very words Renzo had used when they were under siege at the warehouse.

It was time to say goodbye. Elisabetta mimicked Alberti, patting Stephen on the shoulder. 'So long, Scotland Yard.'

'You'll come and visit when next you're in London, won't you?' Stephen had said.

'I want that tour of the pubs you've promised me,' Elisabetta had said, waving goodbye. Stephen turned around one last time. 'It's a deal.'

* * *

A red, white and green checked tablecloth was laid over two tables joined together and set with the best china and glassware. The chairs around the table were of various sizes and styles. The mantelpiece was cluttered with Golden Wedding cards. Next to these was the family photo of great-granddad in his Cacciatori delle Alpi uniform from Garibaldi's days and the vial of holy water blessed by the Pope. On the wall, in pride of place, was St Jerome and the Lion, the lion holding his paw aloft as the saint tended to him.

As the family sat down to eat and they were ready to toast the couple, the eldest daughter glanced up at the painting. 'Mamma, you kept it.'

'It grows on you,' she said. 'I still don't like that heavy frame.'

* * *

Java, Indonesia

Cara hovered outside a roadside stall selling fruit and stopped to buy a papaya juice. The seller, a man in his forties, acknowledged her with a nod.

'He's still working on it,' he said, directing her to the internet cafe next door. 'We'll give you a call when it's ready.'

Cara walked through to the back where there were six desks with computers down one side of a lime green wall and six on the other.

She sat down and logged on. It had been a while since she'd sent that evidence to Tariq about Greg Palmer and his connection to organised crime. She hoped he'd passed the news along to Stephen. Normally she didn't like cops. Sometimes they could be handy to have around. She tapped in the name of Palmer's company, Dream Large USA.

There was story after story about "PR man Greg Palmer." He'd been arrested in London, had known links with mobster Joe Russo and was awaiting extradition to the USA.

Cara threw her head back and laughed hard enough to startle not only the backpackers and locals seated at the terminals, but the people who worked out the back of the internet cafe.

An Indonesian man in his sixties popped his head round the door.

'Natalie, you okay?'

Cara beamed. 'Sorry Joyo. Something incredible has happened that I never thought I'd live to see.'

Joyo beckoned her. 'I have it here for you.'

Joyo held the door ajar and she followed him inside the cave-like space. The room was a treasure trove of fake IDs, travel documents and passports, in piles of various nationalities.

Joyo sat down at his desk and pulled out the seat opposite. As Cara sat down, Joyo peered at every last detail on a newly made passport through a jeweller's monocle. Beside him was a high-tech scanner and printer.

'Irish, okay?'

'Yeah, Irish is great, thank you.'

'A thousand dollars as agreed.' Cara pulled out a wallet of US dollars and counted them out. The forger held each one up to the light.

'You know I'm pretty good at telling what's real and what's fake, don't you?' he chuckled. 'Everything's in order,' he said as he passed over the newly created passport.

Cara flicked through the pages. Her picture showed her with her new long bob.

'Thanks Joyo. Know where I can buy a reconditioned laptop? I need one for my travels.'

Joyo looked up.

'Right here.'

'How much?'

'Three hundred and fifty because it's you. I throw in my labour for free. Ready for you in an hour.'

'Thanks,' Cara said. 'I'll be in here,' she gestured, as she opened the door back into the internet cafe area.

While she was waiting for the laptop, she went back online. Who had Tariq tipped off? If it was Stephen, she wanted to find him again, tell him what it meant to her to have the man who she held responsible for her kidnapping to be behind bars. Where was Stephen now?

She did an internet search and up popped a newspaper article with a photograph of him, in a story from Italy about looted treasures recovered from a tomb. He was smiling broadly, standing next to a pile of old pots, alongside a female colleague.

"The priceless artefacts were recovered in a joint operation with the London Metropolitan Police," the piece said. Then there was another report, this time about artworks stolen from the Isabella Stewart Gardner museum in Boston in the 1990s. Twelve works of art were found in the home of notorious underworld gangster Joe Russo, thanks to another anonymous tip-off.

Cara couldn't take credit for that one, but nonetheless, felt satisfaction that she had played a small part in stopping evil in its tracks.

Greg Palmer, once the king of spin, would forever more find his name associated with the mafia boss who had committed the world's biggest art heist. Could life get any better?

'Natalie, I've finished,' Joyo called.

She walked back in, with a spring in her step. She held out her hand and whispered, 'Thanks for everything. But I think it's safe for me to go home now.'

The old forger looked up at her and patted her arm.

'You stay safe, Natalie,' Joyo said, gruffly. He turned away, but she'd already seen the tears in his eyes.

* * *

Rome, Italy

Paolo climbed down his stepladder, paint pot and brush in hand. 'What do you think happened to Fat Tony?'

Geppo, who was cleaning his paintbrushes, turned to his nephew. 'He was too greedy. He got what was coming to him.'

Paolo stared at his uncle. 'What do you mean?'

Geppo looked straight into his nephew's eyes.

'I had nothing to do with it. So don't ask me again,' Geppo said.

Paolo was speechless.

'Why do you think we were offered witness protection and a chance to make a new life in Australia?'

Paolo shook his head. 'You're not going, are you? You turned them down.' He looked at his paint-splattered overalls. 'For this. Where we make a third of the money we did back then.'

'I did it for you. To make you proud of your old uncle. We could have taken that offer up but there'd be no going back. We'd be cut off from our old life forever.'

Paolo shot back. 'You're not going because you're scared.'

'I'm not going because I'd be stuck with you and all that shit about left-wing billionaires and celebrities running the world.'

'Alright, I get it Uncle.' Paolo sulked.

'Get used to it. Come on let's load the van before we get a parking ticket.' Geppo started carrying cans of paint through the empty shop and onto the street where a white van with a painted sign, Corri & Nephew Painters and Decorators was parked. He unclicked the doors, which swung open and started loading paint pots and step ladders into the back while Paolo was cleaning up.

'The dust sheet comes out last,' Geppo called out.

Paolo yelled back. 'You don't have to tell me.'

As they were talking a Lambretta scooter roared around the corner.

Paolo jumped up as he heard the noise. He ran outside.

The driver and the pillion passenger were in full visors and black leathers.

'Uncle,' Paolo screamed. 'Get back.'

Geppo swung around, bewildered.

Paolo grabbed Geppo and pushed him down next to the kerb, with the van between them and the bike riders as the pillion passenger raised a pump-action shotgun and sprayed the van with bullets. The scooter stopped, its engine still running.

Paolo crept around the side of the van, pounced and pushed the scooter over, unseating the two riders. He grabbed the gun.

The gangsters picked themselves up and ran straight into the path of two police cars, sirens blaring which flew around the corner and into the street. There was a screech of tyres as the car in front hit one of the assassins a glancing blow and the other flew over the top and landed on the windscreen of the police car behind.

Geppo sat on the side of the pavement, cowering. Paolo had his arm protectively around his uncle.

'You saved my life.'

'I didn't mean what I said before,' Paolo said.

'I know you didn't, son.'

'But these guys, they don't give up.'

Geppo looked at his nephew, tears in his eyes.

'I'm too old. Australia is for the likes of you. I'll take my chances.'

'But, Uncle. You'll have to run the business on your own.'

Geppo went in for one last hug.

'I'll manage. I'm going to sit here and talk to the cops. You better make yourself scarce.'

Paolo was about to say something more. Geppo interrupted him.

'I know. You don't have to say it. On your way, kid.'

Paolo turned and called out one last time, 'watch out for the deep state,' before he shuffled off sorrowfully through the growing crowd.

* * *

London, England

Stephen had chosen the long way round to get to Tottenham Court Road tube, via Soho Square, rather than along the busy main road. He loved the square at this time of year. He had barely been back a couple of days and was still surprised to be fielding calls from daytime TV and chat shows to come in and talk about his part in discovering looted artworks.

He must have been talking too loudly on his phone to the last journalist who called him, as out of the corner of his eye he could see a woman with a bemused expression on her face, looking at him. He finished the call and then rang Tariq.

Headphones jammed into his ears, he walked along, listening to his friend.

'Can you make your next jaunt closer to home? Where your disabled mate could visit, without having to battle tourists waving selfie sticks at every ancient monument?'

Stephen stopped and paused for a moment, leaning against a gap in the railings.

'Where to next, Steve?' Tariq asked.

'Don't know exactly, yet. Organised crime? People smuggling? I haven't made up my mind.'

'The boss gave you a choice?'

'Reynolds is the one who doesn't have the choice. I'm officially back in the fold. I didn't screw up or make her look bad in front of her Europol pals. She even told me I'd finally pulled my head out of my arse, which is as close to a compliment as she'll ever get.'

As Stephen was talking, he saw in his peripheral vision the same woman who had been looking at him before. He hadn't noticed she was a cyclist and was now waiting to park her bike in the very spot he was leaning against.

'Steve, are you there?'

'Sorry mate, hang on.'

The woman called out, her tone light-hearted.

'There must be a law against that, isn't there?'

He recognised her voice in an instant. Stephen tried hard not to stare. She was the right height, around one sixty-five to one seventy centimetres and looked about the right age. But a shoulder-length bob and a fringe? And then there was the bicycle—beige with white tyres and a basket in the front, more suited to carting a baguette and a small dog around a French village than travelling city streets. And her outfit of grey tapered trousers, white shirt and short grey jacket would have drawn a pithy comment from the woman from his past who she resembled, the gamine, spiky-haired courier who always dressed in top-to-toe black.

'Tariq, can I call you back?'

The cyclist grabbed his phone.

'Tariq?' A jolt of electricity shot through Stephen at the sound of her voice. He pictured Tariq's face on the other end of the line.

'He wants to speak to you,' the woman said, passing the phone back. Their hands touched.

'Am I hearing things?' Tariq said.

'No, you heard correctly,' Stephen said.

'It's Natalie, now.' Cara spoke before Stephen could say her name. 'I'm back for a few days.' She paused. 'And I thought I'd look up a couple of old friends,' she said with more than a hint of irony.

Before he could ask her back from where, and what was with the new identity, she was reaching for his phone. 'Here she is again.'

'Hey Tariq. How's that office of yours? Are the windows still so dirty you can't see out of them?' As she was talking, Stephen thought of the last time he'd seen her, when he'd had to push her onto a plane at Geelong and told her to get herself out of Australia and harm's way.

'I'm on my way to Tariq's as it happens,' he said as Cara, (he couldn't get his head around Natalie yet), handed him his phone. 'Want to come?'

'Yeah, I'd like that. It's been too long.'

'Let's get a cab. Special occasion and all that.' As Cara locked up her bike, Stephen glanced down at his phone and saw that Ginny had left a message. His Catholic guilt nagged at him. Not so long ago he'd have called her straight back. He still had work to do there. Elisabetta may have let him off the hook. Ginny wouldn't be quite so forgiving. He put his phone back in his pocket.

'You've been spying on me?' Stephen said, his face breaking into a smile.

'You didn't make it easy. But then you went and found those missing artefacts and your face was splashed all over the newspapers.'

'Then we're even.'

Cara's face fell.

'You saw the broadcast?'

'I wasn't sure it was you. But I never gave up hope. You know, for Tariq.'

Cara turned away, tears in her eyes.

Stephen fumbled in his pocket for a tissue and passed it to her.

'It's grand to have you back.'

Cara dabbed her eyes and smiled at him.

'Thanks for looking out for me.'

Once they'd flagged down a taxi and were inside, Stephen had a million questions to ask, where she'd been, how she'd coped. He knew that her disappearance had haunted Tariq. Every time they met for a drink she'd come up in the conversation. Although he'd never said it to his face, Tariq blamed him for abandoning Cara. And the guilt Stephen had felt was difficult to bear. But for now, he was grateful that at least Tariq might finally forgive him for that split-second decision back in Australia. She'd survived. And, he realised, so had he. That was all that mattered.

* * *

Thanks so much for reading this book. If you enjoyed it, we would love it if you would leave a review on Amazon or another book review website. It doesn't have to be a long one. Even a line or two makes all the difference. Click on the link below to go straight to the review page. https://www.amazon.com/review/create-review?& asin=B08WYQ117Q

Acknowledgments

At the end of 2017, when I was living in Boston, I realised this book would never see the light of day, unless I put my hand up and asked for help. I was looking for a mentor to help me shape the novel from the ground up. When I came across Jenny Nash and her book coaching company, Author Accelerator I knew I'd found kindred spirits. I started their intensive coaching programme in 2018 and with the help of book coach Kelly Hartog, came up with a first and final chapter. Once I knew the start and the end, I finally figured out how to get there.

Thanks go to Robert Devcic and Charles Gollop for accompanying us on a research trip into the entrails of the global art market.

Averill Buchanan's developmental edit helped me shape an early draft; Eden Sharp's subsequent edit got me over the finish line. My beta reader Stephanie Light saved me from making more embarrassing mistakes. Thanks also to Sarah Carradine for both beta reading and proofreading.

Thank also to Andrew Brown of Design for Writers for his imaginative book cover which perfectly captures the tone of the novel.

And to my family, Susan Ripley and Philip Taylor for being our rock of support, now and always.

About the Author

Lambert Nagle is the pen-name for Alison Ripley Cubitt and Sean Cubitt, co-writers of international thrillers, mystery and crime.

Alison is a former television production executive who worked for Walt Disney and the BBC before pivoting to become a multi-genre author and screenwriter. Her short film drama *Waves* (with Maciek Pisarek) won the Special Jury Prize, Worldfest, Houston.

Sean's day job is Professor of Film and Television, University of Melbourne, Australia. He writes about film and media for leading academic publishers.

With six passports between them, they set their books in the far-away places they live and work.

Find us on social media and on our website: https://www.lambertnagle.com

Also by Lambert Nagle

Revolution Earth

Capital Crimes: with a foreword by Peter James